CATALINA ROMANCE

A REALITY TV ROMANCE

ANASTASIA ALEXANDER

Catalina Romance

Published by Elegant Elephant

Copyright © 2021 by Anastasia Alexander

Cover and ebook design by Molly Phipps

ISBN: 978-1948410069

Printed in the United States of America

Year of first printing: 2014

BOOKS BY ANASTASIA ALEXANDER

MILLIONAIRE ROMANCE SERIES

CHAPTER 1

Charissa

*P*eople up for all the battle wounds of love should continue to be offered that opportunity until death. I wasn't one of those people. I quit on love, as well as people, for that matter.

Instead of dealing with love and people, I hauled my stuff into my new cabin in Island Park, Idaho. I'd gone there to have the Walden Pond experience. The air held a chill and wrapped around the steady lodge-pole pines. It was impossible to not step on weeds in various shades, and I passed a few wildflowers clinging onto their last hee-haw. A dog barked in the distance, and the unexpected cadence of a woman's voice caught my attention. I tried to figure out where it came from.

Grey reservoir water splashed in small ripples against the rocky weedy shoreline. The cabins next door remained empty silent containers. Up at the top of the property where the dirt road ran, something flickered. A few seconds later, a tall figure wrapped in a long black fur coat and trendy boots tromped toward me. She waved her hands above her head in the fading afternoon gray light.

"Hello," she called out as a poodle with a diamond collar pranced in front of her. "I'm Nia, and I'm here on vacation staying in a friend's cabin."

A glint of setting sunlight behind her outlined her tall and wide Afro, creating the impression an angel had floated in until I heard her breathing. She was huffing something fierce. But that didn't stop her from calling out in a cheerful small-town way as she thumped through knee-high weeds and delicate wildflowers. "It's so good to see I have a neighbor in this lonely place."

I plastered on a smile. It wouldn't hurt to be friendly. "Hello, there," I called out.

This encouraged her. Before I knew it, a middle-aged black woman with short stylish hair stood in front of me. Nia pressed her hands to her chest. "Gosh, I'm sure out of shape." She leaned forward, gasping for more of the clean air, sounding like a vacuum inhaling. Her white poodle stood there blinking, fur draping in his eyes as though he didn't think much of these weeds and overactive humans.

The woman's breathing slowed, and she looked up at my face with her large, deep-brown eyes. Her eyes immediately widened as she took me in. "You're... you're, Charissa!"

Really? Seriously, I had come out to the most remote place my budget could afford to get away from gawking people who watch the show, and *boom!* Here's another one in the middle of nowhere. I could never, ever escape. I crossed my arms over my chest.

Nia screamed, "From *Millionaire Engagement!*"

Prickly heat danced down my skull. I'd never get used to this. I nodded to the loud vacationer. It would do me no good to deny it. I'd just feel guilty, and she wouldn't believe me. Yes, I had tried that many times before. This was the curse of looking too much like yourself.

"You were one of my favorites," she rattled on. "I know everything about you."

My guard clicked up. If she did know stuff not already blasted in the media, that would make her a stalker, and that would be creepy.

"You were the first person to receive a flower."

She was unfazed by my defensive body stance, with my shoulders and chest pumped up. I needed to chill. She was just an excited fan. The chances of her meaning me to harm measured almost zero.

I had grown too defensive lately since appearing on the show. I kept expected everyone to try to hurt or use me. She was right. I was the first person to receive the impact flower, which meant JT had an interest in me from our thirty-second chat, and I had gained the right to stay on the show for another week. Most people in America knew that accomplishment. The clip of JT presenting me the daisy had been played over and over on commercials, or flash-back recounts. Ironically, JT told me a daisy meant friend-ship and, over the course of the show, I stayed exactly there —in the "friend zone," no matter what efforts I made to climb out.

"You were on every single group date. No other girl managed to do that." Nia smirked.

I loved how people felt compelled to tell me about my accomplishments like I didn't know them. Despite the handicap of landing in the quicksand friend zone, I did manage to be "chosen" for all the group dates. Lucky me, getting to go on a date with him with a bunch of other girls. Fun. That achievement splattered me across magazine covers, too.

Nia beamed like she was seeing her long-lost beloved sister after years of separation. "I can't believe I'm meeting you. This is so cool. I can't wait to call my friends and tell them." She frantically dug into her black coat pocket. "Oh, would you mind taking a picture with me?"

All those hours, I had put into finding this place, frantic to be hidden from this fan reaction, bristled against my patience. I wasn't about to have everything unravel with one damn photo, probably with a geo-locator attached identifying where I hid.

I stumbled backward. "Yes, I would mind."

The lady looked like a wounded girl with a big quivering lower lip and glassy eyes.

I put my hands up as if to reassure her. "I'm sorry. I didn't mean to snap."

Her eyes narrowed in on me.

"I just don't like the media."

The lady's huffed. "Then you shouldn't have gone on TV."

I gasped from that jab. That was a low blow and hit me right in the gut.

"Come, Candlewick, let's go on with our vacation." She

tugged on her dog's leash. "We are out of here. Charissa's got a reputation with a gun, and there's no telling if she has one hidden in her jacket."

No way did she really believe I hid a gun in my sweater pocket. She was jabbing at me about those not-so-flattering magazine articles.

On one of the group dates, we had gone shooting. I showed a little vigor with a gun in my hands. The target dared me to blast a hole in it, and all I could think about were all the guys in my past. *Bang! Bang! Bang!* Those bullets flew. Sweet satisfaction. My unusual intensity caught the producer's eye, and prompted more commercials, and replays of me shooting with a crooked smile.

Magazines touted headlines like, *"Watch Out Boys—She* Will *Shoot."*

That promotion didn't bother me. In fact, I was a little proud. It sent a clear message to not mess with me. A girl couldn't ever be too safe. Apparently, it worked, too, considering this very disappointed fan struggling to retreat. If possible, she breathed even more heavily as she went back on the same path, her shoulders slumped.

Thank heavens she'd not mentioned my most embarrassing moment, on the "meet the family" episode, where I starred as one of the final three. It also so happened to be my first one-on-one date with JT.

I had thought we were in love, even though we'd barely talked a few times. For days prior to the big event, I had planned out the menu for our get together, practiced cooking the spiced meats, created elaborate desserts, and debated on the various salad choices. I acted as though if I cooked the perfect meal, all my dreams of being in love would come true.

"*Dropped Before Dinner,*" the headlines read.

Those lines haunted me in my nightmares and trailed me into the daytime. I had charged out into the big old world and made a name for myself. An embarrassing one, granted, but one nonetheless. I could cross fame off my list of things to experience, even though I never actually wanted it.

* * *

HOURS LATER, after the passing-neighbor incident, I managed to finish hauling my clothes and sewing materials into the cabin. The frames for the quilts spilled over against a far wall, taking up more room than felt right in proportion to the rest of the place.

I should start on the quilt orders I was lucky enough to secure with the craft store. Tiredness weighed on me. Maybe I would just set them up tonight so I could hit it strong tomorrow.

As I unpacked my sewing machine and fabric cabinet, my cell phone rang. My sister. Her daily check-in.

"Just unpacking," I answered before she asked.

"Are you loving it there?" She spoke in her fake, bubbly tone.

"Chelsey, can you please remind me why I went on that darn show anyway?"

The hum of the treadmill in the background filled the phone waves. "You're still thinking about it?" She sounded breathless—her daily workout. "You have to stop that.

You're going to defeat the whole purpose of this move. But, to answer your question, you went to people, please."

"People, please, who?" I asked.

"Your boss. Remember, you weren't strong enough to stand up to her."

"That couldn't be it," I murmured.

Granted, my boss at the time did pressure me to do the show, suggesting I'd make more cosmetic sales that way. I distinctly recall telling her to do it herself. She snapped back she would but was married, even if unfortunately so. She was right. Cosmetics sales did go up, but I was fairly certain that wasn't why I went. Maybe I thought I'd really find love, or that by being on the show I'd help someone.

"I just want to understand myself," I blurted out. "It's just isn't like me."

Chelsey laughed. "It wasn't, but you really wanted to do it. You'd let no one and nothing get in your way. You thought it would be a great way to meet a nice guy. I worried about the underbelly of Hollywood and how you struggled standing up to people. I told you it'd get you in trouble. You wouldn't listen."

My stomach fluttered. It was true. I did have a hard time standing up for myself, even when people were using me. That was why I lost JT. I was sure of it. He told me as much on the reunion show—fortunately, off-air.

"Charissa, you became too caught up in trying to be perfect. Just relax."

Easy for him to say with his millions of dollars. If I had millions of dollars, I could look as relaxed as he. Plus, he didn't always live in his sister's shadow like I did. If I ever stood up when we were kids, she'd flare up mad. She wasn't that way now, but it made an impression on me. Even though I sold a lot of skin care after the show, I hated the questions that came with it.

"Are you so embarrassed for being dumped even before dinner?"

"What is reality TV like?"

"Is JT as cute and charming in real life as on TV?"

Time for me to change the subject with my sister. "How's Ava? Is the treatment still working?"

Chelsey laughed. "She's fine, and yes, it's still working. She's actually taking a dance class. Modern jazz. She's loving it."

"That's so good to hear." I wiped at my eyes. "It has to be a result of the new diet we have her on." I used the word "we" to be generous. It was actually me who had her try a whole new protocol. I had done a ton of research on which diets had the best chance of helping to cure cancer, or at least put it in remission.

"Maybe." Chelsey had always been resistant to the idea that eating a certain way could cure Ava, but to humor me, she allowed me control of Ava's diet if my niece was willing and the doctors didn't oppose it. The doctors didn't exactly approve. They said ridiculous things like, "I can't see how it would hurt," and "If you want to try, go ahead."

Ava thought it made sense that our food affected us and was natural medicine, so she was willing. Thankfully. Not often does a twelve-year-old listen to her aunt, even if her aunt is as cool as me.

"So," Chelsey said, "what's your cabin like?"

It's perfect." I peered out the big windows to the choppy

Snake River. "It's in the middle of nowhere. Perfect," I repeated.

My heart swelled with gratitude that I could afford to rent a small two-bedroom cabin in the center of lodgepole pines and, most often, snow. I wasn't rolling in dough, but I had been paid for making it close to the top of the reality TV show ranking, had residual money from previous sales of the skincare products, and was finally earning money off my quilts.

My phone beeped, indicating a call on the other line. Pulling the phone from my ear, I glanced to see if it was one of the stores selling my quilts. I blinked at the phone number. It was *Millionaire Engagement*. My chest tightened as though big burly arms had suddenly seized me to squeeze all the air from my lungs.

What could they possibly want? I had already refused to be on the follow-up show or on news reports, TV, or social media. I was going completely off-line until the memory of me skated into obscurity. Maybe they wanted information for taxes or some other final annoying detail. A little air seeped back into my lungs. Taxes. That had to be it. If I didn't answer now, I'd be stuck calling them back.

"Chelsey, I need to get this call."

Fumbling with the buttons on my cell, I heard, "Charissa?"

Shoot. That was the voice of Dee. I had made it a goal in my life never to cross this intense lady. I always tried to avoid talking to her and generally stayed out of her way. She had lived the skuzzy life of a producer too long and had thrived.

Too late to hang up. "Why are you calling me?" I asked,

not wanting to be too friendly. This woman fed on kindness and would wield it against a person.

"I have great news for you."

Whatever she said next wasn't going to be good. I leaned against the white fridge so the solid structure would hold me. I said nothing, hoping to discourage her, to have her rethink whatever it was that she wanted. The silence didn't slow her down. I doubted she even noticed my lack of enthusiasm. "As you may have heard, *Millionaire Engagement* was renewed for another season. And, this time around, a girl will be the focus. To keep the 'millionaire' part of the show, there won't be as many men wooing the woman because there aren't that many millionaires available. But, still, the men will be great candidates because each one will be vetted to have at least a couple million dollars, if not more."

This woman rambled on about something that didn't have any effect on me. "Dee, I'm happy for you guys and the show and everything. I read about this in the articles. Why call me?"

"Oh, you still do care about us. You're following us."

I shouldn't have done that. I let curiosity get ahold of me, and now I was paying the price.

"Because you were the one we voted for to be the star of the new season."

CHAPTER 2

Andrew

*H*ere we go again. I could tell from the look on my sister Gina's face she was on a mission to make my life miserable. It wasn't her intention. She just had a knack for it. I suspected she drove everyone she cared about crazy.

Her large grey-blue eyes bored into me across the wooden dinner table. "Are you going to be an insurance guy forever?" Her lips curled downward as if she found even *saying* those words disgusting.

I didn't like feeling like a schoolboy in trouble with the teacher. I leaned back to escape the reach of her fire. I puckered my mouth into fish lips at my year-old nephew sitting in a highchair next to her.

Alex struggled to pucker his lips back. Drool flowed

from his mouth, and a "bah" sound slipped through. I couldn't help but laugh.

Gina's eyes narrowed more fiercely onto me, demanding an answer.

Maybe if I acted casual and didn't address what she was really saying under her words, I could make it to the pie faster. I hoped there was still ice cream left, too. "Sis, it's the thrill of the deal. There's nothing like it."

She put her fork down and wiped her hands on a napkin. "You sound like an addict. What's more boring than selling insurance?"

"A tax man," I offered, to be helpful, of course.

She shook her head.

"Gina," I said, feeling suckered into defending myself. I had silently promised I wouldn't justify my job to my sister, but I couldn't help it. "Insurance isn't boring when you think about how I'm helping people." I made the mistake of glancing over at her when I said that. She looked like she might pounce on me as soon as I finished. "The other day, I met with a client whose husband worked on a highway road crew. A driver wasn't paying attention and hit him. He died instantly."

Gina gasped. "That's awful."

It was, and the part I hated most about my career... hearing things like that and not knowing what to say. I had liked that guy. Four months earlier, he had joked through the whole process of getting life insurance. His wife begged him to stop teasing. He never did.

Hands together, I leaned into the table. "I was able to help that poor lady and her children have space to start healing. He was the breadwinner, and she has a three-month-old baby. She doesn't immediately need to secure a job. She has time."

Gina stood and started collecting dishes. "I'm sorry. I'm not saying your job isn't important. Of course, it is. I'm glad that family talked to you instead of some other insurance man who's in it just for the money."

She headed over to the sink to put the dishes in it. It looked like I had said the right words, and the pie was on its way.

She picked up a dishcloth and wiped her hands. "It's just you're such a nice guy. I love having you here every Sunday. Don't get me wrong, but I want to see you with your own family. You'd make such a great dad."

I didn't know about that. Children seemed complicated. I sat back in my chair and said, "Well, if only the right girl would come along."

"You act like you are helpless and don't have any control over that."

I'd prefer eating mud pies instead of listening to this. "It's not like I haven't tried."

"Not hard enough."

Sometimes my sister was too bossy. It was because she cared… still, it needed to stop. "You haven't seen what's out there," I said. "A lot of LA and San Diego women are plastic. They brim with entitlement, insisting on going to expensive restaurants and drinking pricey wines. They even attend workshops on how to manipulate men with money into relationships. No, thank you. Rather be lonely."

Gina opened the oven and pulled out the warm apple pie. She set it on the stovetop, cut a big heaping slice, and slid it on a plate. The children, like magic, scurried around her legs

"I want some," they called out in unison.

She set the slice of pie with a fork in front of me and sighed. "I believe you, but that's not all there is. There are women who aren't like that. I know a few in my yoga class. I know you're busy with work, and you're a great catch. So, maybe… I was wondering since you're so busy, would you be willing to accept help to find a nice girl?"

The more scared my sister became about her own life, the more intensely she focused on mine. Her way of escaping her pain. I walked over to her and put my arm around her. "Have a hard day?"

She nodded. "Thank you for coming over here. I don't like to always being alone. I don't know how you can stand it after all these years."

I pulled her close, and she rested her head on my chest. "You don't need to worry about me."

* * *

TWO DAYS LATER, the throb in my shoulders had raced up my neck, causing stiffness and a light headache with a flickering sensation in my eyes. I had been hunched over my laptop for too long. After I completed two more insurance policies, I would find something to eat to calm the increasing growl in my stomach. Today had been extremely productive but long.

The phone rang. My sister, again. Every few hours, she had called today. Had to hand it to her. She was persistent.

She'd make a good insurance salesman. I'd want her on my team. Definitely, she'd make bank.

I had ignored her calls to the point she'd become insulted and start crying on her messages. I pushed back my chair from my desk and answered this time.

"Yeah?"

Black had crept into my apartment, filling in the empty spaces. I wandered into the hallway to flip on the lights.

"Are you hiding from me?"

That was not a good question to answer. Anything I said would just piss her off. "Of course, work has been intense." I yawned.

"Um hum," she said. "Want to know what I think?"

No, but if I said so, I'd never escape this conversation.

"What?"

I wandered into my kitchen. What could pass for dinner? Mail and magazines once stacked all over the counter had spilled onto the floor. My feet stepped onto something sticky. I sighed. Today was the first time in a long time I had arrived home at a decent hour. My glare took in all the dirty dishes piled throughout my apartment.

"Since you agreed I should look for a girl, you've been hiding from me."

I needed an aspirin but, before that, something to eat. I opened my fridge to discover empty shelves except for a half-eaten bag of carrots and a bottle of ketchup.

"Andrew, aren't you going to say anything?"

Words with women only got men in trouble. We men should become mute. I glanced at my watch. McDonald's would still be open.

"Andrew."

Her voice held a grating edge.

This wasn't going well. "What?"

"I have roasted chicken, seasoned rice, and a large chocolate cake waiting for you."

Yum. "What's the catch?"

This habit of baiting me with food used to happen once every couple of months when she was married to that Bozo. Now it was progressing to multiple times a week. She really hated to be alone, and I knew it scared her. Plus, she was overwhelmed with the young ones. But, now, it seemed like she was up to more than trying not to be lonely all the time.

"You watch a video of a girl who would be perfect for you."

I walked to the kitchen counter to lean against it for strength. "She isn't there waiting to spring on me?"

"What?"

"Is this a surprise attack? Are you trying to lure me in with food?"

"Of course, I always do, and it always works. You're the worst at taking care of yourself. And, no, I'm not surprised attacking you. I want you to watch video clips, that's it."

I strummed my fingers against the counter and tried to figure out what other ways Gina might be trapping me. "What are you not telling me?"

"Nothing," she snapped. "The food goes to the dog if you aren't here in twenty minutes."

* * *

I LIVE IN TEMECULA, California, wine country. The best wine in the state, but don't let the snooty Northerners know that because they like to pretend, they are the only ones who know how to cultivate grapes.

The town earned its name after the Temecula Native Americans who, according to legend, believe life began here in this valley. The Natives call it "Exva Temeeku," or the place of the union of Sky-father and Earthmother.

So far, living in a place with so much *union* energy, I hadn't seen the union part transpire. My sister lived one town away—Murrieta. A quiet place first developed by Ezequiel Murrieta to establish a sheep business.

By the time I pulled up to her house, the moon had spilled over the rugged mountains. When I opened the metal, forest-green house door, it squeaked. It needed oil. I'd pick some up tomorrow and take care of it for her. Her pond-scum husband asked for a separation eight months ago and left her to raise the three young kids with only an occasional check.

"I'm home," I called out to be funny.

My nephew and niece ran to me and grabbed my calves, eyes wide. I laughed as I shuffled and groaned like a mummy. They clung onto my leg.

"Andrew!" they cried out as one voice.

I rubbed both of them on the top of their heads, enjoying our ritual.

Gina hustled out of the kitchen with a sneaky smile I had learned long ago to mistrust. "You made it."

I strolled toward the dinner table, noticing everything had been cleaned off, and the table was shiny—too clean.

"Sis, what is it?" I turned to her. "Did you lie about the food?"

She patted my forearm. "Don't worry. I kept it in the oven." She gave a light floaty laugh as she headed into the kitchen. I followed after her, my stomach growling with the thought of dinner.

She pulled out a plate of chicken and rice with rosemary, onion, and other delicious-smelling spices, and she poured me some local wine.

"Looks great." I rubbed my hands together.

She handed the plate to me and pulled out a fork and knife from the dishwasher. "Since I want you to watch clips from this TV show. You can eat your dinner while we watch."

That sounded harmless, but I knew it couldn't be. I trailed after Gina into the living room like a clueless sheep from Murrieta of the past. The children followed, squawking and fighting.

"Kids, why don't you go play outside?" she asked.

"Yeah!" they cried in unison and hurried away.

She laughed. "They know it's getting close to their bedtime."

I had never before witnessed my sister not honor the sacred ritual of putting them to bed exactly at bedtime. She had to be up to something with this video. She skipped over to the remote like a happy school girl, trying to suppress her giggles as she cued up the television. I sat up to eat and watch. Before long, music interrupted our quiet evening, and the television flickered with the words, *Millionaire Engagement*. An irritating reality show where people made fools of themselves on TV.

"Not happening." I struggled to rise from my seat.

Gina swiveled to face me and pointed. "Sit. I spent a lot of time on that dinner, and I expect you to do what you said you'd do."

Fire fueled her eyes, reminding me of Mom right before she ripped someone to shreds. I sat—biting into the juicy, spicy chicken—and soon found myself watching these women jump into catfights over a man. This was a man's worse nightmare—fighting emotional women.

I yawned and looked at my watch. Yep, it was past the children's' bedtime. I'd be up late if I wanted to finish the policy orders tonight.

Among the women on the show, one stood out. She had beautiful smooth olive skin, gentle eyes, and she avoided the cat fights. She moved softly and showed she cared about others through thoughtful gestures: getting them a glass of water or letting them walk in the door first. The camera didn't follow her often, but I always liked hearing what she had to say. Plus, there was something about her that drew me to her. I found it impossible *not* to watch her.

Gina's focus remained glued to the television set. Her tight jaw line meant she was under more pressure than she was saying, not to mention the dark bags under her eyes.

Something was weighing her down, and she wasn't going to tell me what it was. Instead, she'd pretend everything was alright and distract herself from her woes by focusing on me. I had myself a good sister who always meant well. Her delivery could use some improvement, but her heart was there. I wished I could wave away all the pain her idiot husband created.

She zoomed through the commercials, probably feeling

my impatience. She pushed pause on a soda-pop ad and shifted her whole body to face me. "Well, what do you think?"

I swallowed a savory bite of rich-flavored brown rice and coughed nervously. My sister had certainly put me on the spot. "That guy has it bad trying to handle all those ladies. I don't know why any man would put himself in a situation like that."

Gina gave a half-smile. "Oh, stop being pious. You know you'd love it if a lot of beautiful women threw themselves at you."

"Well, now that you put it that way," I said. "I don't think it'd be half bad."

As I lifted another piece of chicken to my mouth, she grabbed the couch pillow next to her and smacked my stomach. The hit on my stomach didn't hurt.

"Wipe that smirk off your face."

I shrugged, wiping my mouth onto a napkin, not caring if I was smirking or not.

To my chagrin, she restarted the program. When the quiet woman was no longer on camera, I looked over to Gina.

She pursed her lips. "What do you think of them?"

I picked up my wine glass from the floor and sipped. What did my sister have in mind? I was stepping onto a landmine but clueless about what kind of connection she was trying to create between me and a reality show.

"Did you like any particular one of those girls?" She leaned in like she was still that little girl wanting in on a secret.

Liquid stuck in my throat, and I choked. After I recovered from coughing, I asked, "Are you being a matchmaker, or are you trying to get a feel for my preferences?"

Her smiled lightened. "Relax, Romeo. I want to know if there was anyone on those few clips you felt particularly drawn to."

My chest tightened. "Why?"

"Just answer the question."

I loved my sister, but she was playing games. She proved my point as to why I should stay away from the opposite sex except to sell them insurance. The game was more than old.

"Well, I'd certainly want to stay away from that Maggie girl. What a nightmare."

"She is." Gina flipped the remote around in her hands. "But, if you had to go on a date with one of those women, which one would it be?"

My focus returned to the TV, now paused on a scene shot of all the women gathered around on the porch— except Maggie, who had just escaped out of the hotel. I didn't want to talk about my preferences, or the women, or any other stuff. Apparently, I had agreed to it, though, when I agreed to allow my sister to help me in the dating department. I had thought it would stop the lectures. But, looking at my sister's set jaw, waiting for my answer, I could see just how wrong I had been.

I analyzed the scene shot. A lot of the women were loud and critical. A definite buzz kill. Others were boring or immaturely giggly and acted like they were at a slumber party. No thanks. But, in the corner of the screen, tucked behind the others who fought for airtime, stood a peaceful lady who seemed different.

When her comrades came up to her, she welcomed them with a warm smile. As she talked to them, she'd give them reassuring touches on their forearms and beam with interest. Her smooth, tan skin and large hazel eyes captured me. Not only was she pretty in subtle ways, but kind and caring. She came across as a gentle soul. She mostly nodded as she conversed with others and didn't have a compulsion for endless talk. On one outtake, they had shown her in the kitchen, pulling casseroles out of the oven and saying she missed cooking.

"The olive-skinned woman in the far corner." I gestured to the kind lady, playing down my interest as I felt myself flush. She was certainly one attractive, kind woman. She would make someone a great wife.

Gina looked at the screen. "Oh, you mean Charissa." She clapped her hands together. "I thought so!"

My stomach rotated. I put my fork on the plate, waiting to have the trap sprung on me.

"She was one of the final three."

"Okay."

In response to my blank expression, Gina shook her head. "Since she didn't find love in this season, and she made it so far in the show, she has a high probability of being picked to come back next season."

I stared at Gina. She didn't seriously think I'd understand that. "Dinner was great, Sis. I appreciate it."

She didn't go for the conversation switch. "It means next year all these guys are competing for one girl. I think it's going to be the girl you just pointed out, especially since the show needs to clean up their image after Maggie."

I couldn't imagine that sweet, quiet thing being the

target. That would be a mistake for her. "She'd be eaten alive."

"So, you like her?"

I shrugged and stood, ready to call it an evening and get away from all her questioning.

"Andrew, she made it to one of the last three girls standing, meaning the final three." Gina spoke faster like she wanted to slip in all this information before I left. "It was because she was quiet and stayed out of all the catfights. Your kind of girl. Well, the kind you say you want."

"Good for her." I still didn't know what my sister wanted.

"JT flew out to visit her for her home date. She was so nervous about making everything nice. She cooked up a huge meal and had family over, and was ready to feed JT when he walked off the plane. He spent a couple of hours with her, and before they even made it back to her place to eat dinner, he dumped her."

This woman did sound perfect. "What did she cook?"

Gina shook her head. "You are such a boy. You are ruled by your stomach."

"The problem is?" I picked up my dishes and stacked them. I really did need to leave, and this woman wasn't getting to the point.

Gina stood and followed me into the kitchen, where I put my dirty plates into the sink. "The tabloids went crazy, splashing the headlines all over the country: 'Dumped Before Dinner.'"

That whole reality TV thing was certainly something. "That's a shame." If that woman was as nice as she appeared, that must have really hurt her. She didn't deserve it. With all those other women acting ridiculous and her being so civil, that wasn't fair.

"So?" Gina asked me, her eyes wide and waiting.

I ran warm water over my dirty dishes, rinsing them off as heat bore into my back from my sister's evil glare. My back itched from her unmoving intensity behind me.

"So," I asked, "you mentioned something about choco-late cake?"

Gina shook her head as though I was an elementary school boy being silly.

I wasn't being silly. I was being serious. I looked around the clean kitchen, amazed she could keep up with her household chores when I always fail in that department, even without kids.

Movement from the backyard caught my eye. My niece and nephew were dragging toys into the porch light's glow. They were building a fort using their slide. They streamed a blanket from the top of the structure to the ground. I should go out there and help them with their collapsing roof.

"Andrew."

My eyes snapped down to my older sister. She was actually quite short, even compared to me, who hadn't much merit in the height department.

"You should go on the show this coming year and protect her."

"What?"

Not a chance.

"The show hasn't announced which girl will be the star. They did announce it would be a woman, but I have my bet on Charissa. And, from everything I know about you, and from what I have seen on TV about her and read online... she's absolutely perfect for you. She's who you've been waiting for. Besides, maybe this will help your dream of becoming a video producer. You'd see firsthand how Hollywood works, and maybe you can—"

I dug into my pant pocket and pulled out my car keys. "There's no way."

"Why?" Gina stepped closer to me, blocking my path to the front door. "Don't you think she's attractive?"

"She's attractive." I looked over my sister's head.

"You're worried she'd get eaten alive by the men if she went on the show."

"So? I can't help that. It's her choice."

"You're already feeling protective of her. That means she's the type of girl you want to protect. She's sweet and kind. She sells skin cream, so you're both in the sales industry."

"That doesn't matter."

"It does. You have that in common. I just sense you two would get along really well."

"I do too, but there's no way. I'm not going on reality TV."

Gina flipped a strand of her hair onto her back. "I'm not sure if she'll be the next candidate. Maybe they'll pick someone more dynamic."

"See?" I said. "I bet you're right. They probably want someone who will cause a lot more problems, like that Maggie. That's entertainment. Charissa's too reserved to be a good choice."

Gina continued to plant herself firmly in my path like

she could actually stop me if I wanted to pass her. "You probably would've been right, but Milly won, and then she and JT didn't work out. Rumor has it that Maggie and JT are now an item. If that's the case, Maggie's not eligible. It'd fall to Charissa unless they identified someone else more popular to put on the air. Social media does seem to like Charissa, though."

She walked past me back into the kitchen and pulled from the cupboard a large chocolate cake with only one slice missing. She grabbed a small plate as my mouth watered.

She flashed a smile. "It was established that Charissa was a cook on the show. She enjoys cooking and taking care of the main person in her life."

My gaze moved from the cake to my sister. She was still selling, and all I wanted was dessert. I swallowed a lump in my throat. "But, you just said you don't know if she'll be on the show."

"What if I come up with a way for you to meet her?" Gina asked. "Would you be willing?"

"I'm not appearing on that show."

"When are you going to stop hiding and fight for your dream?"

"Marriage can wait," I said.

"No, I'm talking about your dream of producing TV shows."

"Yeah, well—that takes a lot of money, time, and connections. If you... Gina, I'm not going to woo a lady to make connections."

"I see your longing in your face when you see a couple in love. I know you want a romantic relationship. I wish you'd get over the bimbo. She sure did a number on you. I wish you'd stop hiding and search out your true love. Please stop this..." She swung the chocolate cake in front of me. "And, go on the show?" She raised her eyebrows. "Besides, it wouldn't hurt your insurance sales, either."

I rolled my eyes. She wasn't stopping the sales.

CHAPTER 3

Charissa

*T*he problem with being in the middle of nowhere when the sun goes down, and if the moon decides to slack on its job, the countryside becomes absolutely pitch black with no distant city lights to offer any contrast. That meant, as I stood on the back porch, I stared at nothing but a black void. The hairs rose on my arm, and I took it as a sign to go back inside my cabin.

I had stood firm with Dee. Told her no, over and over, and finally hung up.

A cold sweat crept over me as I thought about it. I'd never been so assertive and to *Dee*. Nobody I knew of ever talked to her that way. People only scurried to obey her.

It made absolutely no sense for the show to have picked me. I didn't have a shining personality. I'd been humiliated last season and certainly couldn't have been the nation's favorite. Most magazines referred to me as the "quiet one," which my sister thought an absolute farce since she often claimed I never shut up.

None of this made sense. My stomach hurt thinking about it. To settle it, I brewed myself a cup of hot chamomile tea, found a homemade quilt, and wrapped it around me. I wandered into the living room and plopped onto the couch in front of the empty fireplace. I should make myself a fire, watch the splendor of colors it produced, and feel the heat of nature's warmth, but I couldn't find the gusto to move into action. Besides, I wasn't sure I could even start a fire. Instead, I stared at the fireplace and thought. This whole proposal made absolutely no sense. Why me?

Dee, of course, had given me lines… "America's heart broke when JT called it off with you." And, "You deserve a second chance and, this time, you'll be in the driver's seat." Plus, "America wants you to find love."

The problem was, I no longer wanted to find love. Even if I did want to find it, reality TV wasn't the place I'd choose to look. It was such a fake way to build relationships—with its pressurized situations and the program always trying to manipulate and dredge up people's feelings. I did it once under pressure, and I wouldn't make the same mistake twice. Millions of other women wanted the adventure. I had no doubt the producers would find plenty of other choices from our season alone. Heck, Maggie might be willing to give up JT just to have a chance to be the center of attention.

Anybody was a better choice than me. I wanted to find peace, a very different thing from participating in a popular reality TV show twice. Going on that show wouldn't earn me happiness, it would bring the exact opposite.

No, I needed to do this *Walden Pond* experiment, living out in the wilderness with no TV, no close restaurants, and lots of quiet to find my core, my center, and to heal myself.

* * *

THE NEXT MORNING BEFORE WORK, I grabbed a hot cup of coffee and drifted onto the back porch to enjoy the waking day. A foggy mist covered the land, casting a chilly gray hue on everything and giving it an appropriate fantasy look. I was living a fantasy life communing with nature. Dew settled around me as I realized *Millionaire Engagement* had *promised* a fantasy, but living in the midst of tall pines and roaming buffalo and elk *was* a fantasy. Thus, another lesson learned to keep life simple. Nearby birds squawked loudly as if in agreement.

"Good morning," came a woman's voice to my right.

I screamed, jumped, and splashed hot coffee all over my jeans, burning the top of my thigh. I turned to the laughing person and found afro lady, Nia, standing there with her poodle. In the gray morning light, the woman didn't look as angelic as she had yesterday. Her hair still bounced and encircled her, but today it made her appear like a new species of the area's wildlife.

"Sorry," she said. "I didn't mean to startle you."

If Nia decided we should become friends or that she could just come around all the time, it could become a big problem.

"How can I help you?" I asked.

She tied the leash of her dog to the deck post and approached. "Your sister called me. There's been an emergency."

She had to be kidding. "You don't know my sister."

"Chelsey Woodland?" Nia asked, just as I took the last sip of my coffee.

I coughed as the liquid ran down the wrong pipe. "Yes. How did she get a hold of you?"

Nia shrugged. "It's a long story. Something about her contacting the person you're renting your cabin from. That realtor contacted me and asked permission for your sister to talk to me since I'm renting a cabin close by."

Maybe this lady hadn't been joking when she said she knew everything about me. Possibly, she'd made up this message to confirm the snooping information she had already collected.

I set my coffee cup on the side of my chair. "Why would she go through all that effort to call you when I have a perfectly good phone?"

Nia shrugged. "I'm just the messenger."

My stomach seized as I thought about Chelsey and what could be wrong. Please don't be Ava. Not again. Please. That girl deserved a break. She had been through too much for someone so young.

I CAME out to the wilderness thinking no one would call, but that certainly hadn't been the case. Go figure.

I thanked Nia and assured her I would call my sister as soon as possible. She ambled off down the hill.

I wasn't sure where I had tossed my cell after talking to Dee. It took searching in box after box, and under dishes and clothes that still needed to be put away. Finally, I had to do the famous "re-trace my steps" trick. Dee had been the last person I talked to. I was in the living room unpacking sewing supplies when we talked. I looked into the deep box of materials and threads and found my very dead phone next to my yarn display. With a growing sickness in my stomach, I hurried to the wall socket and plugged it in.

It took forever for the phone to boot up enough to call. My heart pounded wildly by the time I pushed the star icon for my sister. "Please be okay. Please. Please," I whispered.

Panic must have gotten the best of me because tears coursed down my face. I had no doubt what this call was. I had been dreading it for years. The room remained still as I waited for the other line to pick up. Through my tears, I noticed the morning light had lit up all my stuff, crowding the space.

My throat constricted. I really hoped I *was* wrong. If my sister went to all the trouble to track me down, though...

Chelsey picked up. "Why haven't you been answering?"

"Is she okay?"

"No." She burst into sobs.

I leaned against the wall; the cluttered room spun.

Chelsey's voice continued in the background. "She collapsed at the dance. We rushed her to the hospital, where they've been running tests all night. The cancer is back with a vengeance." She slipped into another round of heart-shattering tears. "I'm losing my baby girl."

Those words landed far away in my consciousness like I was wandering in a dark tunnel. Ava couldn't just die. That couldn't be.

There had to be a way.

My sister sniffed. "I guess I always knew deep down inside that this would eventually happen. That she was living on borrowed time."

"It's not over yet." I stood up straight. I would figure out what needed to be done. "This can turn around."

"I don't think so," Chelsey murmured. "Either way, I think you should come."

"Yes, of course. I'll get there as soon as I can."

We said our goodbyes, and I hung up the phone to find the room darkening as cloud cover rolled over the sun.

In the grey light, I searched for the box with all my research. Ever since Ava's first diagnosis, I had studied ways to heal her. Some people would argue that you can't heal cancer. Well, they would argue wrong. I had read too many case studies and too many articles on what could be done.

I found that box, plus my email folder filled with helpful articles on what to do to help the body do its magic. If you removed enough of the toxins, drained the acid, and made your body more alkaline, it would heal. There was just too much evidence showing any cancer could be reversed, no matter how bad it got. I wouldn't accept the death sentence like my sister.

* * *

THE SMALL CABIN pressed against me, crowding me in with boxes everywhere... on the floor, on the kitchen table, on the couches. My sweaters, tee-shirts, jeans, books, stainless steel pots and pans spilled out, creating heaping piles throughout the rooms. I blinked as I looked at the mess through my tears. I had no desire to clean it up. I had no desire to care about quilts due to expectant customers. Nothing else mattered if Ava was sick and in the hospital with that horrible foe of cancer devouring her body and stealing her life.

Ava was life itself, with her yellow-blonde hair and the way she smiled with vigor and brilliance, even when her face paled, and her health wasn't vibrant. She had so much to live for, so much she wanted to experience.

I needed to get to her. I needed to forget my retreat. I had been silly thinking I could play Walden. Why hadn't I stayed in Idaho Falls to be with my sister and be closer to my niece?

I had assured myself Ava had a whole life in front of her, a full existence, even though the doctors warned us it could reoccur. I expected a full life in which I had plenty of time to spend with her. The diet I had her on hadn't been enough. I had read many case studies where it worked for others. Why not Ava?

Standing in the living room, angry at the world, I kicked the object closest to me. My foot met the heavy box with a thump. A spasm vibrated up my ankle. Bending over in pain, I noted the box had barely budged from my effort. Curious about what I kicked, I looked inside to discover my sewing machine. It made sense. That was probably the heaviest thing I had packed. It also made sense, symbolically, of how unsuccessful I have been patching up my life and Ava's.

I grew hot and sweaty as I searched for where I packed the computer. Time ticked, and I was on a scavenger hunt. More than thirty minutes later, I finally found my laptop at the bottom of a blanket box.

Grasping it, I sank onto the rope rug covering the wooden floor in the living room. Leaning my back against the bottom of the couch, I sat cross-legged.

Shadows reached across my living room floor as I hunted online to find a way to save Ava. My head pounded, I scoured online for my frequently visited, alternative health forum. I posted: *"Cancer has returned. Need solutions on how to stop it. Please. I don't care the cost or how radical..."*

I stared at the bright screen in the cloud-darkened room until responses clicked in. Among other comments, ten people responded that *Healing House* was the answer, located in a small remote town in Mexico. I dug into their splashy site. It showed patients lying on tables receiving sound therapy, light therapy, daily colonics, and other treatments I didn't really understand, but many, many people claimed success.

Trying to be wise about this, I Googled their name to see if "spam" or "fraud" or other negative reviews appeared in the search results. Out of the hundreds who had commented, I saw only five complaints, well within the norm.

Strangely, it took a lot of scouring to find the Healing House phone number, which I found flat irritating. Why did so many companies bury their contact information? People who created websites needed to learn to do the basics, like making the phone number prevalent. When I finally found it, I scribbled it on paper, just as series of loud bangs sounded on the back door.

I flinched, looking up through the window to see smiling lips and afro hair in the fading afternoon light. Nia wouldn't leave me alone.

Not now.

She peered right at me. Pretending I wasn't home or didn't hear her knock wasn't going to work.

She waved with a big friendly smile. I closed the lid on my laptop and struggled to my feet. My lower back twinged, and my knees struggled to unfold. I opened the door a crack. A chilly breeze rushed over me.

"Hi, Nia again, I'm here to check up on you, Sweetheart. I'm sure you got bad news earlier, and I wanted to make sure you're okay."

She stepped in and passed by me into the cabin before I could say a word.

She headed toward the kitchen but then faced me. Only then did I noticed she carried a hot pot of something.

"I brought dinner." She smiled. "Where do you want me to put it?"

A hot spicy chili smell filled the room. I looked around for where she could set it in the midst of messiness. Half-empty boxes filled with cooking utensils covered the kitchen floor. The counters were just as bad. The only spot left unscathed was the oven.

"Um, the stovetop." I blinked, not sure how to take all this. She was going out of her way to be kind and yet extremely intrusive.

She laughed. "That's the only available horizontal space

in the whole place." She set the pot on the stove, placing her hot pad on the counter, and faced me. "Are you okay?"

I was in her debt for coming over and letting me know about the call, bringing dinner, and now she was trying to be supportive, but my body shook.

"Thank you for the food." I couldn't look her in the eye as I spoke. "It was thoughtful."

"Do you want to talk about it?" she asked.

I backed toward the door and put my hand on the metal handle. "Family crisis." I opened the door, allowing a breeze of cold to slip into my tiny room. "Thank you for cooking dinner. You really shouldn't have."

She shouldn't have, but the spices and flavors of the food stirring my stomach let me know I hadn't eaten anything all day.

Nia smiled. "It's just chili. It's all I could throw together."

"It's fine," I said. "I appreciate it." I pushed the door wider. It was sunset time, and the sky lit up in magical pastel colors.

Nia beamed, revealing her pearly whites. "Oh, I'm not going anywhere. Clearly, you need help and to talk. I'm a good listener and a hard worker."

She heard my bad news that someone in my family was sick, gave her condolences. She scanned the cabin, which looked like a wild animal had been in there, with my belongings scattered everywhere, and told me she'd help out. Not long afterward, she had made a lot of progress putting order to my mess. Twenty minutes into her dazzle, she stopped and insisted I eat the chili.

I tried a few bites, but my throat was so constricted I

couldn't swallow more. I set my spoon down in the bowl and pushed it farther away from me. "I'll eat more later. I need to make a call before it becomes too late."

Nia nodded to my explanation and resumed unpacking.

I couldn't afford to be distracted by her or anyone else. I hurried out onto the back porch for some much-needed privacy. My hands shook in an uncomfortable jitter as I dialed. Soon, a voicemail began playing, first in Spanish, then in English. I left my number and hung up. I vowed to call back every twenty minutes all night long if I had to until they answered. In my third round of waiting twenty minutes and calling, someone finally picked up the phone.

By this time, my kitchen had slipped into order by Nia, and she had moved on to set up my bathroom. She hummed as she worked but, the moment she heard me talking, she stopped and wandered into the living room, listening.

The person on the other end of the phone had a thick Hispanic accent, and I struggled to figure out what he said.

I finally resorted to begging. "English. English. Please."

I was put on hold until a younger voice answered in English. I asked questions about the place and explained my situation. The man, on the other end, sounded friendly and knowledgeable. He spoke with perfect English. He said the center had treated many people in similar positions. They offered lab testing, ultrasound, and microscopic blood analysis—often used to determine how to best treat cancer. He told me about ozone therapy—which I had heard wonders about—and about twenty other types of treatments, therapies, and cutting-edge fancy machines known to yield incredible results. Plus, they provided on-staff nutrition specialists, a psychological therapist, and fitness classes. Organic meals were included—free of gluten, dairy, and corn.

As the young man talked, I opened my computer and flipped to pictures of the place. One snapshot captured a paradise, with palm trees taking on a dark hue in the evening and buildings with glowing arches outlining the different rooms. Another showed a green forest hill rolling upward with a large palm tree spreading its glory wide in the afternoon sun. Next appeared a long-distance shot of residents in the glistening, clear-blue pool, with ocean waves splashing about five-hundred feet away.

The stunning location oozed with healing, and I could see Ava there with a smile on her face as she held my hand. "Aunt Charissa, this place is amazing. Thank you so much."

Not only was it a great getaway but, more importantly, a place where a person could heal. The doctors and the treatments might make a real difference. This was exactly what Ava needed. I could feel intuition swelling in my chest.

This was right. This was the answer. From all my research over the years, the things I saw in this place were exactly what people online found to be helpful.

"Okay, what do I need to do to sign up my niece?" I asked.

"The range for a three-week visit is between one-hundred thousand and two-hundred thousand dollars, depending on what the doctors think is necessary. We would need fifty thousand dollars to reserve your spot. Please note this doesn't include transportation costs to get to Rosarito, but it does include medical attention and room and board."

"You have got to be kidding me!" I practically yelled into the phone.

"Sorry?" the man said. "I don't understand."

I was going too American on him. "That's really expensive," I said. "Do you take a payment plan?" Like for the next hundred years.

"It's a nice place and worth it. You get health. No payment plans."

My hope sank. "Okay, I'll get back to you."

My knees went weak as I hung up the phone. I burst into tears. The price didn't even include the airplane flights or anything additional that might be needed. I buried my head in my hands.

Nia hurried to me. "What's wrong?"

"I failed my niece, and now she's going to die." I did not look up.

She stroked my hair and hushed me as I broke into another round of sobs. That continued for probably another ten minutes before I wiped my nose and rubbed my eyes.

I owed this pseudo-stalker an explanation now. "My niece is back in the hospital. Her cancer has returned. It's aggressive."

That sparred another round of tears.

Nia gasped. "I'm so sorry. You love your niece very much."

I nodded. "I practically raised her for a while. My sister was a single mother, and she wanted to go back to school." I wiped at my eyes in a hopeless attempt to rid myself of tears. "So, I moved to Idaho Falls to be with her and to watch Ava while Chelsey was in nursing school." I looked up at Nia, who listened intently with soft deep-brown eyes. "That program was intense, and there were times Chelsey almost never saw Ava. She was a toddler at the time, and ever since then, she has been like my own daughter."

My voice choked with emotion. I stopped talking to regain composure.

"I couldn't love a person more than I love that girl." I wiped at tears that started pouring again. "She's so courageous. She has been battling cancer off and on since she was ten." I looked at the ground, remembering all those years. All the fear. All the hugs. All the tears. All the hope. "She's now fifteen. I thought it was finally gone. I really did, and now it's back, and unless we do something dramatic, we're going to lose her."

"Then do something dramatic," Nia said.

I looked into her eyes. They told me to not give up, and there was still hope. I brushed at the tears one more time and squared my shoulders. That was exactly what I would do.

CHAPTER 4

Charissa

*Y*arn, sewing needles, clothes, and jars of food spilled out everywhere inside my car as I drove wildly toward Chelsey's. I would find an absolute mess to sort through once I arrived. I hadn't had time to sort out anything, so Nia had helped me throw everything I own, including what she had just put away, into the car and my rented moving trailer and constantly waved until I no longer saw her in my rear-view mirror.

When I finally arrived at my sister's apartment in Idaho Falls, I pulled up to the side of the building. She didn't know I was coming. I had talked to her just a bit earlier, though, so I knew she had left Ava in the hospital, then run home to shower and regroup.

Chelsey's voice had shaken so much, I knew it would be best not to ask about Ava's condition. When Chelsey went through things like this, my job was to stop talking and show up by her side, so she knew she wasn't facing it alone.

I peered into the visor mirror to make sure I didn't have any smudged mascara or other tell-tale signs of my emotional condition. The last thing she needed was something else to worry about. Swiping my hands on my jeans to rid them of sweat, I climbed out of my car. I was as ready as I was ever going to be. I marched up to the white door and knocked, hurting my knuckles against the wood.

A distant bird chirped, and a dog barked as scrambling sounds came from inside the house. I shifted my weight as the noise grew closer. When Chelsey opened the door, my heart lurched. She had tossed her dark hair into a sloppy bun, and her eyes were large and red from crying. Her clothes looked as disheveled as her face. She wore jeans under a wrinkled cotton white shirt with spills down the front.

She appeared like a shell of a person. Desperately wanting to make it better, I grabbed her by the shoulders and pulled her to me. She unleashed a torrent of tears. Shaking like an earthquake in my arms. I tightened my hug around her as she nearly collapsed, sobbing.

My grasp tightened on her shoulders as I fought back the tears. "Let's get you inside, so the neighbors don't see," I whispered.

I wanted to avoid any chance pictures of me splattered across magazines. It had been a while since I had been newsworthy, and, granted, this was Idaho, so I was probably being a bit paranoid.

Once safely inside, I guided her to the front room couch, pushed off a pile of newspapers, and sat her down.

Chelsey continued to cry as I wrapped my arms around her.

"It's going to be okay." I gently stroked her back, hot from perspiration.

"She's my baby." Her weak voice cracked.

I continued to rub her back. "I'm going to send her to a place in Mexico that's world-renown for helping people like her. They have healed a lot of patient's conditions. They're going to do the same for Ava."

Chelsey wiped her tears. "What?"

I flushed. I had rushed the news too quickly. It was too late now. "I'm sending Ava to Mexico to be healed."

She shook her head, no. "Now isn't the time for your crazy schemes."

"I have heard of this place again and again." My words came out way too fast like they always do when I become anxious.

"They have a huge proven track record. Let me show you on the computer." Before she could protest, I grabbed her by the wrist and tugged her toward her desk in the kitchen nook.

She stumbled along with me, clearly without enough strength to fight me, and muttered, "I need to go back to the hospital and see what the doctors say."

"We will." I planted her on the bar stool in front of her computer and held up a halting hand before she could speak again. "There are doctors in Mexico, too. Plus, many are educated in the U.S. and other international universities. A lot of them are traditional doctors. I checked all that stuff out. I know you're worried about hack places. It isn't that. This is a top-of-the-line treatment center and beautiful."

To bring up the site, I bent in front of her to reach the keyboard and clicked the mouse. "And, yes, you'll get come, too. I've arranged for both of you."

Her mouth opened, and I could feel her stare, but I didn't pull my gaze away from the computer screen. Her shock would be a distraction.

Several minutes later, I pulled up the site on the computer, showing lush green vegetation and giant, full palm trees.

She gasped. "It looks like a vacation destination, not a cancer center."

"This is where the very wealthy go when they have cancer."

Her brows furrowed. "This is all very kind, and I know you're trying to do everything you can to save Ava. I appreciate it, but I simply can't afford it."

I reached over and caressed her arm. "You aren't going to pay for it. I am."

She jerked her arm away from me. "I can't allow you to do that. You don't have that kind of money either."

I stood and faced her, heart beating hard. Now was the time to tell her what I had done. I had no idea what she would say, especially in her current emotional condition. "I'm going to do it, and I do have that kind of money."

Heat flushed through me as we stared at each other. I could see the pain of the current situation fading temporarily as her thoughts churned, considering my next words.

"What did you do?"

"What I needed to do to save Ava." I crossed my arms over my chest.

She bit her lip. "Tell me. What did you do?"

"It's fine." I looked away from her gaze. "It's all legal."

"Tell me."

I could not put this off for much longer. Besides, I had a plane to catch, not to mention a trip to pack for, and stuff to figure out where to store.

"I took *Millionaire Engagement* up on their offer... with one condition. Instead of paying me, they agreed to pay for you and Ava to stay at a treatment program for as long as the doctors determined it best for Ava."

"You *what?*"

"There's one catch," I continued.

"You did what!" Chelsey repeated.

"I agreed to have an episode shot at the Healing House. I believe the production company made a promotional deal with them. I don't care. This means Ava is going to have the best treatment in the world. That's what matters, and that what's important."

* * *

WE REMAINED quiet for the five-minute drive to the hospital. I couldn't leave without saying goodbye to Ava, even if my visit had to be short before I caught the plane. I was never good at pretending not to see the tubes running in and out of her or hearing the machine counting her vital signs as it stole away her innocence. Not to mention the harshness of the white hospital walls imprisoning us in these little rooms as if to mock us. Despite all these feelings, I needed to find my hope and smile, no matter how hard, before I entered Ava's room.

Somewhere in the parking lot Chelsey and I had silently hooked up arm-in-arm, clinging together in our unspoken pact as we faced the world and fought for our girl. The grey daylight and nippy weather respected our predicament as Chelsey's heels tapped against the asphalt of the parking lot. It brought back memories of our arm-in-arm walk in the cemetery toward our parents' burial plot. They had died in a horrific boating accident, and we had been thrust into full-fledged adulthood together—Chelsey nineteen and me seventeen.

Now, still braving life's cruelties together, we slipped through the hospital into Ava's room on the far east corner of the children's wing. Ava lay on the bed, a tiny dot swallowed up with tubes, a large mattress, and beeping machines.

My little girl had curled up in a tiny ball as though to protect herself. Her skin had faded to a light shade of green, as it often did when she didn't feel well. The doctor followed us into the room. Chelsey dropped my arm and turned to him for the latest update and prognosis.I left them to their discussion and slipped over to my baby.

Ava's hair was a tossed mess, probably from all the testing they had put her through. I reached out and stroked it, straightening it, shocked at how long it had grown. It seemed at least two inches longer since I last saw her. She was beautiful with her mom's pinched nose, even with her olive skin, a sickly green pallor, and her too-thin frame, thanks to cancer.

"Ava," I whispered.

She looked at me with a hazy gaze. "Chars, you're here."

I kissed her softly on the cheek. "I am, baby. I am. You're so beautiful. You must make it really hard for your mother to chase away all the boys."

She smiled. "I try." She closed her eyes.

"Baby, I'm going to go away for a while, but I want you to know I love you." I tried to say that without tears running down my face, but it was impossible. A few had started since the moment I saw my helpless baby lying there on those crisp white sheets.

Her hazel eyes opened. "Where are you going?"

"To be more famous."

She laughed as I had hoped. "What? Didn't you get on enough magazine covers last time?"

Now, it was my turn to laugh, knowing now I'd be on a lot more. I'd soon become a household name to many Americans. That hit me in the chest.

I could do it, though. For Ava. "A girl can never be featured on too many magazine covers. This time, I thought I'll stop being so stingy and have you on the cover of some of them, too. How do you feel about that?"

Ava laughed. "Really?"

The media would eat up my story, and I could wing it. I knew I could. I wasn't sure if I wanted Ava exploited like that, and I'd have to get her mom to agree.

"Would you want to be?" I asked.

"Of course!" A big smile spread before the energy drained out of her face. "What's it for this time?"

We had a staring contest until a small smile slipped onto her face. "Did they pick you to be the bachelorette that the guys pursue?"

I nodded.

She squealed. "Oh my gosh, that's so cool. Seriously?"

I nodded again to her contagious smile.

"Oh my gosh, my aunt's going to fall in love in front of the whole world and have the hottest guys compete for her. I can't wait."

The news had surely given her energy. At the same time, it started overwhelming me with the reality of what I had signed up for. Ava was right, guys would be competing. Not for me, really, but more like I was a tool for them to win fame and fortune. My neck tensed at the thought.

"Can I help you pick the guys?" Ava's eyes sparkled, looking at me, making my knees weak.

"Whatever you want, sweetheart."

"I can call you, right?" she asked.

"Of course, don't hesitate, morning or night."

"I'll watch the show and tell you which ones you should send home. You have to listen to me because I don't want you to be one of those dumb people who keeps the bad guy on the show so long, and all America is going, 'Why is that girl so stupid?' I'll tell you like it is."

I laughed. "I have no doubt of that."

"Plus, I want to be there when the two guys meet the family. I want to have my private talk where I drill them with hard-hitting questions, and I'll detect who's the jerk. I'll find you the hero, Auntie. I'm good at reading people. You've got to listen to me."

As she made plans, I stroked her hair. "Don't I always listen to you?"

"What?" Ava perked up. "You never listen. But you have

to this time. I get to be the maid of honor at your wedding. Promise me."

"I promise."

"And I get to babysit your twin babies. They're going to be so cute because your future hubby is a guaranteed hotty."

I flushed again, laughing.

Chesley walked back into the room and watched us with red-rimmed eyes.

More bad news from the doctor. They had to hurry to Mexico immediately if there was to be any chance.

CHAPTER 5

Andrew

$\mathcal{I}$ was in the middle of closing a deal with a young family in San Diego when my phone pinged in a text. I didn't pay it any attention and continued to explain details to the young mother and, eventually, where to sign to complete her application.

She smiled at me sweetly, and I flipped to another page in the back where she also needed to sign. At that point, my phone decided to light on fire. It buzzed and buzzed.

I smiled apologetically. "Sorry about this. I should've turned it off before our appointment." I flipped the silencer switch.

My client brushed it aside, and I launched into the required wrapping-up script. Besides the client signing up for the products, this was the second most important thing I did on a visit. Ask for referrals.

"Do you have any friends or family you think could also benefit from insurance?" I asked in my casual, off-the-cuff tone.

My phone vibrated. I shuddered. It did another round of intense shaking. "Good grief." I dug my phone out of my pocket. All the texts were from Gina.

I shut it off and continued the last three minutes of the sale. They didn't go so well, as I was rattled and edgy. I completely lost my natural, comforting air, and the lady had been jolted out of the magic of buying insurance and kept glancing at her refrigerator as I finished my spiel. Might as well not bother trying to secure referrals right now.

I took a deep breath, smiled at the young mother, and extended my hand. "I look forward to seeing you soon."

She avoided eye contact.

I dodged all the toys on the carpet and headed to the car, noticing our warm evenings were fading toward winter. I would've completely lost the chance to close any sale at all had the interruptions happened any earlier.

The door shut behind me, and I slapped my paperwork against my hand. What could Gina want? She knew I was often in a meeting and couldn't respond right away. I hustled to my car and put off returning her calls until I had comfortably merged into the heavy traffic.

Twenty minutes later, my car crawled onto the freeway, heading toward home. I expected a long journey during the peak of evening traffic, so I flipped on the radio. I made it about five hundred feet before I came to a complete stop. As I turned my phone back on, I debated whether to read

She jumped. "What?"

"You're trying to get me to go on a love reality TV show!"

She blushed. "Am. It's the audition. I need you to go there, or you won't meet her."

Her kids swooped into the room, bringing with them a lot of chatter and noise. Gina beelined for her young son and hugged him. "Wouldn't you want to see Uncle Andrew on TV?" she asked with a twisted smile, using her baby as emotional protection.

"Yes!" the kids cried out in unison.

I shook my head. "You've got to be joking."

* * *

THE DARKNESS of the past evening still loomed over the horizon as I parked in the two-thirds-full parking lot. Today would be the day. A good win against Charles on the racquetball court would clear my mind and give me the edge to focus on driving my sales quota higher than my racquetball partner and manager's.

Beating him on or off the court was never an easy feat. Off the court, he milked his British accent and tall, dark, good looks that drove clients to him, especially the women. A happily married man, he never yielded to the flirtations of women, other than to sell insurance policies. On the court, his advantage was crushing the ball out of my reach.

Today, I needed to find my groove and get back to where I controlled the ball and hit his weak spot—far left and about a foot away from the wall. For such an early hour, the traffic had been heavy and filled with half-crazed drivers determined to reach San Diego before the congestion became unmovable.

With the heater shut down, the cold seeped into the car, quickly making me regret not grabbing my sweatshirt on the way out of my apartment. Before climbing out of my car, I paused to look at my phone. It had buzzed happily on my way over to the gym. The caller was my sister. Rarely was she up at this hour.

Some chatty young ladies with bobbing ponytails, wearing long sweats and sweatshirts, sauntered past my car toward the entrance. I tossed my cell to the backseat, ready to be free of its electronic chain.

I checked-in at the front desk to find out which court was assigned... the farthest one back. I headed that way, passed the pop and chip machine, and noted empty courts sat available at this popular time of the morning. Soon, the courts would fill with grunting middle-aged men trying to reclaim their youth by hitting a ball.

The ugly brown carpet lined the court, probably put there to hide the dirt, but it looked tired and begged for replacement. Charles stood atop it, in mid stretching routine... he'd beaten me to the court again. He looked like a fitness guru, untouched by the weight of his two-point-five children and weekends filled with soccer games and honey-do lists. He was ready to prove he could manage his busy life and still easily declare victory over the single guy. He offered a welcoming smile, but I wasn't going to let him disarm me even for a second. I had fallen prey to too many of his low shots.

In no time, I had missed two easy shoots in a row. I shook my shoulders and gave myself an inner pep talk. I needed to keep my eye on the ball and not allow my thoughts to wander to my sister's silly suggestion. We were well into the second set—with me behind but fighting hard and ruthlessly—when Charles grabbed the blue ball and stared at me head-on.

My chest rose up and down as I gasped for a steadier flow of air. Unwanted thoughts of Charissa plagued me. What would she be like to talk to? Could I easily make her smile? What did her meals taste like? More practical thoughts intruded, too. How would she handle all the fame seekers if she did go on that show? Would she even consent to go on it? And, if she did, what would that say about her?

"Damn." Charles shocked my attention back to the game. "Something bothering you?"

"I'm fine."

"You're not fine. You're distracted. More than usual, anyway. What's eating at you? Your sales are fine this month, so what is it?"

Cold sweat pressed against my back. "It's nothing. It's just my sister's on my case. She has this crazy idea in her head, and she's bugging me about it. You know how women get."

Charles bounced the ball hard against the court wall and caught it. "I do. What's she fixated on?"

I hustled over to the corner to prepare for his serve. "She wants me to get caught up with some reality TV star."

Charles's whole face lit up. "You're kidding. That's awesome. Go for it."

"Why?" I loosened my grip on my racquetball racket.

"It's different." He took a breath. "Is she cute?"

I stood up out of a squat. This was going to take a while. "Yes."

"Do you like her?"

I spun my racket in my hand, getting tired of all the questions. "From what I can tell."

"Then go for it."

"Why?" I asked again.

"'Cause you don't want to live with the question of what would've happened if you didn't."

He hit his deadly low ball, taking me completely unaware.

THE CALLS, emails, and videos from Gina became unrelenting. She sent me clips of Charissa from the show. She sent me texts begging me to please audition. She reminded me that I promised.

Endless times, I pointed out the big difference between agreeing to meet someone and putting my life on hold for weeks by going on reality TV.

Another slew of texts buzzed in while I was at the office. I had taken to turning off my phone at appointments but didn't always turn it off here.

My supervisor, Charles, smiled as my phone buzzed from her lengthy texts. "Dating someone cute?" he asked.

"Nope," I said.

"Well," he said with his eyebrows raised. "Someone has a lot to say."

"My sister. She still thinks I should go on the show."

"Really?" Charles perked up as he scratched his head. "Well, it is out there. How popular is the show?"

"Very."

"No, kidding?" he asked.

I nodded. "Really. Can you imagine a more stupid thing to do?"

My manager shrugged. That wasn't the response I had expected. "Are the girls good-looking?"

"Girl," I said. "All these guys compete for the hand of one girl."

Charles burst into a huge grin. "Like fighting for the princess. I like it. You are a fierce competitor."

"True." I opened my files to make sure I took the right forms with me before heading out in the field.

"Do you know what she's like?"

I continued to flip through the forms, searching to find the one missing one. "I actually do. My sister keeps sending me video clips of her."

"Let me see," Charles said.

He was getting nosey. I pulled up a clip on my phone.

"Here. Look." I showed him the one with Charissa talking about JT and how she hoped he'd like the dinner she had cooked. She smiled her engaging grin, explained how she made everything from scratch and had been preparing it for days. She couldn't wait to give him a home-cooked meal because he certainly had eaten enough restaurant food. She was definitely quirky. She brushed at a few loose hairs tickling her face and wrinkled her nose in a charming way.

"She's great," Charles said.

I smiled and stared at Charissa. "I know. She's the type

of girl I'd want to bring home to Mom, if my mom was still alive."

Charles nudged me. "Go on the show."

Wide-eyed, I flipped my gaze to him. "What?"

"Go on the show."

"No way. You're as bad as Gina."

"It's an order," Charles said.

I laughed. "You can't order me. I'm not in the military."

"Fine, do it, or I'm firing you."

"I'm an independent agent. I'd just find a different supervisor."

"Look, man, I'm telling you to go on that show. You need a kick in the kabootski. Besides, the visibility will make it a lot easier for you to sell life insurance policies."

An older woman dressed in a tweed suit walked by and gave us a strange, inquisitive glance. He waited until she was out of hearing distance. "Would you listen? I'm trying to give you an easy out here. It's obvious you're into this girl. You couldn't blush any redder if you tried. You get this totally cheesy expression every time you look at her. Do you really want to watch her on national TV falling in love with someone else when you know it should be you?"

"No." Of course, I didn't want that. He was trying to scare me into doing it, and it was working.

He slapped my arm with the back of his hand. "She even cooks. I'll hold down the fort for you here. No excuses."

My supervisor was really pushing this. He was doing a fine sales job at it, too. It looked like I was headed for fame or losing my pride. At least this would make my sister happy.

* * *

A WEEK after I received the call-back, Gina hired a babysitter so she could drive me to the Long Beach ferry without the children. I didn't blame her. No one in LA traffic likes getting stuck in the car with fussy kids.

"You going to be okay driving back by yourself?" I rested my arm on the car door handle. "You'll be in the thick of rush hour."

Gina tapped her fingers on the steering wheeling as she slowed the car to a crawl. "Going to meet a friend down here for dinner and wait it out."

That sounded like my sister and wasn't a half-bad idea. The closer we came to the ferry port, the more the traffic increased. Interstate 405 was a bear. For as long as I had been in California, I had never seen this freeway uncongested.

She eased her foot on the brake. We had come to a standstill. I should have driven.

"I can't believe you talked me into this."

"When you marry her, I expect a big thank you. I expect you to name your first daughter after me. And, gratitude for being so happy every year."

I took a sip from my water bottle. "When I come home with my head between my knees, and I've made a fool of myself in front of America, I expect you to be satisfied and never set me up again."

Gina laughed. "That'll never happen."

"What!" I tightened my grip on the water bottle. "How would you even know that?"

I guess it was a good thing to have a sister who loved

me so much she believed in me accomplishing close to impossible. Today, though, it was irritating.

"First off," she said, "you two are meant to be together. I can feel it, and, as proof, so did your supervisor. It was all so perfect... he joined forces with me to get you to your future wife."

My shoulders lowered to release the tension I didn't know I was carrying. It was good to be loved, cared for, and to hear those closest to me verbalize the same thing I didn't dare admit to out loud. "Of course you think that. I find it damn annoying."

"Just so you know, baby brother, I care too much about you to ever give up. As I said, you two *not* hooking up... never going to happen."

She was never going to stop annoying me about hooking up with someone until I was finally married. Time to think about something else. "I won't be able to communicate with you to tell you how it's going."

A large pout covered her face. "That's terrible."

"Do you think you can live without knowing?"

The car went quiet. I focused on the swaying fronds of a palm tree in the distance. There was something about the California coast, despite it hosting ten percent of the United States population... a place modeled for vacation pictures with the sand, palm trees, and pastel sunsets. The people, the gangs, the fires, and mudslides couldn't rob this land of its beauty.

I looked over at my sister. Tears streamed down her face.

I reached out and tapped her on the shoulder. "Why are

you crying? I'm going to be okay. I promise. I'll try my best. I was just teasing you."

She sniffed. "I know."

Still... tears. I hated it when women cried. "What are the tears about?" I shifted my weight. "Come on, tell me."

She shrugged. "It's just that you're going to be gone. We won't be able to talk for weeks." Her voice broke. She wiped at her face and pressed on the gas as the cars in front of her started crawling forward. "It's no big deal. I'm being silly."

More tears. This time lots of them.

I squeezed her shoulder. My sister depended on me more than she'd ever admitted. I found it kind of endearing. "You're going to be all right. It's going to be okay."

She nodded as though she believed me, but the tears didn't stop.

Gina had been like this ever since our parents died. She had gotten worse since her stupid husband up and left. She liked to act like she was all tough and strong, and she was the one taking caring of me but, in truth, I was the one who helped her.

If I didn't come around often enough, her anxiety would grow until she slipped into a full attack, clinging to me with breathless crying. Or, when she couldn't sleep, she'd call in a panic late at night.

That's when I hinted I was starving and needed her home-cooked meals. It gave me the pretext to pay her grocery bill but also gave me an excuse to hang around. The more I showed up, the less late-night panicked phone calls I'd receive. So, in the long run, it amounted to self-protection.

"Look…" I stroked her arm, knowing it would be hard for her with me gone, and not knowing how long I might be away. "I left money for my groceries on the kitchen counter. You're going to have plenty of money to make me lots of food. If you can, just freeze my dinners in your freezer until I come home, I'd appreciate it."

Gina laughed. That was a good sign.

"Plus, I promise I'll sneak away and call you during the show. I'm going to check up on you. I won't tell you anything that's going on behind the scenes. I'll give you no clues, so don't bother asking, but I'll call to make sure you're okay. Plus, if I make it to hometown visits, we will both come and visit you."

She sniffed. "Mom would be proud that you're doing this. Just don't do anything she wouldn't be happy with."

Of course, a parting with a healthy slap of guilt. That was certainly one way to say goodbye. It didn't matter… I knew somewhere deep down inside me Charissa would be worth it.

CHAPTER 6

Charissa

he uneventful flight lurched and bounced, as most charter planes tend to do. I held a book in my lap, but I didn't bother to open it up once. My thoughts spun. I had called the store I owed the quilts to and told them I wouldn't be able to make them. They had been accepting about the fact and were excited about me being on the show again. I guess that was good.

Seeing Ava lying on the hospital bed, pale and weak, had hurt my heart. I hated it. A tear slipped down my face. Young people should never be in the hospital. That should be reserved for the old.

When I finally landed in LA, and the show's crew drove me to my hotel room, Dee burst into my room. She found a chair, flopped down, and kicked her feet up on the table.

She wore the same garb as last year. Jeans, black tee-shirt, and backward baseball cap complete with a dangling ponytail. She still chewed gum.

"There have been dramatic changes to the format of the show," she said as a greeting. "You'll be happy with most of them."

Business. Production. The intensity of this show was a completely different world than my Walden-like existence of only twenty-four hours ago. Still, I wanted to know the dynamics of the lion's den I had just stepped into.

"So, why were you in such a hurry to get me here?"

Dee looked at me, snapping gum, while she clearly pondered whether to answer my question. "We had a different star picked. Kendra. She agreed to do it but, at the last minute, backed out. According to her, she found love."

Feeling foolish standing, I slithered over to the couch opposite Dee and took a seat. "You don't believe her?"

Snap, snap went the gum. That would drive me crazy if I focused on it.

Dee grimaced. "Who gives up this kind of fame and national celebrity for love?"

"You don't believe in the whole premise of the show?" I asked.

She flashed her brown eyes at me. "Some people do find love along the way. JT and Maggie seemed happy together, even though they weren't the couple we showed the happy-ever-after scene with. Just remember," her gaze locked onto mine, "you have to break a lot of hearts along the way."

I looked into this woman's cold, hardened eyes. She

wasn't the easiest person to work with. She was reminding me of that… setting the tone. I understood. She was there to make TV, and that was what we were going to do. The faster we got this thing done, the faster I returned to Chelsey and Ava.

"Enough chitchat," Dee said. "There have been a lot of changes to the format. You're gonna to like them. First off, you won't be flying all over the southwest."

It was my understanding the reason we did that last year was because JT had a lot of business he needed to do while shooting the show. Since he was an important millionaire and famous, they had agreed to work around him.

"We aren't going all over the world either. We're going to put you on an island, and we'll fly men to you."

That sounded sexy.

"Okay," was all I said, in an effort to keep the meeting professional.

"We need to keep the *Millionaire Engagement* title, so all the men we'll fly in will have at least several million dollars. Since that dramatically cuts down the pool of available men, you won't have as many to pick from."

Great. Fewer hearts to break. Fewer decisions. So far, it seemed these changes were only good. "What island are we going to be on?" I ran my finger over the slick wooden table.

"Catalina Island. It's off of Long Beach. The only way to it is either by ferry or helicopter. You'll take the ferry, and so will the men."

"I like it." What else could I say?

Dee's face remained emotionless. "Also… here's another change you probably won't like. When the men first meet you, they'll have the right to decide if they're interested in you. They can simply choose to return home."

So, I was going to be experiencing more rejection on national TV. Of course, the show producers thought of this. After all, they were shooting the "dumped before dinner" gal. This time I was going to be the "dumped before dating" gal.

I blinked, then looked at Dee, obviously waiting for me to fight it. "That's fine. That's only right. It gives the guys a voice and opinion on this. The worst thing would be some guy pretending he liked me just because that's the role he felt he should play."

"Also," Dee continued as if I had not commented, "you'll not wear fancy dress, nor the men wear suits, like last season in Tucson. You're going to meet on an island, not in a mansion. You'll dress appropriately for a summer date on the beach."

"Which is what?" My stomach clenched.

Deciding on attire for the last show had been a brutal experience, but, lucky for me, Chelsey had helped me beforehand. She had put together a whole array of outfits. Not only that, she made me try them on before I flew out to be humiliated on national TV. She took a picture and printed each of them so I'd know and remember what went with what and what jewelry to wear.

Dee laughed. "Don't worry. You can get that goofy expression off your face. You won't be wearing your own clothes. You'll have your own personal stylist. She's going to do all the work, so you look good on TV. She'll provide all the clothes and accessories."

"Seriously?"

"Seriously," Dee said, with her first smile of our interaction. "Thank heaven I'm not in charge of it."

I erupted into laughter. "I think *I'm* more grateful for that than you are."

Her eyes snapped at me, but she thought about it momentarily. "I can see that. Now, we need to get busy. We have to build your backstory, so when you're introduced, you'll be interesting. For the next week, we have scheduled promotional ads for you to do."

I shifted in my seat. "Should I show you the picture of my niece, so you have a better idea of who I'm talking about? She's a great kid. America is going to fall in love with her."

"What?" Dee pinched her nose.

"My niece. The reason I'm here is so she can have the best cancer treatment in the world."

Dee rubbed her eye. "Oh, I remember hearing something about that. No, that isn't going to work. We have to keep the focus on love, not on some dying kid."

I doubled over, feeling like I had just received a punch in my stomach. How uncaring and ruthless can this woman get? My heart rate and breathing raced.

She momentarily stopped popping her gum. "Oh, sorry. I didn't mean to say it like that. I'm sure she's wonderful, but that'll depress America. It'd be best for her, and you and all the guys involved if we keep that a secret. America wants to see a love story, and we have work to do with you to make you interesting."

Waves of nausea poured over me. All of this came back to me. This was what I hated about the last show. The fakeness. The deception and manipulation. The producers' complete lack of morals and willingness to ruin normal people's lives. They had no trouble doing that. Those who made the decisions ate that kind of thing up like a snack, and would look around for more victims to destroy for dinner.

"No, we're definitely starting with the 'dumped before dinner' gal."

I folded my arms across my chest. "I won't do that." My breathing had increased.

"Did you put that in your contract?"

I felt my resolve give in. I couldn't fight that. "No."

"Should have. We're doing it."

I glared at this woman in her black baseball cap. I had been so focused on getting Ava the treatment I didn't pay attention to any of the other details. It didn't matter. Ava was going to get better. That was the important part. I needed to keep my focus. I zeroed my gaze onto her and clenched my jaw. My pride didn't matter.

*　*　*

TIME TO BARE my soul to the camera. I peered into the clear lens. The production crew stood outside the ferry ticket building on the dock, waiting for the next boat to transport us over to the island. The weather—of course—was perfect. After all, we were in Southern California, whose residents only tolerated seventy-five-degree weather. The afternoon glare slipped into my eyes, causing me to squint.

"No squinting!" shouted a cameraman.

I forced my eyes to open wide as I stared into the translucent mysteries of the camera.

Dee hunkered down next to the main camera. Her sunglasses, with the black baseball cap shoved down tight on her head, concealed most of the intensity on her face, but it couldn't hide the tightness of her jaw. The snapping of her gum competed against the call of the seagulls flying above.

"Construct your answers with the subject of the question in it," she ordered.

The light in the corner of the camera flashed red as I stood blinking, trying not to. What was I supposed to do with my hands? Fold them? No, that would be defensive. Hold them behind my back? No, too much "come and get me" posture. Shove them in my pockets? That would add weight—making the pockets bulge.

"So, what do you think about going to Catalina Island?"

What to say? Everyone's gaze rested on me, waiting. They should've prepped me, Maybe they thought if they did I would come off too rehearsed. I swallowed down the lump in my throat, closed my eyes, and pictured Chelsey standing in front of me. Talk to Chelsey. Pretend she asked me the question and just answer it.

I cleared my throat. "I've never been to Catalina Island before. Never heard of it. But, people have told me it's the Island of Love. Sounds like an appropriate place to begin my new journey."

My chest tightened. This was really happening. Don't think about that. Talk about last year. People relate to last year's experience. Remind them I'm something more than the girl who was dumped before dinner.

"I had the opportunity to go to cool places all over the west and southwest on JT's season, but I never had the opportunity to be on an island. I look forward to seeing such a beautiful location. So much so, that Wrigley, from the gum company, bought a part of the island sight unseen. Then, when he came out for a visit to see what he had purchased, he decided to buy the whole island."

When I did that part over, I couldn't help but chuckle and look at Dee. "Can you imagine being rich enough to say, 'Oh, I think I'll buy an island today?'"

Dee smiled. "Some of the guys you're meeting on this show might be. Maybe that'll be your life, too."

I brushed that aside. I didn't want an island. I wanted health for Ava.

"That's a take," Dee called.

For the next twenty-four minutes, I was off camera until we boarded the ferry. When it was time, I smiled and walked onto the boat as the crew filmed me from both front and back angles.

I only had to stroll onto the boat three times before they declared that shot "a wrap."

The sun was setting. We took the last ferry of the day out to the island. The men would be coming on a ferry tomorrow. I wondered how that worked for the natives. There would be no running to LA to party and catch a ferry later that night to return home.

No, if they came to the city, they'd be stuck for the evening. The sky streaked with color—royal blue on top, fading into shades of lighter blue until the color ended in a thin strip of yellow. The shading of the evening made the rippling water take on a grayish-blue. Other ferries floated in the distance. Buildings in Long Beach intermixed with palm trees and colored sky. The boat hummed from the motors working hard.

As time passed, the buildings of the mainland faded away, replaced by white ruffling water made by the boat's wake over the choppy surface. The glare of the golden ball of the sun lowering into the horizon bounced and roiled between wind-tossed waves.

The production crew left me alone for the time being, and I sat in the window seat in the main cabin area, which held only a scattering of people. My stomach had turned into butter from the rough sea. I closed my eyes and tried to breathe.

The production company interrupted the attempt to tell me the importance of shooting me on the ferry, gazing across the ocean toward the island with a longing expression.

If that was what they wanted, that was what they'd get.

I took several deep breaths and walked unsteadily from the main cabin, and headed to the staircase. Touching the wrought iron handrail felt like grabbing a sheet of ice as gusts of damp, nippy wind snaked around me. And, we hadn't even launched completely into the ocean yet.

Once upstairs, I folded my arms, wrapping them around my stomach as the wind tousled my hair. The film crew instructed me to stand, gazing hopefully at the upcoming island. I struggled not to shiver, but the wind, absorbing the ocean chill, pierced me. I muttered to the film crew that no one informed me I'd have to become an Eskimo.

My trembling progressed from jitters to full-force shaking in a matter of minutes. A young twenty-something gofer hustled around fellow crew members to secure me a thick black sweater. I hurriedly slipped into it, grateful for its warmth and the fact it was black, which appeared more slimming on camera.

"We're losing the sun. We've to get this shot now!" the director cried out.

This shifted everyone into action. The grip people fussed with the camera. My stylist, Monique, fiddled with my hair, which did little good in the constant breeze. I blinked my eyes, irritated from the fake eyelashes. My eyes watered in rebellion, and my eyeballs had become extremely itchy. These darn lashes would make me look like I was crying through this whole show. I didn't want to have a reputation for being a crier, like other girls on reality TV shows.

Dee hurried over to me. "For this shot, we want you to see the island for the first time. This is where you can see your dreams coming true. I want to see hope and longing. I want to see you believing you'll meet Prince Charming. It's now your time. Got it?"

Another cold gust of wind whipped by us. I had no idea how anyone was supposed to get all of what Dee just said into an expression, not to mention controlling the extreme nerves I was feeling. Besides that fact, I wasn't an actor, and I had begun to understand on a deep level, how much I seriously never wanted to be one.

Dee pointed to the spot where I would stand. To my

surprise, the boat roiled from the battering waves, which required me to use my abs and legs to stand sturdily.

They wanted me close to the guardrail, but not too close, to leave room for the cameras. I wanted to wrap my hands around the bar, but the camera couldn't capture my face that way, so I needed to stand a couple of feet back. Standing away from my crutch made me feel even more shaky.

"Look out to the mountain and the town in the distance," someone called out.

The spotlight shone. I collected my composure and stared in the direction they instructed. This was ridiculous. The crew wanted me to think about men and love, dating, and all that stuff, when my thoughts were on Ava and whether she had made it to Mexico safely. I hadn't received a message yet that they'd arrived. I should've heard by now. No, wait. Their plane left at... I started calculating.

"That isn't hopeful," Dee called out, interrupting my thoughts. "You look like you're going to the bathroom. Come on, the man of your dreams is being flown to you right now. You've been waiting for this your whole life. Let's make love happen, people."

Wow. I shook my hands. I needed to be careful what I thought about when the camera zoomed up close and personal. Apparently, it picked up on my emotions. More wind encircled me, causing me to shiver.

"Ready! Action." The camera's light flipped to red.

I still couldn't think of men and finding *the one* and all that other silly stuff. There were things much more important. I did need to get this job done, though. I looked out in front of me and the boat. This time I really stared out and saw the grayish-blue ocean with hundreds of rippling waves. The wind had picked up and stirred the water into motion.

Behind the grey water loomed a dark violet-hued mountain. A dab of orange light above the mountain on the right spread into a color scheme of yellow. White clouds layered on top of the pastel display, contrasting with the ever-darkening sky.

The view was magical. Nature at its best. Mesmerizing. So different from the nature display in Island Park, but still as impressive. The universe had its own unique power to create beyond what any of us mere mortals could capture. If nature could paint a picture like that every single night, which was exactly what it did, then there was a unique power to be able to tap into nature's ability to heal any condition, even people overtaken with cancer.

All was not yet lost. Mexico had powerful energy. Well, at least that's what I was told by people who knew those kinds of things. I stared at the dark blues and the power of the mountains. The next time I stood here, looking at them, I would be leaving this island, parting as a different person. It was highly unlikely I'd be filled with the love of video work or adventure. Instead, I'd be filled with an incredible yearning to go hang out with my favorite niece. She'd itch to embrace all it meant to be a young woman. I'd be more than ready to support her through whatever lay in store for her.

"Perfect!" Dee yelled. She hurried over to me and slapped me on the shoulder, almost dropping her clipboard. "You did it. At the beginning there, you had me doubting. I wasn't quite sure what we were going to do. I thought of taking nature shots, creating a voiceover, and leaving you out of the picture. That definitely wouldn't be as good as what we just captured."

Dee... Scary Dee... with her sour face most of the time, had just complimented me. I didn't even know what to do or say, so I blinked. This would be a long journey with my heart not in it.

CHAPTER 7

Andrew

*I*n the gentle California sun, Gina trembled in my arms as I hugged her goodbye. She shook like a frightened baby kitten, clearly dreading being completely on her own without me in town. I didn't want to think about the why behind her reaction, it would only make leaving harder.

My fingers twitched as she slumped back into her car, crying. Moments later, she drove jerkily away onto the backed-up freeway. She probably shouldn't be behind the wheel until she had gained some sort of composure.

Next up for me were ferries, islands, other guys, and national TV, all because I was attracted to a woman. I didn't want to think too much about what was going on for me, either. I glanced at my watch. I had arrived at the wharf fifteen minutes early. That would give me time to figure out the scope of the place. I paused to absorb the soft breeze fluttering through the large palm trees. Today, we had perfect weather, which never grew old. Taking a deep breath, I entered the musty-smelling building and approached a few staff members until I found someone who knew about the show and where to go.

A little later, as I plowed through another thick stack of waivers, a crew member informed me the ferry would leave in about thirty minutes. They asked me to please stay inside the station, so the production team could gather us quickly when the other men arrived.

More downtime.

A big display off to the side of the room caught my attention. A sign with shiny gold letters across the top read, *"Explore Wild Catalina."* I stepped closer to its rough terrain map, capturing miles of roaming wilderness. I hadn't given much thought to the location. I had only thought of meeting Charissa: pondering whether I'd find her big hazel eyes as captivating in real life, what type of food she enjoyed eating, and what she liked to cook.

Visiting an island with lots of wilderness to explore was cool. The map showed distinct variations in elevation. Next to the terrain map, a display showcased the vegetation and wildlife. The place hosted flowers, lots of desert plants, insects, birds, foxes, and buffalo. Buffalo struck me as curious. Did a Native American, way back when, haul in a baby buffalo in a canoe? Not likely, so how did such a large animal make it onto the island?

A six-foot statue of a bald eagle perched next to the display. A totem-pole painting on his body showed the ocean, island, shoreline, both land and ocean creatures, plus vegetation. This was a good omen of a fruitful life. I wondered how much I'd see, and if fruitful symbolism would work better for me than the "union" energy of Temecula. Before I could take that thought any further, a muscular dark-skinned man approached. He sported a crew cut and moved with military exactness and fierceness.

He extended his beefy hand. "Forester."

The guy must be going on the show, too. His grip felt firm, confident, and held nothing back, revealing a solid man.

"Andrew," I said, "*Millionaire Engagement?*"

"Yep. Great way to take a vacation."

He acted friendly enough. It would serve me to make the next couple of weeks more bearable if I buddied up. "Needed the savings?" I asked.

He stood solid, clearly not finding my comment funny. Maybe it wasn't, since we were all vetted millionaires. No question women would like him. In fact, out of the corner of my eye, I could see women already gawking at him. Hopefully, Charissa put more weight into other things besides looks, or I wouldn't last long.

"Where you from?" I asked.

"San Diego. Lawyer."

Made sense. He talked with precise confidence and did a lot more assessing than speaking. He leaned back and gave me an overall glance. "And, you?"

I tightened my hand on my suitcase handle. "Temecula. Insurance."

He nodded like that made sense. "Must be good." His blank expression slipped slowly into a huge smile, revealing white, perfect teeth. He slapped me on the shoulder. "Sorry, pal, that sounds boring. I mean, I buy the stuff because I have to, but I have the hardest time staying awake during my insurance guy's presentation. Glad somebody sells it."

I hiked my backpack higher on my shoulder. We were going to get along.

"Seriously? That coming from a lawyer?" I asked with a large smile of my own.

"Maybe." He laughed. "Let the competition begin. So, why are you here? Come to the island to get famous?"

"No, to meet Charissa."

He gave me the once-over. "The proper expression is 'to find love.'"

I shook my head. "We'll see."

"What's wrong with the girls back home? You look like an attractive enough guy. I'm sure somebody would be into you."

The guy knew how to push buttons. "Nothing's wrong with them. Want them?"

He smiled his big, white, toothy grin. "Naw, I'd rather take Charissa away from you. I'll save the women in Temecula, so you'll have someone to go home to. I'm a real giver that way."

I smacked him on his solid shoulder with an open palm. "So, with your oozing charm and natural good looks, why don't you currently have a girl draped on each arm?"

His eyes brightened. "Too picky. What's your excuse?"

Too much a workaholic. Too heartbroken. Too isolated.

"The same," I said.

* * *

I'M A COLLECTOR OF SECRETS: mostly people's fears, their worries, what haunts them. Sometimes I also collect their dreams, but that doesn't happen as often. Being a collector of secrets means I'm often engaged with others and pull their truths out of them. It makes me good at what I do and, because people trust me with their secrets, they trust me with protection policies. My tendency to engage with others and, in the process, gather their secrets wasn't something I planned to purposefully pursue before we landed on the island. In fact, I went mostly mute while the other contestants gathered and traveled on the ferry.

Once on the island, I noticed how the contestants didn't trust one another or the game we were about to enter. I handled it by keeping my mouth shut as we dragged our suitcases and/or duffle bags off to one side and gathered in the orientation meeting. The space looked like any hotel meeting room in the United States: blah carpet, cushioned metal folding chairs, and walls painted a muted brown. The only thing that stood out in the room was the commotion of the production.

Several production crew members moved round, disheveled, with stained jeans, holey t-shirts, and messy hair. Others scanned the room with wired coffee-eyes and clipboards in hand.

The closest contestant to me wore a cowboy hat over short traditionally styled hair, stood an average height, and wore a blue flannel shirt. The weather seemed too warm for flannel, but I guess it reflected a country-boy vibe. His voice carried as he talked with the staff about a football game played a long ago.

Just beyond him, by the doughnuts and coffee, hunched a shorter man with a head full of thick silver hair. He pressed his lips together as he took inventory of the pastries. He wore a pale blue dress shirt, just like so many financial planners. He had to be one. When he talked, he brought up the current political situation. Everything he said about it oozed with clichés.

Forester's booming voice came from across the room, joking with the staff. I hadn't noticed before, but a small soul patch dotted his chin. Not sure if that was a good move or not. Women were opinionated about those. He wore a thick golden watch and a linked-chain necklace around his neck.

Time to stop playing mute and figure this gig out. "So," I said loudly into the room, "are there only five of us?"

The men perked up to see who responded.

"Don't know," Forester said. He strolled over to my side, carrying a mug of steaming coffee and the scent of a heavy musk cologne.

"Andrew from Temecula," I said, gesturing toward my chest and glancing at each of the other men.

"How about you?" Forester called out to doughnut man from behind his newspaper.

The financial guy, balancing four doughnuts on his napkin, wandered over to our informal semi-circle. He paused to secure his treats. "Brett," he muttered.

The man in broken-in jeans and a flannel shirt strolled over to the group. He had a deep sunkissed face. "Shawn, from Wisconsin, a dairy farmer. Gotta love the cheese."

A man with buzzed brown hair, Army cut, in a red tee-shirt cleared his throat and walked up. "Trevor. Ohio, construction."

"Then there's Forester here… was it LA?" I asked.

He nodded and waved. "Pleased to meet everyone."

"Is that all of us?" I asked again. "From the clips of the shows I watched, tons of girls went after the guy. I expected there to be at least twenty of us. If there's only five, it isn't going to make much of a show."

"That's where you are wrong," came a strong, high-pitched, female voice echoing behind me.

I turned to find a very short lady with a black ponytail poking out of a baseball cap. She was wired to the gills, chewed gum, and sparked with attitude.

I moved my palm up in a questioning gesture. "Say again?"

"Each week, more men will fly in, and two guys will ship home."

"Two, which makes the chances to stay about fifty/fifty," someone said behind me. It sounded like Trevor… he'd done the math to figure out the odds.

Everyone here seemed bright, accomplished, and attractive. There would be no standing out in this crowd.

The firecracker nodded. "Yes, two. So, you need to be on your game the whole time. There's not going to be as much competition, but you have higher odds of going home sooner than in previous shows."

"Why the change?" asked Forester.

"We wanted to mix the show up from the way the other shows operate to make ours stand out, besides the fact we have older contestants," ponytail lady said. "By the way, I'm Dee."

So, production was on a tighter budget and not supported as much. "That's not the real reason." I knew all to well how corporations worked and the talk they used to cover their butts. When a company had money constraints, but wanted to look like they were doing well, they made "changes."

Dee flipped on me. "You better watch it. I can make your life hell."

A cold chill spread through me… my gieger counter for recognizing secrets. She was hiding something.

"Or, perhaps not enough multi-millionaire single men applied for the show?" Forester hurriedly offered.

Ponytail about-faced and scanned him up and down. "Yes, GQ, that's true. Do you have a problem with that?"

He dashed her a large smile with lots of white teeth. "Nope. Don't. I don't mind being one of the few. I got game." He winked.

The firecracker raised her eyebrow. "I'm sure you do. Why don't you save it for the contestant?" She moved her attention back to the rest of us. "Everyone gather around, so I don't have to shout." She gestured at the table next to her.

We trudged over and sat, spread out a healthy distance from one another.

"Now," the firecracker said, slapping her hands together, "like I said before, my name is Dee, and I'm the producer. I'll be walking you through what's going to happen and the rules of the show in a few minutes. Then we'll start shooting. Got that?"

Mumbled "yeahs" rippled through the room. Trevor's fingers started fidgeting by his side, and Forester's smile grew even bigger if that was possible. Shawn remained neutral to the news. I suppose that was how I looked, too, even though it jolted me to think the time had finally come.

"First, we're going to move to the wait station set up down on the beach. Once we get there, one of my assistants will escort you individually to meet our bachelorette." Dee droned on like she did this every day. "You'll have exactly four minutes to chat with her before you promptly trot down the deck."

"Four minutes isn't long enough." That came from Forester, again.

Dee raised her dark eyebrows giving him the warning signal that he better tread carefully. "It's a hell of a lot longer than what the contestants had on the other shows. No whining," Dee said.

She shrugged off her annoyance by shaking her shoulders, and drew her attention back to us. Her pointed gaze questioned if any of us wanted to push her further.

Note to self, don't mess with this gal. She had 'tude and seemed potentially dangerous.

"At the end of the dock," she said, as though she hadn't been interrupted, "you'll see two signs. One sign will say 'yes' and the other sign will say no.' You decide if you're interested in Charissa and if you think the two of you could be together."

"What happens if we decide we aren't interested?" I asked.

It was late in the afternoon, and they'd be pushing it to

have us catch a ferry back tonight, so it didn't make sense to send us straight home. Maybe they'd have us meet other women? "Do we get a shot with another lady?"

Dee's eyes narrowed in on me. "No. You'll be taken home. No questions asked, just a final goodbye to the camera that you're under contract to give, and then you'll be swept away to return to your normal life, no worse for the wear."

I pushed my chair back from the table and stood. "I'll go first," I said, not liking to wait for things.

Dee pointed over to Shawn. "He's first." She said in a tone to establish just how much power she held.

"Why him?" I asked to learn how operations worked.

"We had a nationwide pre-show vote. Shawn won. Best to lead with the nation's favorite."

CHAPTER 8

Charissa

*J*ust as they summoned me to the make-up and wardrobe station, the long-awaited text finally beeped in from Chelsey. Ava and she had arrived in Mexico safely. No major hiccups and, from the way she described the spa, it was even better than the ads. The trip wore Ava out, which was expected, but Chelsey couldn't think of a better place to rest.

Resting called to me, too, but I had to ignore its lure. It was time to meet my first batch of men. That sounded so weird—my men. My chin quivered, thinking about the attention and adoration focused on me.

The make-up room took over a hotel room, with supplies set out on every hard surface, and a chair plopped in the middle of the open space. After picking out a rather casual outfit for this whole affair with the wardrobe consultant, I perched onto the high salon chair as the make-up artist, Monique, examined my bone structure and skin tone. She squinted her eyes, deciding on the color my cheeks should be.

"We're going to be spending a lot of time together," Monique said.

I had suspected that. "I am glad you are going on this ride with me."

"What look do you want for the first meeting—smoky eyes, nude lips, dewy skin, or maybe a golden shadow and enticing red lips with full lashes? Or, strong brow creating an air of female empowerment?"

My stomach seized. If I didn't speak up, I'd have to live with the replays forever. My chest pounded. "No to a sex kitty, no to beach bum, no to GI Jane."

Monique stepped back, eyes narrowing as if to determine other possibilities.

Feeling an intense need to define myself, I said, "I don't want the men going after an image. I'd rather not look too sexy. Instead, be more who I really am."

She said nothing.

Had I offended her? Her attention flashed back to my brows. "Soft peach makeup it is. That will go well with your tan skin tone. I'll pull the same hue from your hair tones. It'll be an understated sexy. I'll combine the earthiness of bronze with the innocence of coral. Tones of brown will pull out your eyes. It won't be splashy like you're worried about, but more of a quiet allure."

My stomach had started to ease its grip when the hotel door opened. Dee stormed through the doorway. "This is how it's going to go down..."

I wasn't sure if she spoke to me or someone on her walkie talkie.

"You will sit where the guys will approach you one at a time." She walked over to the chest-of-drawers and leaned against it as she talked at me.

Guess she was speaking to me.

"You get exactly four minutes with each guy. That way, both of you will have an impression, but nothing more."

This seemed surreal. Everything was being thrown at me at once. I tried to take a deep breath, but my throat was too tight.

"After talking to you..." The smirk edging Dee's lips wasn't calming me any. "The guys will walk out of view and decide which way to go. If they go right, that means they want to get to know you better."

She acted like she expected me to be upset about this or something. "It gives the men some power. I suspect most of them will stay, whether interested or not." She shrugged. "They wouldn't want to give up their chance at fame."

I flinched when Monique tugged hard on my hair. "You'd be surprised." She flashed a sharp look at Dee. "I saw a similar set-up on other shows. One guy did choose the end of the road... a good, honest upright guy."

I closed my eyes for a few seconds to ground myself. I was going to look stupid one way or another. The show would find a way.

Monique stepped back, surveying her work. "Ready to meet your first prospect?"

She spun the chair so I could see myself in the specially lit mirror. I had transformed from the scraggly appearance of tumbling out of bed, to shiny hair that moved in a flattering way around my face. The makeup, soft and subtle, brought out my eyes and lips. My new look complimented my earth-toned, sweepy blouse and skinny jeans.

"Great job."

I gave her an appreciative hug.

As we pulled apart, she winked at me. I stumbled down off the stool and headed out of the room, following Dee, who apparently wasn't in the mood for dawdling.

The afternoon had turned overcast grey from the morning layer in this tropical paradise, but I couldn't take time to pay much attention as I scurried to keep up in my three-inch heels. Dee talked as we walked down the uneven cobbled road toward the rippling ocean.

"Here comes Nancy." She pointed in the distance. "She's the former Miss America and your show's host."

Great. I would "win" standing next to Miss America. Perfect. That would be a fun contrast for the guys. It definitely would highlight how pedestrian I was. It would be a miracle if any guy expressed an interest after this.

I hustled the hundred feet on the sidewalk until, at the end, it changed into dirt. My high heels wobbled under my weight, and I struggled toward the sunshade, where I would meet the men. Behind the filming set sprawled a deck, right on the ocean with a bar at its end. My absolute inexperience walking on flimsy stilts showed. I never even thought of wearing them last time I was on the show, but now, as the star—and based on advice from my new stylist —I felt unspoken pressure to wear those things. I would probably have been in fear of spraining my ankle, but the horror of the upcoming moments stole my thoughts.

"Charissa, you need to sit under the awning," Dee called

at me from behind a camera. She pointed in the direction of the set. "Millionaire number one is one his way."

That sounded sexy, but I didn't have time to give it any attention. I hurried as fast as my shoes would allow and stumbled onto the bench. My stomach twisted, and I tried not to think about how badly my heart pounded. Maybe I hadn't done enough recovery from last time. Maybe I wasn't ready for this. I reached into my pocket and felt the edges of Ava's photo. Maybe none of that mattered. I took it out and looked up from the picture to a tall man, slender and a bit lanky. He approached in cowboy boots, Wrangler jeans, and a long-sleeve plaid shirt and moved with the grace of a giraffe.

Without taking my gaze off him, I turned the picture over and slipped it into my back pocket. I struggled to swallow the lump in my throat as a gentle breeze tickled my neck. Seeing him strolling so casually made me even more jittery.

I don't think I had talked to a guy since, well... since the last time the cameras rolled on me. Several cameras followed the first contestant. I shouldn't have, but I glanced around and spotted three other cameras aimed at me. Seeing their filming lights shining bright red didn't help my nerves any.

Time for me to step into the dreaded spotlight. I hated that every twitch of my face recorded on camera. I clenched my hands into fists and watched the cowboy approaching. The closer he came, the better the view with his sandy brown hair... short, but not enough to hide its sexy waves. An afternoon shadow made him look extremely masculine. His broad smile captured my breath as he extended a hand long before he came to me. It made me realize I shouldn't be sitting on the bench waiting for people. The proper thing would be to rise to my feet and greet him, which I struggled to do on my heels. I stumbled up to him. He more caught me than shook my hand. Heat flushed through me, and a bolt of energy shot through us as we touched.

His crystal blue eyes gazed down on me. That large goofy grin made him adorable and highlighted his brilliant white teeth. "Are you okay?"

I nodded, feeling even more embarrassed.

He eyed my feet. "Those are quite some trees you have for shoes there."

I looked down and realized he was making fun of my shoes. He wanted to play. I should go along with him. "Well, obviously, you have never had short people problems."

He laughed. "You're right. I never had. I'm Shawn, by the way. I'm from Wisconsin."

He took my hand and sat me next to him on the bench.

"We are a place filled with cheese and good people with old-fashioned values."

"So," I said, liking his catchy, flirtatious nature, "Shawn, from Wisconsin, what are you doing here on the Island of Romance?"

He smiled one of those smiles that revealed dimples and his ability to steal just about any girl's heart. He must be really popular among the women.

"I'm here to woo you."

I burst into laughter. I was pretty sure it was nervous

laughter because he had been so blunt. I'd never had a guy talk like that to me before.

"Really?" I tried to pretend like I still had dignity. "And, how do you plan on doing that?"

He squeezed my hands. "By catching you when you fall, among other things."

This man was clever. "Touché," I said. "So, when you are not flying across the country to woo girls on TV, what do you do?"

"Dairy farmer." Pride filled his tone.

He must embrace some of those old-fashioned values he bragged about. I didn't know dairy farmers could make that kind of money. He must have a large farm.

"Well, Shawn, I get the sense that you're good at what you do."

He smiled. "You mean dairy farming or wooing? I demand excellence in everything I do."

"Next," called the producers. They signaled it was time for me to move on to meet another guy. I didn't want to move on. I wanted to talk to Shawn. I could talk to him for a long time. I wanted to look into those blue eyes. I could get lost in them. They were incredibly mesmerizing. Plus, I sensed we had a lot in common.

"Looks like my cue to go." He pulled my hands closer to his chest.

The warmth of his touch seeped into my fingers and radiated up my arm. My whole body felt on fire. I couldn't hold his gaze, so I tipped my chin downward, feeling sweat pop onto my neck. A drop trickled down my back. This man was super hot and charming and had an intensity about him. Because of the way he looked at me, I simply didn't know how to react.

I froze.

This didn't stop him. He gently brought my hand up to his lips and kissed it. His afternoon shadow brushing against my skin sent more tingles through me.

"Well, until next time." He winked.

I was glad I was sitting because I was pretty sure my knees would have given out from that last move.

He stood and left. I slumped back in the bench with a sigh, fanning my hand against my chest, and muttered. "Now, that was hot. I hope he stays."

My face exploded from the heat exchanged between us. I didn't care, because I thought I had already found my man.

The fact that Shawn walked away from me caused my heart to twist. I had not been charming, or smart, or funny, or flattering, or any of the things men liked. No, I just sat on this bench like a bump on a log, and the one time I stood to greet him, I almost fell. He had to come to my "rescue" like I was a helpless little princess.

Ugh.

Ava would be watching this. How could I face her after being so dorky and awkward?

A dark shadow appeared in the distance. The camera light flipped to red. A huge wave of nerves flushed through me. I needed to meet someone else. This man would, likely, be good looking, too. Not possibly as attractive as the first, but he *had* been selected for the show. Americans weren't like the Brits. America had a tendency to like to watch only beautiful people on their television screens.

The approaching man was shorter than Shawn but solid. The clouds shifted, and the sun slipped through to spill over him. He wore jeans, dress shoes, and what appeared to be a light pink polo shirt.

I blushed. He was very attractive, too.

It took a brave man to wear pink. The social media feed would light up from his choice. There would be articles written. Can real men wear pink? What does it say about a contestant who shows up in a pink shirt? I would say they were extremely good-looking and had the confidence to wear it.

Despite the distraction of potential social media commentary flooding through my head, my body shook. This man sported a large smile that drew me in. He also had thick, longer hair that fell into waves, enticing a brave woman to string her fingers through it.

"Hello, there," he called out in a friendly way, his voice deep and sophisticated, like a classical trumpet.

I stood, my knees shaking as much as the first time. Good-looking guys made me nervous, and the super high heels didn't help. The clouds traveled over the sun again, casting relief from the blaze. Wanting to learn my lesson from the last suitor, I needed to be welcoming.

"Hi." I extended my arms to him. It took me a few seconds to realize I extended my arms too soon. He was still quite a distance away.

Recognizing my mistake, he broke into a jog and hurried to me, wrapping me in his strong arms. A woodsy, rustic smell washed over me, causing me to almost swoon. I closed my eyes and breathed it in. I could curl up in that scent forever.

He pulled from our embrace.

"Nice to meet you." I looked into his gray eyes for the first time, as clear as a perfect water-skiing day. They sparkled with life, energy and held a flicker of what I hoped was interest. He kept his hands on my arms, radiating warmth where he touched. I had grown as hot as I had with the Shawn, maybe even warmer.

"You're even more beautiful in real life than you are on TV."

Complete flush. Yep, I could see the headlines now, declaring I was the reddest bachelorette of all time. I needed to say something but had to force words out. I was the focus of this show, after all. I had promised I wouldn't be boring. But, his eyes, the interest he showed in me, caused a definite head rush.

"You watched the show last year?" I squeaked out.

He shrugged. "No. It's not my thing, but when my sister saw you, she recorded part of the show you were in and had me watch. She declared you were the perfect woman for my soul mate and me."

He had just said the words "soul mate" less than two minutes after meeting me. That was intense. He didn't seem to notice my alarm because he continued.

"So, after a lot of pressure, I'm here to check you out myself."

I slunk to the bench, needing its wooden strength to steady me through this. "Hmm," I said, at a loss for words. "I hope you don't feel pressured to stay if you don't want to."

Now, was his turn to become beet red. "I didn't mean it that way. It's good I'm here. I'm glad. I had to meet you. I couldn't get you out of my head after seeing you on TV. I have so many questions, plus, I really think we could be a good match." He sighed. "I'm rambling. Sorry. I'm a lot more nervous than I thought I'd be. It's been a long time since I've tried dating. I'm never nervous, but here I am, blithering to the most beautiful and amazing woman..."

He studied my face. "You're a good person. Your heart is beautiful. Come on." He grabbed my hand, sending sparks through me. "I have already messed up most of my time with you, but I don't want to ruin the whole thing."

He tugged me up and pulled me to him with firm determination. I fell onto his chest, his cologne washing over me, luring me. I had to fight the urge to snuggle up to him. He grabbed my other hand and dove into a waltz. I stumbled into a rhythm with him, despite my shoes, as he moved me across the pebbled ground. It made me laugh and like him even more. He was funny, awkward, and not well-rehearsed, which I found irresistible. Maybe because he seemed vulnerable and real like me.

"Time," the producers called.

"Time," he whispered, his hot breath tickling my skin. "I need more time with you. By the way, my name is Andrew."

CHAPTER 9

Charissa

*A*ndrew begged me for more time with wide searching, gray eyes and a shaky voice, at his very last moment with me. Two men. Both extremely attractive and both blessed with startling eyes. I needed to have another look at both of them to decipher the different shades.

Shawn had such an easy air about him. It was like he knew he was a country man, not a boy, and he was comfortable with it. He acted like he had all the time in the world. With Andrew, I was more aware of a ticking clock. It was strange that a man so attractive and wealthy could be so nervous. That, I hadn't expected. He must be a computer programmer or something else with zero connection to people. He gave me the impression he didn't get out much.

I sat back on the bench, thinking about what had just taken place. The producers wanted me to say something so they could put it on the air. I glanced at one of the camera people.

"Did you see how nervous Andrew was? That was cute. He seemed too embarrassed to admit his sister was the one who'd encouraged him to come. Poor guy." I shook my head and laughed.

"Do you hope he chooses to stay?" a director asked.

I couldn't hold back my smile. "Yes! Did you see the way he asked me for more time? And, how he thought I was so beautiful? He's funny, real, and super attractive. Who could resist that?"

There was something about Andrew, even though he clearly wasn't as polished as Shawn. Though blunt, he had been so honest. I wondered about his sister. Why she was so proactive in picking a girl for him? Why she thought I'd be a good choice?

Soul mate. He had actually used the words "soul mate." That was completely shocking. And funny. He seemed so embarrassed about it when he realized what he'd said.

I was still smiling when I looked up to see another gentleman heading my way. This was getting intense. I thought about jumping up and doing a dance and singing, "It's Raining Men," but instead, my curiosity took over.

Immediately, I could tell this man was different from the other two. He had broad shoulders—super wide—and dark skin. He carried himself with power like he was aware of his girth and proud of it. The afternoon was slipping into the evening as I watched. He wore a nice, quality-looking black shirt and jeans.

Squinting in the sun—which had popped out again—I smiled at him as I stood. His hair was cropped super short, like his nicely trimmed soul-patch He strolled up to me as if he owned the place and extended his hand. "Forester." His voice sounded extremely deep.

He could probably crush me with one hand if he wanted to.

"Charissa," I said, surprised at the difference between each of these men. "Nice to meet you."

I tried once again to control my sweating. This man caused my heart to race. I wanted to squirm out of my skin. Instead, I shuffled my feet, a mistake because I wobbled again and tried to catch myself by extending my arms.

He stepped up to steady me and laughed as he looked down. "Not used to those heels, huh?"

"No, not really."

"I like a woman who can wear a good heel."

I nodded, not sure what to do with that statement, other than to realize I was striking out. A fleeting thought warned me he seemed full of himself and was the type of man who wanted his woman to conform to his tastes.

"Okay. I have to admit I don't find the need to wear them much."

He took a seat on the bench, head shaking, signaling I should try to stop balancing on my stilts. I had planned to take these shoes off before he arrived. If I had, maybe our exchange wouldn't be so awkward.

I stumbled into my seat.

He looked at me. "So, what do you do if you don't wear heels much? Don't you need them for work?"

This reminded me of being in trouble when I was little. "First off, I live in Idaho," I said, heart pounding, "so heels aren't really practical. Second, I work from home, making quilts. And, third, where do you live, and what do you do that makes you think heels are so important?"

His eyes turned harder. "A country girl. I don't think we have anything in common."

Aware of the camera still rolling and that this was supposed to be an introductory meeting, I gulped.

"Maybe not." I forced a smile. "Sorry, I didn't catch your name or where you are from?"

"A lawyer in LA. I work on a lot of social justice issues, and my name is Forester."

He was smart and, from the gruff way he was treating me, knew what he wanted. Apparently, I didn't fit the picture. I was going to try to salvage what I could and hope he didn't speak too badly of me.

"I like your name," I said.

He nodded. "Thank you, Madam."

I peered out in front of me at the crew shuffling around. "Sounds like you are up to important work."

He suddenly shifted in his seat. "Look, Charissa, I'm sorry about this, but we can stop all the small talk. I can tell right now this isn't going to work. You and I come from completely different worlds. I'm looking for a woman who gets me and who can support me in my mission for social justice. No offense, but you live in Idaho, and I doubt you have any idea about what I do. I have a lot of important legal cases I walked away from in order to be here, and I can already tell from our first meeting this was a mistake. I don't want to waste your time, the producers', or those guys who are here to date you seriously."

He paused to take a breath. "I'm going home to return back to my work, but thank you for meeting with me. You might not know it, but our meeting has been helpful in getting me clear with what I want in a relationship."

He stood and sauntered off into the sunset.

Good riddance. I couldn't believe he had said all that. He had just barely met me, and he was making all sorts of judgments. I didn't know what set him off. Shoes?

"Say something," one of the producers called out to me. "Tell us how you feel about what just went down."

I nestled my hands in my lap like a prim and proper lady. "Well," I said, blinking as I looked at the camera on the right, "Forester was... is a very attractive man. He seemed like he was intelligent and had an interesting mission in life. One I might like to know more about."

Tears rose in my eyes. "Apparently, I'm not going to have that chance." My heart pounded in my chest, reminding me of my vulnerability and of the pain currently spiking my heart from rejection.

"That goes to show that I'm not for everyone. He completely had every right not to be attracted to me. I'm glad he told me now and had the integrity not to string me along. It's a two-way street."

"Take," called Dee. She marched up to me as I wiped at the corner of my eyes. "Charissa, here's what's going happen next. You have more guys to meet. After you do your exchanges, which hopefully goes a little better than the last one, I'll escort you to the patio where the guys who choose yes will be waiting."

"Great," I said. "So, I get to see and talk to them more."

"We'll see," she said with an air of mystery. I thought she did that to annoy me. If she did, it worked.

Embarrassed heat spread through me. I hoped Shawn and Andrew had picked me.

At that moment, I saw a businessman in the distance decked out in a suit. Dee scurried away from me. So many men. This place *was* raining men. I squared my shoulders to be ready this time. I was already standing, so I got that part right. I waited until I could look him right into his blue eyes to extend my hand.

"Hi, I'm Charissa," I said once he got the right distance from me.

"Trevor," he said.

We shot questions back and forth, and I learned he was from Ohio; owned a construction company; and liked sports, playing pool, and listening to music. As we talked, I felt like I was answering a live dating questionnaire. We hadn't gotten to anything real when the time was up.

After Trevor left, Dee came back. She launched into where she had left off. "While you're there, you get to pick the three men you want to spend the most time with, and they'll stay with you and hang out in the hotel for another week. The remaining men, if there are any, will be flown home in a chopper." She pointed in the direction that the chopper must be in.

The producers of the show probably stayed up late thinking about how cool it would be to create camera angle shots of a chopper at night. It would be dramatic to film close-ups of the rejected men one-by-one climbing into the chopper to be whisked away from me and the

Island of Romance. Women around the world would be sad to watch the men go.

"How will men find out if they're staying or not?"

"We have a mini ceremony set up on the patio. You'll give a shell to the three men you choose to stay. The other men, if four or five men have elected to continue the journey with you, will know they haven't been chosen if they remain empty-handed."

A noise echoed from Dee's walkie-talkie. She held up her finger. "Just a minute," she muttered into the device. "I'm prepping the star. I'll be over there in three."

The wind had settled to complete stillness, but my insides stirred up a storm. I couldn't even picture looking each guy in the eye and telling him I didn't want to continue a relationship. When JT had done that to me, it was like he had taken a razor blade and sliced me. The flesh wound still remained, raw and red, and now I must do that to somebody else.

I could be nice to the guys and as gentle and under-standing as I could when I rejected them but, from personal experience, that didn't mean it wouldn't leave wounds and scars. I was extra sensitive, more so than others, but still, I'd have to look at these men—who put their lives and income on hold—just to see if there was a chance. That was flattering. That was kind. And something I didn't take lightly. That was something no other man had done for me before.

"After handing out the last shell, you'll wait to see if there are any who want to talk to you. You're more than welcome to walk them out and over to the helicopter. That way, you can explain why they weren't picked," Dee said. She obviously did not care about the upcoming pain.

"But, I just met them," I cried out.

Those could be really awkward conversations. I couldn't even do it with JT when I was on the other side. It would be unimaginably hard for me to explain my selections, even one-on-one.

"It'll be the same drill week-in and week-out, so you might as well get used to it," Dee said, with what almost looked like an evil smirk.

This wasn't going to be fun.

Dee sneered at my shoes. "You're awful in heels. You'd better tell the wardrobe lady to keep you in low-heeled shoes. This is me being nice to you."

She said that phrase with so much seriousness it made me think the gesture wasn't normal, and I should be grateful. She tilted her head back, and her jaw clenched tight. She shifted her weight. "You're so bad at standing in those shoes, it'd be completely funny to have you in extremely high-heeled shoes throughout the rest of the show, *bu-u-ut…*"

My shoe buckles pressed into my foot. I had no idea how anyone wore these things for an extended amount of time. I kicked them off, and they tumbled onto their sides like they'd decided they were done for the evening.

"Since I do feel bad for you about what happened during your last debut, and since this show is actually supposed to be about love, I'm giving you this break."

Pity from Dee? I involuntarily bristled. "Thanks," I muttered. The throbbing of my feet increased like a little heart had been inserted into my sole. *Thump. Thump.* That increased my need to pee. Meeting these men was a lot more stressful than expected.

I rolled my shoulders in circles. They crackled. I must've had them jacked up to my ears for them to hurt like that. I yawned.

Dee slapped me on my shoulder. "None of that. You need to look super excited. Let's get you to wardrobe, then off to see the *men* again." She said "men" in an irritatingly suggestive way, like they were human toys to purchase. "You will make it in time for the sunset if you stay on schedule, so hurry to hair and makeup. I want to shoot in the next half hour. The men have been waiting long enough. We're going to lose the natural lighting. I know it is a lot for one day, but that is the way it rolls. "

I dashed toward the bathroom. Once inside and away from all distractions, I took a breath. Most of the men were very attractive, smart, and interesting. I used my secret phone, hidden in my pocket, and called my sister, even though I didn't know the time where she was.

She answered on the third ring. "How is it?"

I hustled into the stall, not able to hold back the need to pee any longer. Chelsey was just going to have to put up with the sounds in-between me pushing the mute button. "Can't talk long," I whispered. "Are you guys doing okay?"

"We're having a wonderful time. It's very healing. Ava did a lot of sleeping after we first arrived. I've been sitting out here on the porch, letting the breeze wash over me and journaling. I almost feel like I'm on vacation."

My shoulder lowered, releasing tension. "Good. You need it."

"How're the men?" Chelsey asked.

I paused before answering. I shouldn't say much. I wasn't supposed to have the phone, and if, for some radical reason, someone found a way to tap either of our phones, that would be bad for the show.

"Better than expected," I said. "I don't have much time, and I can't say much. I just wanted to see if the two of you were all right."

"You don't sound like yourself. What's wrong?"

That was just like her, to pick up on my uneasiness. "I'm having a hard time getting my head in the game."

"Feeling guilty?"

I hurried out of the stall and over to the sink to wash my hands. "How did you know?"

"That's your pattern. What is it this time? Is it saying goodbye to some of the guys?"

That, too.

"No. It's 'cause I'm not with you. I should be with you and Ava."

Chelsey's sigh erupted loudly in the earpiece. "Should have thought of that one. Look, we wouldn't be here if you weren't there. Enjoy the men, the attention, the food, the cool events. Sis, you of all people deserve it. You've been a saint through all this, and now is the time to enjoy the spotlight on you."

Pressure built in my chest.

"Charissa," she said in her bossy, older sister way.

My attention snapped back to the phone. I was done washing my hands and needed to have my hair done. "Yeah?"

"You messed up your chance last time because you were so focused on others and what you could do for them that you completely left yourself out of the picture. JT didn't see the real you, so he couldn't fall in love with you. Don't make that mistake this time. We need you to succeed so we can secure the treatment for Ava."

I hadn't thought of that. The more I was loved, the more support for Ava I'd be able to achieve. We had no idea how long this healing process would take, and if she needed more treatment, I would probably be able to cover it by doing the show.

"Guilt's gone," I said too loudly. "Thanks, you're the best. I have to dash."

I loved having a sister who knew me so well. It was awesome to have her just a phone call away, no matter where she was in the world. With my anxiety level lowered, I hurried over to have my hair done. I smiled at Monique.

"Up do," I said.

She raised one eyebrow in approval. "You want to break their hearts in style?"

Well, if I had to break their hearts… "Yep."

My stomach knotted. I really didn't want to think about what that would be like, but I did need to decide who I'd keep.

"Well," Monique said long and drawn out. "What do you think?"

I lifted my hand out from under the hairdressers' cloak. "Hot. Every one of them was very good looking and smart." I waved my hand at my lips for emphasis.

She smiled. "Now that's a problem I'd like to have. Who are your favorites?"

My jaw dropped. "I'm not supposed to say."

She leaned into my ear. "Actually, I'm really the only one you can say anything to." She combed through my hair. "I hear all sorts of things. So, what do you think?"

I couldn't wait to talk. "There are definitely two of them I'm super excited about."

My enthusiasm continued as I talked endlessly about the men. We did take a break from the guy talk to discuss more reasonable shoes and a new style for tonight, going from sweet girl of the afternoon to a sexy evening look. I wanted the relationship to be built on who I was first. I wanted to see who'd stay around for that.

CHAPTER 10

Andrew

*W*hy did I just confess everything the moment I met the woman? Seriously, that was awful. I had made a complete fool of myself on national TV. Now, we had something in common.

I don't think I have ever been so nervous around a female... or so attracted. That wasn't normal. What had me so freaked out? Cameras? The pressure of other guys? Or, was it her? The way she looked at me with those big, beautiful eyes closed my throat and scrambled my brain.

I sauntered down the dock, aware that cameras zoomed in tight on me, ready for my next move. At times like these, it was best just to own it, so I shook my head and muttered. "Now, that was stupid."

I looked up and saw the dock path had ended. In front of me perched two-foot-wide, wooden signs. Dee's instructions had been to stop in front of them. Look at both. One painted with the word "Yes" in white, and the other "No" in black. Pause. Then we were to take a step and say out loud why we made our choice.

Following the orders, I stopped and looked at the "Yes" sign pointing to my right. If I chose to continue on this journey, I'd walk down that path and go to an outdoor bar where I'd wait to see Charissa once more. I'd also possibly be hanging out with other guys who thought it'd be a good idea to continue this journey with her. Or, guys who simply just wanted more airtime. Hard to tell.

My eyes flickered to the "No" sign. If I turned left, I could stroll right out of this mess. My sister would just have to accept that it didn't work out. She wouldn't be happy, but what could she do but set me up with someone else... which she certainly would do.

A breeze spilled over me, smelling of fresh cool sea air. Seagulls squawked in the background, highlighting the urgency to pick something. I needed to come to the ocean more often.

"Clock is ticking. Decide," called out one of the show people.

Red crawled up the back of my neck. I wasn't doing myself any favors standing there looking dumb, frozen, not able to make a decision. I understood on a whole new level how easy it was to look bad on reality TV—compassion for Charissa and what she must be experiencing swelled in me.

I looked out along the endless miles of ocean. The wind stopped blowing. It had nothing to say—not unlike Charissa, who had been mostly quiet. She just peered up at me with those hazel eyes of hers and shook like she was scared.

Of course, I had to stay.

* * *

IT DIDN'T TAKE LONG to walk down the right deck to find the bar and Shawn. Naturally, the farmer had taken the path to learn more about Charissa. Why wouldn't he? Charissa was a strikingly beautiful woman, charming and smart with a simpleness about her that made her irresistible, as I had just expressed for the cameras.

It wouldn't surprise me if all four guys said yes to her. She would be incredibly hard to say no to, even if I *had* made a fool of myself on national TV.

Shawn sat at one of the tables with a cocktail topped with a little umbrella poked through a green olive.

"How did it go?" he asked with a smile of confidence.

I donned my poker face. "Fine," I said. "And, you?"

"She's definitely what I'm looking for."

Not sure what to do with that, I nodded. "Didn't Trevor go right after you?"

"No, he went after Forester." Shawn looked around. "But, now that you mention it, where is he?"

"Did he decide he wasn't into her?" I asked.

Shawn shrugged.

I was pretty sure what his absence meant. "One less guy to compete against." But, this didn't set well with me. I don't like winning by default.

Shawn smiled and rubbed his hands. "Yep."

I motioned to the bartender. "A water, please."

The bartender looked between Shawn and me and nodded. I strummed my fingers against the table. "Wonder how Charissa will feel about it."

Shawn furrowed his brows. "That will suck. She seems to take things personally."

He swirled his drink, watching as the liquid moved in a dizzying pattern. This was definitely an awkward situation the producers put us in. Guinea pigs were placed in an experiment to watch through a camera lens and record how we reacted in ever-changing circumstances.

Studying Shawn and listening to the waves crashing against the dock pillars below us, I thought about what to do. "You seem to like Charissa, really."

Shawn's head bent, watching his drink spin. "I do."

I nodded. "I do, too. How about we make a deal?" I scanned the bar to make sure no one from the show lurked nearby. They were sneaky and might have someone hidden out of sight.

His eyes flashed up at me. "What kind of deal?"

"No matter what happens, we both always put Charissa's needs first. If there's some crummy guy here, we watch out for her and take care of her."

Shawn's eyes narrowed. "I would do that, anyway, even without cameras." He puffed up, offended.

"So would I, but if we could be friends, it would be easier for Charissa."

He took a sip of the drink, tipped his chin back, and studied me. "That's true. Friends then." He extended his hand, which I gripped and shook hard.

The sky turned darker as we waited. Soon after the deal

was made, Forester showed up looking a bit startled, for the lack of a better word.

It didn't take long for Shawn, Forester, and I to become absorbed in a good discussion. Raised in Compton, Forester had proven himself and worked himself out of one of the roughest cities in California.

Forester just started talking like something was on his mind, and he needed to get it out. "When I met Charissa, I thought our differences would definitely be a no go. I tried already to leave, but Dee was on me like used gum. She would hear nothing of it. She thinks I should give it a chance because we could create a unique relationship coming from such different backgrounds. She said Charissa could give me a completely different perspective that might really benefit my life. I am not sure what to think about it. But, if by a small chance Dee is right, I decided to give it a go."

That sucked to hear that Dee was fighting so hard for Forester and Charissa's relationship. That certainly wasn't good news.

"Do sports?" Shawn asked him.

He shook his head no.

"Wow," I said, surprised. "Thought you had to play sometime. You look like a top athlete."

He nodded. "You aren't the only one who has assumed that. I'm in the top one percent of physical shape in the nation for my age bracket."

"Good for you. Now, what is it that you do that qualifies you for the show?" Shawn prodded.

He must have forgotten Forester told us when we first met him.

"Lawyer."

I jabbed Shawn in the ribs. "We better watch out."

Our attention turned to Shawn, and we discovered his dairy farm business used some bold business ideas to grow. I was impressed and could tell he had a good head.

"Did you always want to raise cows?"

A dark shadow caught my attention out of the corner of my eye. Up the walkway strolled a man in a business suit with short-cropped blond hair.

"Hello, guys," he said.

Shawn stood from the table. "Remind me your name?"

The newcomer gave an easy smile. "Brett. I had to bug out for an unexpected business emergency and am now just getting back into the game."

"We met earlier, but you didn't meet Charissa like we did. You're still part of the show?" I asked. He was good looking, too, if a person liked the banker type.

"Yep. I had a business deal I had to attend to before I arrived, and my plane was delayed because of fog." He shook his head. "I told the pilot not to worry about it. I would get here when I got here, besides he had to wait for me to pack." He laughed. "I had no idea what to bring."

"Do you always disregard the rules?" I asked.

He shrugged. "I do what I want when I want. I always get what I want. Charissa might not know it yet, but she will be mine."

* * *

THE SPLASHING of waves under the outdoor bar created a calming effect. Maybe the production staff thought it would aid crowd control. Even though there weren't many of us, I could see the board determining it as an effective method to keep our impatience to a minimum, or maybe they wanted to evoke impatience, but it appear like that wasn't what they were up to.

More than half an hour had gone by since Brett tricked his way into our exclusive party on the ocean. He talked surface stuff, which bored the secret-finder in me. So, I watched the deep grey waves twist to their own rhythms. It tempted me to dip my toes in. If I did indulge, my touch would access a part of the Pacific, which made its way to the southern ocean, dripped into the Indian and then the Atlantic, and eventually journeyed up to the Arctic. My touch would become a part of a world-wide connection. A shiver of awe dispersed through me at the thought of such an expansive contact with the world.

Nature established calm with its predictable rhythms. The sun always rose and set. The waves of the ocean always splashed and gripped the shore before retreating. The sky always painted a fantastic display of mystery. Every day and every evening a different canvas. Nature was constantly creating, expressing, and moving.

I stood on the corner of the bar's porch, peering at the gray depths of the ocean. I could be getting plenty of work done, but no, I had to wait. I peered out over the water at the dense varying shades of clouds.

Finally, I moved closer to the group, and I lowered myself into the chair across from Forester.

"Do you know what happened to Trevor?"

"Apparently, he opted out," Shawn reaffirmed, looking to Forester for his reaction.

"I guess *some* people are allowed to do that," Forester muttered, rubbing his shoe on the ground.

I stroked my hands against the tablecloth. Shawn seemed like a good guy who was more content with sitting around drinking than I was. Before I could think of a question to ask him, I heard footsteps.

Charissa appeared, with her jaw drawn tight. Everyone stopped talking and watched her shaky approach. She no longer wore the high heels. The trembling must be due to something else. I saw her glance nervously at the cameras a couple of times, so it could be just the fact she was on camera. She clearly dreaded what she had to do... I could tell from the awkward way she moved.

She had changed her hair since we last saw her. It piled up appealingly on her head, exposing her neck. She now wore a long dress, a wonderful light shade of green which complimented her eyes and her lightly tanned skin. She was stunning.

Forester whistled.

"Hi, guys!" She smiled, the white of her teeth popping.

Chairs scraped against the deck as each man rose to his feet. We all moved away from the table and gathered in a semi-circle around her, me closest to her. I looked down at the flats she now wore. That was smart. I still planned to stick close to her, though.

"I'm glad so many of you have chosen to continue this journey with me," she said. She glanced down, then looked up shyly, but directly into each of our eyes. When it came my turn, our gazes connected in a soulful way. Maybe I imagined it, but I swore she held my gaze longer than the others'. I couldn't take my eyes off her. She was one gorgeous woman.

"Wow, only one person who decided this was a no-go," she said, revealing nervousness about us rejecting her.

Trevor. Stupid man. I was sure he would not have problems finding other women. His sophistication might be a mismatch for Charissa anyway.

"So," she said, staring at the space in front of her, "It's now my turn to pick who I'd like to join me for a fine dining experience the show has planned."

My chest tightened. Charissa looked like a child forced by a parent to apologize for something she didn't want to.

Her fingers twisted together as her face pinkened. "With that, I want to thank everyone for taking their time to travel here and for the opportunity for me to meet you."

She was considerate of us and our sacrifice. She felt gratitude. All of these things were good signs. She stopped talking, and everyone grew quiet, emphasizing the sound of the waves.

A flash of red light caught my eye. I turned to my side to see the recording light illuminated on the camera, which focused on me.

"Keep going," Dee called out.

I wanted to snap at Dee and tell her to stop pressuring Charissa, but that would make things worse. Charissa's large, scared gaze landed on me. Now was my chance. I winked at her.

A small flicker of response came from her, and she started talking again. "I don't take lightly the sacrifices you all have to make. I was in your shoes last year, and I know how hard it can be. All of us have family at home, and sometimes family who needs us." Her voice broke.

All her nerves spread to me, and I felt them for her. I winked again. I doubted she saw, but the cameras did.

A well-dressed lady with shining brown hair stepped up and smiled at all of us, like a professional coming in to save the show. She was clearly the more polished lady of the two. This must be the host Dee told us about... Nancy, I think.

The newcomer placed one hand on Charissa's arm. "As a symbol of Charissa's affection, she has chosen to give out shells to the three lucky men who she wants to continue with her in the show."

She waited for the cameraman to zoom in closer. "If you do not receive a conch shell, I'm sorry, but your journey will end here. We have a helicopter waiting," she gestured to the north "to fly you back home."

A helicopter? They made us take a ferry here, and now a helicopter to highlight our failure. I calculated the travel time. I could make it back to my bed by two or three a.m., depending on how bad the traffic shaped up at that hour.

"Charissa," Nancy said, gesturing to her. "It's time for you to hand out your conch shells."

All light had faded from Charissa's face. "Before I do that," she said, voice shaking, "I wanted to explain to you why I am using conch shells. Yes, we're on a romantic island, and yes, it is good reflection of the island, but there is more to it."

She stopped to finger away a section of hair that had blown onto her thin shining lips.

"The Buddhists use conch shells as a symbol of truth

speaking. With a relationship, communication is an important determiner to make it work. I certainly made my mistakes with that last year."

She paused and took a breath. "Not that I didn't tell the truth, but I didn't speak up and really share who I am. I don't plan to make that mistake with you. Also, the Buddhists see the conch shell as a symbol of strength. If we're going to do this journey together, all of us are going to need strength. This might get messy at times, and I want strength to be with each of us."

I liked how philosophical this woman was. She was a thinker like me. I smiled, and maybe had a sparkle in my eye, but I couldn't help it. So far, I thought Gina had made a good choice in selecting Charissa.

"The Hindus refer to the conch shell in their tradition of prayer. Also, it was one of that culture's weapons of choice. They thought the conch provided strength and fortitude. That is my wish for all of you."

This woman had a tender heart despite life's problems. That was rare. Even though she was the center of attention, she thought about us. I smiled again at her, letting her know I appreciated her words.

On the table next to her, she grabbed the first conch and held it up. "This is the most ancient musical instrument from the beginning of time. It's a gift from the ocean that connects us to the whole world, so I give this to you as an invitation for us to make music together."

Dee yelled from behind us. "Charissa, one man has to go home. Get on with it."

She looked up past us at Dee. Her fingers trembled

more, and higher color rose to her face. She gave a gentle nod as though she was used to it.

"I have a hard time telling people no," she choked out. "I like to make people happy, and make sure they're having a good time. This is going to be hard." She cleared her throat.

A tear shimmered in the outside corners of her eyes. The poor thing was struggling. If she didn't choose me, I needed to be cool with it for her sake. I didn't want to make this any worse for her.

Holding out the conch shell-like she didn't know what to say, she said, "Shawn."

Shawn? She had said "Shawn," the okay-looking dairy farmer. Maybe he had been right about his connection with her.

I had felt a dynamic connection myself, but maybe she didn't. My vision blurred. I was already more into this woman than I ever expected to be, but was happy about it.

I wiped the sweat from my hands onto my blue jeans as I felt the damn camera lock onto me, wanting to capture my reaction. That was the fun of the show for everyone else. Maybe I should've listened to myself and stayed in Temecula. I could be closing a deal right now. That thought sounded lame, even to myself.

Shawn strolled up to her. He moved too close, and she seemed to subconsciously lean on him. It wasn't good for my psyche.

She looked at him timidly, her eyes soft and kind. "Will you take this shell?" she asked.

He laughed. "That's funny… a shell instead of a flower. I get it. And, yes." He took it and pulled her in into a tight hug. He held her for what I deemed as too long and strode over to the allotted victory corner.

This was worse than playing football. I forced myself not to look at Shawn or the conch shell anymore. Instead, I studied Charissa. A toughness seemed to ooze from her face. I hadn't seen that strength before. Maybe she *could* handle this.

She picked up another conch shell and smiled at the remaining three of us. Brett stood next to me. His breathing grew loud, nearly like a fog horn. It was disturbing, but I chose to ignore it. If he was such a big businessman, he should be used to this kind of stress. It might be too late for him to start caring, but I didn't blame him for starting to worry. After all, we were on national TV, and nobody wanted to be dumped under these circumstances. But, if she was not going to choose me, I'd prefer it happen now than later. I'd much rather get back to my real life and sell more insurance policies than stand around drinking, waiting, and sharing a few brief moments with her.

Her hazel-brown eyes looked up at us all as she held out the shell. I tried to catch her attention, but she concentrated on her task. She looked past us all. Maybe this was her way of coping and being able to do what she knew she had to. Her fingers rubbed against the shell, probably to calm herself.

"Forester," she said, eyes snapping onto him.

My gaze zapped to the lawyer in huge surprise. He looked at me, and I gestured with my head for him to go up and take the conch shell.

He hurried over to Charissa and stood in front of her,

blocking her from my sight. But, I had no doubt the cameras were all over their exchange.

"Really?" Forester asked.

"If you want to." She spoke with an edge to her voice.

Something wasn't right between the two. I looked over at the other remaining man, Brett. I hadn't spent much time getting to know him, so I had no idea what I was up against. Certainly more uptight than me, he wore slacks and a collared shirt well. From appearances and a few word exchanges, though, I had the feeling we were really different from each other.

He raised his eyebrows at me as though to suggest, "Here we go."

Forester had moved over to the victory area, appearing more dazed than anything. I suspected he really didn't want to be here and hid a different reason to come onto the show than to find love. Maybe Dee's interest in him remaining on the show sparked his ambition. Or, maybe she'd convinced him Charissa might be a better match than he originally thought. So far, I didn't know why he'd decided to stay after all. So much for my secret-finding skills.

By the time my attention returned to Charissa, she had another shell in her hand, which shook even more than before. She would be saying goodbye to someone with this shell.

It was either Brett or me. This was worse than waiting to see if I had closed on a big sale. She was a beautiful woman, but it was more than that. I could tell she was big-hearted. I wanted that. She was so different from the callous women who lined my past. She also had said something similar about the ocean… that had to mean something. She seemed to think deeply and reflect on life. Not many women I met thought any more deeply than about which new purse to buy.

Her face went pale as she peered down. I thought I saw a tear fall. Behind her, the sky had bent into an almost pitch black, coated with grayish clouds that spread out over the horizon. A gust of wind swept in and blew against us, and she held out the conch.

"Andrew."

CHAPTER 11

Charissa

The headlines were going to read, "Trembling Charissa." There was no way they wouldn't. I doubted my hands and legs could've shaken any harder. There was an intensity to having all those very good-looking guys staring at me, all sending me energy to pick them. They had all chosen me, and they wanted the same in return.

"Wow," I said to the hairdresser. "That was intense and upsetting. I'm sorry I'm so sweaty."

She smiled. "You're fine. Don't worry about it. Let's pin-up the few strands of hair that fell out and get you back to dating."

My stomach tightened. "I doubt I'll be able to eat. How does a girl date three men at once, not to mention the one who flat out told me off? I don't even want to look at him. I can't believe Dee made me keep him."

Monique smiled. "She does that… Now, think about it, gurrl, you're about to eat dinner with three attractive men. I'd sincerely adore that problem."

I swung the back of my hand at her as she fixed my hair. We were instantly becoming good friends. "Knock it off. I'm serious. How am I supposed to do this?"

She narrowed her eyes. "Okay, since I like you, and you're doing this for a good cause, I'll help you out. I want you to know this is rare. I certainly didn't help the last few stars."

Relief washed over me. "Thank you," I whispered. Now, two staffers had told me they were doing me favors. Odd.

"No, don't go thanking me. You aren't going to like what I have to say."

A chill crept over me, and I sat taller in the hairdresser's chair, bracing myself.

"You gotta go in there with confidence, like you know you're the catch, and each one of the men is lucky you chose them. Men love confident women. Also… and this is even more important for you to remember, men are built to want to please women. They want to be our heroes."

She tugged hard on a section of hair on the back of my neck.

"Ouch," I muttered.

Monique didn't pay my whimpers any attention. "You need to give them a standard. You have to make it obvious you expect them to perform up to, and even exceed, that bar. Challenge them. Make them rise to be your hero. They'll respond. Promise."

Her lips swished back and forth as she moved to the side of my head to examine my hair. When I had thought she was done dishing out the advice, she added, "Also, if you don't go in there blazing, they'll turn against each other and fight among themselves to prove who's the king of the castle." She grabbed hairspray and squirted.

The blood drained from my head. She was right, I didn't like her advice. These were tall orders, though I suspected she gave me just what I needed to hear. I wasn't sure if I even could pull off bold, let alone confident.

"Great," I said, noticing for the first time that Monique had a picture of Ava placed in the corner of the mirror. "You put up Ava! How did you get her photo?"

Monique's whole face lit up with her bright smile. "Sure thing, I put up Ava's picture. We could use her courage." She reached for a spray bottle and squirted the back of my head. "I grabbed your 'hidden' phone from the pocket of your previous outfit while you were changing, and sent a picture of her to the printer." She laughed. "You never know what I will do."

That was like Trevor. Though attractive and nice, I hadn't had the foggiest idea of what he intended to do either. I had been a no go for him. He seemed like a family guy, but our conversation had definitely been strained and awkward. That alone would explain his choice to not stay around. Despite that fact, though, he left me with a twinge of annoyance.

Ava would say, "Never mind him."

Knowing her, she'd leave it at that. But, how could I when Forester still hung around? He had stormed off yet showed up, claiming he chose me. What was that about? I had to find out.

Monique's fingers worked their magic in a matter of seconds, taming my hair into a shape it had never been in, ever. She did all this before I even noticed. I said goodbye to her and hurried to my next location, a small upscale steakhouse overlooking the sea.

Its furniture was small traditional southwestern with a splash of strong red and orange. Impressionistic paintings of people and landscapes with a modern twist dotted the walls.

The ocean breeze, palm trees, and sailboats calmed me. Then Dee came into view. She peered at me with a raised eyebrow, daring me to speak. I cleared my throat, realizing sooner than later I'd have to get over my intimidation.

"Why is Forester here? Why was I instructed to keep him?"

She gave me a blank stare.

"He said I wasn't the right woman to have by his side. I wasn't 'social justice' enough."

She shifted her weight. "He had a change of mind and decided to give you a chance."

"Give me a chance?" I squawked. Blood pounded in my head. "You've got to give me a break. Like he's some God's gift to women."

She crossed her arms over her chest. "To a lot of women, he is. He's used to getting his way. Do you want to upset his world?"

"What?" I asked. This woman was working me, and I was too angry to figure out a way to stop her.

"Do you want to get even with him and teach him a lesson?"

I blinked. "No."

Waiters passed by us, giving us curious glances. I wasn't going to allow myself to be embarrassed in front of other people. I wouldn't fall for her egging. She wanted to make great TV. Whatever that was.

"Of course, you do. That's why I had him choose you."

I had climbed into such a toxic environment, I wasn't sure I could navigate it if it became any worse. Poor Brett had the humiliation of being the first one cut when he had simply failed to ignite a sparkly conversation with me. Yet, the rude, judgmental activist stayed. If there would be any justice in this game, I would to have to act more boldly and be willing to stir the pot and go against the rules. Nausea swept through me. I doubted I could do it.

Dee patted me on the arm as if consoling a fussy two-year-old. "Don't worry. This is going to be good for you."

"Then why is Forester still here?"

"At the end of the day, he chose to stay, and you chose to keep him," Dee smirked. "The best thing you can do now is give him a chance."

I glared at the woman. She had some incredible nerve to say that.

Dee repositioned her cap nonchalantly and snapped her gum. "I actually think you two have a lot in common, and it's a shame you haven't had the time to discover it about each other."

I immediately started considering if that might hold any validity. I stopped, cocked my head, and stared at her askance. She was still trying to work me. Dang, she was good.

I shifted my weight and gave her a level look. "What could I possibly have in common with that man? We come from completely different worlds. He comes from edgy Compton. I'm from Idaho Falls… the simple land of snow, potato farmers, and people who waste their lives gossiping."

My breathing came out ragged. Her assumptions were unbelievable. How could she so casually, without even blinking, mess with my life?

"LA scares me. It's a big city. I'm a country girl. He wants someone who'll take on the world. I want to retire from the world, but I haven't been able to yet. What could you possibly find that we have in common?"

She tipped her chin a bit, clearly registering my disdain. "You both are passionate about your own social issues. He's active in the political world, and you're active in the health world. Both those worlds touch on politics. Both those worlds fight for improvements and to make peoples' lives better." One hand propped on her hip. "I've been doing this a long time, and I see and know things you don't have any idea about. This is why I'm the producer. I'm damn good at what I do. So, stop questioning me, and sit at that table up against the wall. I want shots of you gazing at the ocean, thinking about your men before they arrive."

* * *

AFTER DOING THE CAMERA SHOTS, I fiddled with my fork and spoon as I sat tucked away into the corner of the dark steakhouse restaurant. I stared at the off-white tablecloth and the shadows playing across it from the quivering little candle in its center. The men would soon be here, including Forester. He and I needed to talk because I wasn't going to let him be rude and get away with it.

I had calmed since our initial upset and almost reached a place of peaceful contentment as I stared at the cobble-stone roads leading out to the ocean. The blackness of evening blanketed the water, giving it a mystic feel.

When something rattled behind me, I turned to see a crew member walk into the room. He looked middle-aged with streaks of grey in the midst of brown, wore an expen-sive suit, and headed my way with a confident stroll.

I forced a smile.

"Charissa, I wanted to take a moment to introduce myself, if I'm not intruding."

"No, sit."

I gestured to the chair next to me.

He pulled out the chair a few feet away from the table and sat. "I'm Edward, the show's pilot. I know how boring these things are."

I stifled a yawn and laughed. "They are. So, how are you, Edward, the pilot?"

He cracked a partial grin. "We have something in common."

"What's that?"

"We both have loved ones suffering from cancer." His eyes held an immense deep pain.

I gasped. "Oh, I'm so sorry. May I ask who?"

"My wife. Just diagnosed." His eyes teared up. "If you don't mind me asking... If you do, it's okay just to tell me so, but I have to try. Some of the crew said you might have some answers about how to help... ideas that are... well, nontraditional."

My back straightened. I couldn't claim to have answers, but I could share the information and resources I'd found. I taught him what I knew until we received the signal from the crew that the men were on their way.

Edward stood. I rose to hug him goodbye. When we drew apart, he held appreciation in his gaze.

I studied the hurting man. "Come talk to me anytime, Edward. I know how hard it is. Even if you just need someone who understands, I'm here."

CHAPTER 12

Andrew

I made it in. Barely. Charissa waited until the end to give me the shell. Was she sending me a message? Or, was that what the producers wanted? It seemed like they did have a lot of say.

The evening had grown extremely dark, especially with the blackness of the ocean outlining the town. The producers had silently escorted us off the dock when we finished with the shell ceremony. Even the ocean waves seemed to die down to stillness, waiting with me for the next time I would be with her.

"We're going to take you to the restaurant," one of the crew members said but volunteered no other details.

My stomach growled. It had been hours since they last fed us. Maybe they wanted to see how we operated on low blood sugar, hopeful for contention between us.

Feeling grouchy, I followed our escort off the deck with my shoulders hunched and head down. As we made our way into town, I didn't even gaze around. Charissa choosing me last was getting to me more than it should. Finally, I mentally slapped myself. It meant nothing. The way she looked at me was what mattered.

I finally stopped resisting the urge to look around. The dark outline of a mountain range stood as a backdrop to the harbor, which held lines of sailboats rocking gently in the breeze. In the distance, a lighted white circular building bumped up against the mountain. Palm trees, strategically placed around the structure, reminded me we all were searching for love in a tropical paradise. A host of small houses and buildings dotted the hill. Dim light seeped out of the homes, which suggested that, despite the darkness, a lot of life still graced this island.

The director marched ahead with Forester by his side. Shawn trailed them, a few steps ahead of me. The air had calmed, and yet I sensed something behind me. I glanced back to see a rectangular house among the dark shadows, hovering at the edge of a cliff. A few hundred feet below the house perched a larger white residence. More houses dotted the incline until they merged into shops.

Shawn slowed for me to join him. He gestured to the large house. "It's rumored the owner built it for his fiancée, but she never showed up. He sat on his balcony every night watching and waiting for her."

Melancholy settled on me. "Why didn't she come?"

"The rumor has it she was a mail-order-bride and had cold feet."

Love could be so brutal sometimes, like when Vickie—

my former love interest—told me all those bogus stories about her family falling ill. I felt so bad for her and even helped pay the medical bills with money set aside to form my TV production company. It had all been a scam. She stole both my heart and my dreams.

"How do you know all this?" I asked Shawn.

"Read up on it before I came. Wanted to check into any business opportunities while I'm here."

A businessman on the hunt. Doubt he would've fallen, like I had, for a lady who'd snatch his wallet. "Dairy farming isn't enough?"

Shawn chuckled. "It's a risky business. There are good years and bad."

"Going to move to the west coast?"

"Not a chance. I'm just looking for business deals to invest in, like Wrigley did."

My shoes slapped against the cobblestone streets. The town was small and pleasant with a European feel. It must be something to own most of this island. That had to make a man feel like a pseudo-God. He could create and build a world to fit almost anything he could conjure up.

"Wrigley did pretty well," Shawn went on. "He made this a destination point for the Hollywood celebrities of his time. He threw huge A-list parties, plus managed to transport the film crews out here."

So, the gods decided to go for more wealth, connection, and power. Not sure if I would've made that choice with an island to myself, but there was no question this would be a good place to shoot movies.

I noted Shawn had shifted the conversation to neutral ground. No gloating. Our tour guide paraded us by a lot of restaurants. All of them small, and most of them had quite an open feel with outdoor porches and tables. Most touted either seafood or steak. A few were Italian.

Shawn saw an opportunity in this settled island, maybe more than he did with Charissa. Maybe he was here for businesses. But, I couldn't shake the look between Shawn and Charissa when she gave him the shell. There was a connection between them. But, there was one between us, too. She had, after all, kept me around. It was early in the game.

This town was a quaint get-away... a good backdrop to fall in love with Charissa. Some would leave this island, no doubt, broken-hearted. But, the waves continued to splash, and the sun continued to rise and set. The question remained, whose heart would break?

A BIRD SQUAWKED OVERHEAD, drawing my attention. The tour guide stopped so the rest of us could catch up. The bird screeched again. He was right. I needed to squawk at their rules. This wasn't just a game. This could mess with my future life. It was weird, but I felt something different toward Charissa than I had with anyone before. I really, really liked her. That was worth paying attention to and seeing what it meant.

I had never played by the status quo before, not in sports, not in work, and I wasn't going to fall into it now. No, it was time to up the game, no matter what the producers said or the other guys thought.

"Okay, gentlemen, you are here," the tour guide said.

"Go up the stairs, look for Charissa, and enjoy your dinner."

That was my cue. I brushed by Shawn and tried to pass Forester, too, but shuffling by a person who could pass for a former linebacker turned out to be formidable. It didn't happen. Forester barely fit in the extra-narrow staircase. His broad shoulders brushed against the red wallpaper wall.

Who followed two steps behind him? Me. Feeling like adolescent fighting to ride shotgun in a car, I reassured myself I'd secure a seat on one side of Charissa, whichever Forester didn't claim first. Shawn was a nice guy, but he'd have to fend for himself.

At the top of the landing stood a long narrow bar with people watching TV. The lighting was dark to create the mood. We found the place mostly empty with tables waiting for the next patrons. In the far distant corner, Charissa sat gazing out over the ocean with a lit candle in front of her. It flickered shadows on the table and shone on her face with a mysterious light.

For being such a big man, Forester was amazingly quick. He dashed to Charissa's side in record time, with me trailing. I didn't stop to notice what Shawn was doing. I needed to secure my seat for my "date," if you could call it that. Technically a date occurs between two people, not three men and one lady.

Forester spared no time hugging Charissa. She seemed to disappear into his arms. Not wanting to watch them, I studied the table, noting Charissa's pushed-back chair. She greeted Forester on the right side. I leaned over the table, grabbed a water glass, brought it to my lips, then smacked my glass down on the place-setting to the left of Charissa. Spot claimed.

In her evening gown, she extended her arms out to me for a hug. Her hazel eyes softly took me in. My lips curled into the crooked smile high school girls had loved in my day.

"Hey, gorgeous," I said not too loudly. I didn't want the other men to jump into the complimenting game.

"Andrew," she said as we hugged. "I'm so glad you came."

Her tiny body curled into mine like she belonged there and wanted me to protect her, take care of her... love her. I held her tight, feeling her heart beating faster than a little bunny. Heat built between us. Having her there, head resting against my chest felt right.

"Mmm," I whispered in her ear.

Charissa blushed as she pulled away.

She turned to greet Shawn with a brilliant smile and welcoming words. As they spoke, I nudged into position behind them. When she stepped away from Shawn, I moved behind her chair and gestured for her to be seated. I assisted her as she sat.

"Oh, thank you," she said, cranking her head up to look at me.

I flushed.

She flushed, too, and moved her gaze back down at the table. "It's been a long time since I dated. I've never dated so many good-looking men, and never all at once. This feels..."

While she searched for words, I observed Shawn moving my glass of water over to the next spot and claiming the place next to Charissa. He took advantage of my gentlemanly act to one-up me.

Game on.

I took the seat across from Charissa. I could make that work for me.

"Untraditional." Shawn filled in the last word in for her.

That answer drew Charissa's attention as I reluctantly sat one spot removed from her, unable to ignore the intensity between her and Shawn. Their eyes locked, and a soft smile slipped across her mouth. He had just earned points, more than I got for holding her chair.

"Yes," she said. "I guess that's the word."

"So, Charissa," I said, trying to ignore the other connections she was making. "Where do you like to go on your vacations?"

She picked up her napkin and put it on her lap. "Oh, well, let me think." She took a sip of water, or maybe alcohol, provided for her in her wine glass. "That's a hard one. I don't vacation much, but I have recently moved to Island Park, and that might be considered a vacation place, so I really don't need to vacation."

"That's funny," Shawn said, trying to steal my thunder, "I take it you're a country girl, through and through, then?"

Boom. Shawn had masterfully shifted the attention to him and their similarities.

CHAPTER 13

Charissa

I had done substitute teaching in elementary classes a few times to pick up petty cash. I thought it exhausting to pay attention to all the kids veering me away from my focus. Little did I know the experience would prep me for this date.

The men stumbled over each other to secure my attention. I didn't blame them. I remember wanting to do the same thing on the show with JT. I had been too shy to compete and held to an embedded belief the man should chase the girl. One of the problems I had with these shows was they messed with that principle.

With JT, my conscious decision to slip into the background and not command the limelight might have been one of the reasons I lasted so long on the show. He didn't know me and, therefore, still held out hope we'd work.

On the other hand, I wasted a lot of my time with dreams and hopes that we could build a life together. I envisioned taking him on vacations to visit Ava and him taking me on his business trips. I pictured me taking care of him and me… I never made it farther than that. I never really knew what I'd do. When it came time for our first date, he had decided it was no go.

Now, I stood on the other side of the line with these men dreaming and wanting to be picked. It was almost like I was playing Scarlet O'Hara, even though I never wanted to be her. I had always thought that scene was so silly, with her stringing men's hearts along. Didn't she have anything better to do?

Supposedly, I was in charge, but like a modern queen, my authority only extended so far. To my grave disappointment, too, I didn't have power over what everyone ate. Since being on JT's show, I had gone vegetarian from reading so much literature on the harmful effects of meat. I had talked to Edward earlier about what red meat does to the gut. Ever since I knew what eating meat did to one's health, I grew ill just seeing it. Blood sat on both Shawn and Andrew plates. I tried not to look, but it was as hard as not thinking of a purple elephant I was trying to ignore.

To make matters worse, the guys continued jockeying to one-up one another.

When we headed into the dessert, my head pounded like it might after hours of babysitting arguing toddlers. I closed my eyes. If I didn't do something, I'd have to deal with this drama for five weeks. My stomach clenched more tightly. I had to do this. I had to make this experience more bearable. I put my fork and knife on my plate with a clang.

I pushed my plate in front of me so I could rest my elbows on the table.

I cleared my throat, which was becoming my signal I had something to say, and they should listen. All of them hushed.

"I have loved having you here tonight. I do enjoy being with each one of you. With that, I'd like to make a request that you pipe down on the competition. This is supposed to be about finding love, not about who can talk to me the most, or who has the most connections."

I put my hands on the table. "No girl likes to feel like an object. I know you feel pressured, and it seems there isn't enough time to develop a relationship. Remember, I was in your place not long ago. I understand it. But, I promise each of you will have alone time with me this evening. You're not going to be picked or not picked because of how many times you talked to me or how many connection points you were able to establish."

The men's gazes lowered as they listened.

I tilted my head to one side. "Relationships are a lot deeper than that."

Our table fell quiet as the men look awkwardly at each other's flushed faces rather than at me. Sweat poured down my lower back and my heart pounded in my ears. I coughed to break the thick tension.

Thankfully, Andrew spoke up. "Sorry, I think I started it. You're right. You aren't a prize. You're a person. I didn't mean to make you feel like that."

"Me, neither," offered Shawn.

"You are a lady and we need to always remember to treat you like one," Forester said.

That was a shockingly nice thing for Forester to say. Maybe he felt bad for his earlier words. I noticed his light purple shirt at that moment, for whatever reason. It contrasted nicely with his dark skin. Despite what had transpired between us, he was a very attractive man. When he wasn't criticizing me, he was charming.

I smiled, relieved. My lecture, surprisingly, worked. To shift the energy away from the discomfort, I lifted up my water glass. "No worries. I thought I'd just get it out there."

We clinked our glasses, and I sipped from mine. "Here's to getting to know one another."

They repeated what I said. I looked at the men, who had listened to me and were trying to put my words into practice, and I realized Monique might have been right. Men did want to make the lady happy.

A warm buzz seeped through me like a first sip of vodka. I had more power and strength than I realized. Now was the time to see what I was made of. I'd bring that confidence with me as I met and talked with each of these guys tonight. While I was in my strength, I might as well start with the hardest one.

"Forester?" I asked. "Would you like to go talk first?"

His smile filled his whole face, making him look extra charming. "Yes, ma'am."

THE SHOW HAD SET up a room in the hotel next to the restaurant where we could sit. They furnished it with a courtesy couch, formal chair on each side, coffee table with wine glasses, bottle of red wine, two glasses of water, and a camera in front of all the furniture. A large chandelier more than two feet wide hung from the ceiling, spilling a glow on the setting. Camera people, producers, and crew members filled the area.

My legs trembled as I followed one of the crew members, and Forester trailed behind me. He had been rude, said I wasn't good enough, that he was leaving the show. I didn't know why he hadn't done what he said he would do, but I'd find out.

His shadow spilled onto me. A crew member gestured to the couch. I scooted to the farthest corner, signaling I wanted distance. I wanted to pick up the throw pillow and place it on my lap, but that would come across as cold and distant.

Ignoring the chilly vibe I sent out, he sat close to me. His knee remained a few inches from mine. This man was huge and close and smelled like musk on a crisp mountaintop, which drew me to him.

Remembering Monique's advice, I looked Forester straight on. "So, why are you here?"

His brow furrowed as he poured wine into both our glasses. "What do you mean?"

My forehead throbbed. I needed to speak up now. My fingers dug into the throw pillow next to me, and my foot swung rapidly like it had a mind of its own.

For Ava.

"The last time we spoke, you said goodbye and that you didn't have time for me. You wanted someone different by your side."

He glanced at the cameras, then back to me and picked

up his wine glasses and tipped it toward me. "Yeah, well, I decided to give you another chance."

My lips pressed together, then and I pursed them. He was still as irritating as ever.

"Well, *thank you*," I almost sang those words, making sarcasm drip from them.

His musky cologne poured off him. "If you weren't happy about it, why did you pick me to stay?"

He thought I choose him because I was into him so much I overlooked all his behavior. That certainly wasn't why. Shifting in my seat, I squared my shoulders, released my grip on the throw pillow, and stopped swinging my foot.

"Because, to not pick you would be the predictable thing to do, right?"

I saw a spark in his eyes. Before he talked any more about me, I decided to beat him to the punch. "Mr. Forester," I said to be cute, "you know I have plenty of suitors, and more are on their way, so why do you feel you're giving me a chance when I clearly have the upper hand?"

He tipped his head back and laughed. "You're funny."

"What's so funny?" I asked.

"I'm not used to this."

"What are you not used to?"

He shrugged, naturally not responding. Men never admit to their weaknesses, especially if it was going to hurt them.

"If you aren't going to say, let me guess. You are attractive. Look like a football hero, and are well-to-do. You're probably used to women, all types of women, throwing themselves at you."

A sly smile slipped onto his lips. "Hey, if you got it…"

I shook my head, rolling my eyes. "That's great and good for you, and I'm sure you'll have no problem finding someone. I'm just not that gal. I don't care if you play football, didn't play it, or just watched it. I'm the type of woman who would be irritated if a game is always on. I don't care how much money you have or how good looking you are. I'm happy with my life, and I don't need to feed a man's ego. I have more important things to do."

He took a sip of wine. "Like what?" he asked.

Should I tell him the truth? It was a risk, but what would he do with the information that the rest of America wouldn't? It didn't matter. I wasn't going to hide myself from anyone. "I have a beautiful niece who is sick with cancer. My important work is to see she gets healed and lives a productive life."

His head bent forward as he took in the information. He sat there taking a long pause. "That sounds good. After she's healed, then what?"

What did he mean then what? I took his cue and took a sip from a glass of water on the coffee table in front of us as I watched him. Despite the fact that I really didn't like this guy's attitude, I still needed to watch out for him because, clearly, he was a player. He did have gorgeous brown eyes. He also had a way of looking at me that caused my insides to stir. He was giving me such a nervous buzz. I almost forgot what he had just asked me. What would I do after healing Ava?

"I'll spend time with her, and support her, and help her live her life full out."

"Sounds like you want to live her life for her instead of your own."

I grimaced. "That's not true. She's one of the most incredible individuals I have ever known."

Forester took that in. "I bet she is, but you're holding yourself back. Look, it's obvious we might not be a match. We have too many differences and passions, and such, but I do respect what you are doing, and I respect why you want to do it. Sacrificing for your niece like that is really cool, and she's lucky to have you. What I'm saying, even though I don't know you very well yet, is you're a strong lady and that you don't appreciate how incredible you are. You're holding yourself back. There's so much more you can do and so much more you can change."

As I sat there looking at him, trying to take in his words, he leaned over. His large hand touched the side of my face, wrapping around most of my head, and he pulled me to him until his soft lips pressed gently against mine. His afternoon shadow prickled my face.

His seductive aftershave was doing its job. My head spun, and he pulled away a few inches, looking at me. I gazed at him with dreamy eyes. He smiled, proud of himself, then pulled me in closer to press his lips against mine more firmly. This time, his lips sought mine, and a flare of passion erupted within. I started kissing him with aggression. I was hungry for his lips and his connection. I wanted more, and he kissed me back.

He bit gently down on my lower lip, tugging it. That stirred desire deep in my stomach. He tugged again, and his tongue pushed against my lips, insisting they separate and open.

I relented, and our tongues touched like our lips had, gentle and soft at first. The respectful kiss dug deeper, and I pulled back to catch my breath, tingles erupting down my arms and my spine.

He smiled. "Until next time." He stood up and walked away.

I slumped onto the couch as my heart twisted. I had never been kissed like that. He and I might not be a good match, but he could stick around for just a little longer. I needed to experience his kisses one more time.

* * *

MY LEGS WOULDN'T STOP WOBBLING. If they shook any worse, I'd need assistance, and that would be downright humiliating. I followed one of the young crew members who thought it necessary to escort me to retrieve the next guy. She looked back to make sure I kept up.

"That was quite a kiss." She burst into a smile.

Man, she was right about that. I couldn't remove the smell of Forester from my mind, nor his touch—so gentle and confident it stirred desire. If I wasn't careful, I could lose my head with that guy.

"It was."

My escort gave me an encouraging nod, wanting more. I didn't have anything else to say. I just wanted to replay that kiss in my mind over and over again. He was so big, strong, bold, and experienced, so different from anyone I'd ever known. That was the danger and the tipping point for me.

I had to stop thinking about that kiss. It wouldn't be

fair to the other guys. So, I instructed myself to stay focused and give the other two a chance, even though it would be hard to chase that kiss from my head.

From the earlier competition at dinner, I suspected Shawn and Andrew would be jostling for position. When JT left the room, and we girls all remained there waiting, most of the drama unfolded. I always stayed quiet, sipped mostly tea, and watched. How these men handled it would say a lot about who they were as people. I wasn't sure an aggressive male would be the right fit for me.

The steakhouse's shadowy lights cast a dark aura on the room. The only bright light was over the guys' table where we ate dinner. Both men leaned back in their chairs in relaxed poses, wine glasses in their hands, and laughing. They stopped when they spotted me.

Andrew smiled, and Shawn looked at me with an expectant expression. I needed to pick who was up next. Maybe this was what it was like to have more than one child when each kid tries to see, from the slightest actions, who mommy loved best. Since that was the case, I should pick Andrew first, then Shawn, since Shawn was my number one.

Andrew lifted his wine glass. "Why don't you talk to Shawn first, and I'll sit here and continue to enjoy the evening?"

That stopped me in my tracks. Did he not want time with me? Was he putting me off for more alcohol? My heart beat faster as I felt the heat on my face. I shifted my weight. "Are you sure?"

He took a sip from his glass and slowly set it down. "Yes. It's a nice evening, and I want to take in the fresh air."

Shawn stood and rubbed his palms together. "Okay, then. I never miss an opportunity to be with a lovely lady."

My smile felt awkward and forced. Shawn's line had sounded just like a line. My sister had always complained about how men were such great sweet talkers until you married them, then their tongues dried up, and all the attention they granted you at the beginning went "vavoosh," gone. Ava's dad had certainly done that. He disappeared never to be heard of again, the moment he found out my sister was pregnant. That had been horrible. I needed to remind myself of that tendency and not just fall for the guy with the best lines.

Shawn's cobalt crystal-blue eyes sparkled down on me as he smiled. He extended his arm up like a gentleman, and I stepped up and took it. Because of his height, his elbow almost touched my ear as we walked. I tugged on his forearm to bring it down to a more reasonable height. He complied.

Remembering Andrew and the fact he might not like seeing me with another guy even if he was putting me off, I looked back to him. "Your turn next."

He nodded barely and refocused on the ocean. Maybe being with me wasn't where he wanted to be. Maybe he really wasn't that into me.

Shawn asked a number of questions and commented on the scenery as we made our way out of the restaurant. My focus stayed on careful walking to avoid any missteps since my knees couldn't stop shaking. My focus was rewarded by making it back to the other hotel's sitting room without tripping or falling. It was too bad this town didn't have a hotel big enough to host this event. It would've made it nice not to have to go back and forth to the different spots.

Once in the room, I gestured over to the couch where Forester had just kissed me despite his rudeness from before. Shawn sat and draped his arm out over the couch back, so if I sat, I would already be in his arms. I looked at his smile, broad shoulders, and trim build. A lump in my throat grew bigger as nerves consumed me. I dabbed at the sweat bubbling on my brow. I didn't know this guy, and I had just kissed Forester. I wasn't up for any more of that... too confusing.

"Sit," Shawn said with a half-smile. "I'm not going to bite you too hard. I promise."

Taking a cue from what Monique said earlier, I decided to step into my other, more confident, self. "Well, that's too bad," I said, "because I might."

He gave me a blank look.

Okay, he wasn't one for playing much right now.

I sat. His fingers lightly brushed against my shoulder as our chitchat began, brief and casual. He asked how my day was going and if this was everything I had imagined it to be.

I asked him why he came to the show and what he hoped to get out of it, noticing that I kept unconsciously leaning toward him.

He kept it simple. "A wife."

I looked at him, and he explained no more. This was a man who knew what he wanted.

Faster than with Forester, the producers gave us the time-to-wrap-it-up signal. I smiled as his mesmerizing eyes took me in. "I've enjoyed talking to you and getting to know you better, Shawn."

He shifted his position to face me directly, reached out, and took my hands.

Heat exploded between us. He took my palm and brought it to his lips just like he had done earlier today. This time he kissed it with his gaze locked on, swallowing me.

He pulled my hand from his lips. "I've also enjoyed getting to know you." His fingers held onto mine. "I've been searching a long time for a girl with good old-fashioned values who would stand by my side and face the future together."

My heart thundered like a horse at a race track. I forgot to breathe as I waited for what he would say next. Instead of saying anything, he pulled the back of my hand to his lips and kissed it, too.

* * *

How could I have so many feelings stirring for two different guys? This wasn't how it was supposed to work. Forester and his breathtaking kiss that just made me want to dive in and get more... Shawn with his simple charm and manners and his code of ethics of being a gentleman, which was so rare, but deeply attractive... I could stay up all night going back and forth between those two guys, and it would give me plenty to think about and process. But, there was also Andrew, who I needed to chat with, too. Just thinking of his piercing gray eyes and how he looked at me, like he could see deep inside me, made my heart patter.

There was an intensity about him and conviction that gave me confidence.

When I was with him, with other company or not, I knew he cared. He possessed the true-blue loyalty card. The way he stared at me all through dinner... like I was the only woman in his world.

But he didn't want to go first. That confused me. My stomach didn't feel good as I thought about that. Maybe he had changed his mind about me. I didn't get that, but he liked being in his safe bubble. Maybe he figured all this was too much trouble? I hoped not. I hustled back to the restaurant for one last time. Soon, I'd be in my hotel room and diving into my bathtub to soak through all my choices.

At the bottom of the staircase, Andrew stood with a smile and a bouquet of flowers. His piercing eyes sparkled as he handed them to me.

My jaw fell open as I gasped and flushed with pleasure. Roses. Red ones. Classic. Nice touch. I had gotten upset over nothing. He had wanted to do something nice for me, so he went last because he needed time to buy the flowers —such a romantic man.

"How did you have time?" I flushed.

One of the crew members dashed over to take them from me. I brought them to my nose and sniffed their fragrance one more time before parting with them.

Andrew extended his arms out for a hug. He pulled me close to him and whispered, "You're a wild beauty."

A fresh ocean scent washed over us, enticing me. Something about those words, or his breath warming my ears and neck, gave me chills.

"Thank you. I love them."

He grabbed my hand, giving me a jolt of warmth. "Come on," he said, "I'm sure you're tired of that fancy hotel room where you've been talking to the other guys. We're on this charming island. Let's go appreciate the nightlife."

He looked at me with an eyebrow raised to see if I was game. I glanced at the crew, the cameras, the producers.

"Don't worry about them," Andrew whispered as I leaned in closer to him. "They want good footage, and us strolling through town laughing, having a good time, and going against the set structure will make for entertaining clips."

I loved how determined he was and how he paid no attention to the rules. That was strength... something I could respect.

He squeezed my hand as he smiled, his gray gaze diving into me, causing goosebumps to chase one another on my skin.

"We have the whole island waiting."

"But, you're only supposed to have ten minutes," I said lamely. I could hear my own lack of conviction in my voice.

Andrew shrugged and leaned toward me like he was sharing something confidential. "I wouldn't mind if the film crew packed up and returned to their hotel rooms, would you?"

He leaned in close, his lips near mine. Heat rose between us as I stared at his lips.

"I wouldn't," I whispered.

* * *

THE HUMID AIR wrapped around us as we wandered the streets of the small town. A nice blackness had settled, and a half-moon cast a slight glow on everything. The sailboats created dark shadows rocking on the gentle waves. I glanced at the different shops and restaurants that invited romance. The tall palm trees against the sky declared their splendor.

Andrew was friendly, talkative, and funny, dropping into impressions of different famous people to make me laugh.

As we strolled the brick street hand-in-hand, I noted our fingers had intertwined. Chelsey instructed me long before to pay attention to how a man held my hand because it revealed a lot of how they felt. If a man's fingers wrapped around my hand, he was more distant. If he held my hand with his fingers melded in-between mine, it was a tell-tell sign he felt close and wanted more connection.

Yes, Andrew held me with melded fingers. Not only that, his fingers curled around and stroked the back of my hand. As we strolled, our shoulders kept bumping into each other. Naturally, the camera crew followed us, so, in their spotlights, the dark could not hide us.

"Now, I really wish the crew wasn't with us," I whispered.

Andrew stopped walking in the middle of the street, leaned over, and whispered in my ear. "Do you want to lose them?"

I gazed into his intense face, which caused waves of heat to rush through me. He wanted to break the rules further. I gave a barely noticeable shake of my head no.

He smiled, squeezed my hand, and strolled toward the

casino. It was darker on this side of the island and away from the pockets of music spilling out from the bars and parties we passed.

Andrew took big strides, and I had to double-time it to keep up. It wasn't easy. I started breathing hard and pulled his arm lightly.

"Would you mind if we go slower?"

He peered at me with a quick questioning gaze, then looked down to my dress. "Want to go to your place and change into something more comfortable?"

I shook my head no, feeling my face grow hot.

Andrew smiled, showcasing a dimple. "I didn't mean it that way. I'd wait in the hallway like a gentleman. You have to be uncomfortable in that dress."

"I'm fine," I said.

He pulled me off the trail and escorted me onto the sand. "Take off your shoes," he ordered.

I stared at him.

He bent in front of me. "We can go dip our feet in the ocean." He started taking off his wingtips.

"Are you serious?" I asked. "I'm wearing a dress."

He smirked. "It's time for you to live a little and stop confining yourself to all these crazy rules. I'm all for going by the rules if it is going to make your life better, but to confine yourself in a box like you do, you'll never really live."

My mouth dropped open, not knowing what to say. No man had ever talked to me like that before. I couldn't really say he was wrong. It felt like he was right, but I didn't like that either.

He climbed to his feet, shoes in one hand, and reached

over to me. He ran his other hand across my wind-teased hair that was falling out of its up-do. Chills shot through me with his touch. How could I have so many different and positive reactions to so many men?

"One splash through the ocean, so we could say we did it. Since it's almost fall, the water will probably be cold," I said.

"Probably will. Come with me and connect with the water that connects to all the other land in this world."

I looked at him, shocked at him expressing such a romantic idea.

Andrew stood in the surf like a Greek God. I tip-toed my feet into the water and gasped from the chilly, brittle temperature. Shivering, I shuffled over to him, holding my dress up. A huge wave splashed icy water up past my knees and onto my bodice—the cold cut like a thousand little razors.

"Oh, my gosh!" I ran to the shoreline through the piercing ice waves. "That was cold!"

Andrew remained in the water watching me until I made it to shore. He laughed, then finally decided to make his way across the sand to me. He slipped off his jacket. He fluffed it, as if to gain the attention of a charging bull, and laid it onto the sand. "Sit, my lady. Let's stare at the sky and make a wish on the stars."

Nervous laughter spilled from me. "Okay."

Even after I positioned myself on the jacket with my icy feet tucked under my dress, I still shivered. I pulled my sweater tighter around me.

Andrew sat next to me, reached out with his forefinger to tip my chin up, and leaned in for a soft kiss.

CHAPTER 14

Andrew

Kissing Charissa hadn't been my plan. In fact, I had decided to hold back on that and develop more of a friendship. I wanted time to sort through who she was and how we interacted together before I messed with the physical. In the moment, though, moonlight had poured down and cast a glow around her. The dress gave her eyes a rich look of a sea green, which popped when the camera light fell on them. All that would pull at any man's heart.

Her sweet, gentle smile and the way she looked at me with those big trusting eyes... both made it impossible for me not to lean in and kiss her. She had been shy and yet respectful in her response. The kiss started softly, but as I found myself unable to pull away, she moved her lips with more passion. Her hand reached out and touched my hair, her fingers playing with my curls. It caused a deep stirring inside my chest.

This woman could drive me crazy. She wasn't like the others. She was so much kinder, and that kiss communicated her heart and her tenderness. It made me want to protect her and to wrap her in my arms to keep her safe from all the harshness of life.

When we finally pulled apart, I had hugged her and said, "That was nice."

She blushed, and I knew it was time to take her home.

"Let's go back." I stood to collect our shoes. "You have a big day tomorrow."

That snapped her into scurrying around to leave. Once her shoes were on, I extended my hands to help her up. She stumbled to her feet, and I pulled her tight to me. I squeezed her, then pulled back a little from our embrace to see her better.

"Charissa, I don't want to put any pressure on you, but I want you to know I have a good feeling about us. I just love who you are. I've been searching my whole life for someone like you."

She stepped to the side, taking in a few hesitant breaths. "You barely know me."

"I know," I said.

"How can you say that then?" she asked. "We haven't even known each other for a day."

I grabbed her hand, walking her up to the path. "Well, this is what I do know about you. You're sensual."

"What?" she asked through a cough.

"You just melt into my touch. That's a good thing. A very good thing. It means you're sensitive. Some people might not appreciate how sensitive you are, but it's also what makes you so kind and caring. It's a double-edged sword. You can't have one without the other."

She didn't say anything, but did squeeze my hand, letting me know she appreciated my words. That closed the deal for me. I'd always remember the night as sublime.

Later, I tenderly stepped down the narrow, thinly carpeted, old hotel hallway, not wanting to disturb any of the hotel's guests in the wee hours, but the old and achy plywood boards moaned with every step. After releasing a long path of creaks, I made it to my hotel door. I paused to assess what might be waiting for me on the other side. Ideally, the guys would be asleep, with no thoughts about me and what I've been up to. Judging from the low rumble of noise from deep inside, though, that seemed highly doubtful.

Both Shawn and Forester were sprawled out on separate couches in front of a TV with its noise pitched on a dull, low volume.

Shawn was still up. That was a bit of a surprise since he rose so early. Forester, not so much.

"Where have you been?" Forester sat up, his arm muscles flexing, I hope subconsciously.

I hadn't even closed the door yet. It rumbled shut behind me. I shoved the room key in my pocket and shrugged my shoulders.

Forester stood, breathing heavily as if to calm himself. "You're a trickster. We're going to have to keep an eye on you." He expelled air in a loud gust and looked ready to pounce.

My eyes flicked to Shawn to determine his stance as

friend or foe. Shawn also sat up, his eyes wide and moving back and forth between his rivals.

I shrugged. "It's getting late." I headed toward my room.

Forester rose to his feet and move to stand, solid and wide, in my way. "What were you doing with her?"

I dodged to the right to move past him, but he sidestepped, blocking me.

I was too tired to play basketball. "I don't kiss and tell," I muttered.

I stood my ground, chest expanded. I could out-wait his aggression.

He stepped closer until hot breath heated my chest. His considerable height cast a shadow on me.

I dove my hands into my pockets. He might be taller, with forearms the size of my head, legs big as telephone poles, and a whopper of a temper, but I wasn't going to let that get to me.

"You played us so you could have more time. I'm onto you."

"I consider us even. You outplayed me at dinner by claiming a seat by her."

A smile cracked his face. "True."

We, Charissa's suitors, were trapped in suspended time. Minutes ticked by in a bubble not attached to the daily grind's reality that made time drag on. Everything jammed into slow motion except when Charissa was in our sphere, and we took a hard shift into fast-forward time. Before we could adjust, *pop!,* we'd snap back into slow motion, and she'd be gone, taking the dazzle.

The morning's bright light trickled into my room, sprawling rays across my bed, hours before I was willing to open my eyes. I couldn't remember the last time I'd hunkered down and slept in. I was going to make the most of my suspended time.

Ten minutes later, a hungry pit in my stomach decided it was time to get up. I followed its orders, stumbled out of bed, and declared I was up for the day. I made my way to the kitchen, where I heard low voices... Shawn and Forester grumbling as they made protein shakes. Well, actually, Forester was making and instructing. Shawn periodically dashed longing looks at the egg carton pushed to the side on the marble counter, apparently not so happy about giving up his scrambled eggs for a liquid drink.

"Morning," I said. "Any word?"

"Nope," Shawn said. "It's the 'new men' day, and we're put on hold."

Forester shook his protein drink in a thermos with gusto, making a noise like a washing machine on spin cycle.

"What did happen last night?"

His voice sounded calm and even, but the slight rise in his shoulders suggested tension. He wanted to know how far in the game I had gotten with my strategy. Not that human relationships could be boiled down simply, but lawyers clearly looked at the world from a different vantage point than I did.

Forester was jacked up from the idea of what Charissa

and I could've done. We had to live with each other for the next couple of weeks—time to de-escalate him.

I prepared for the confrontation by pulling my shoulders back. "Not much man. The cameras were on us the whole time. We just strolled around the island. She yawned at a lot from being tired, and we took off our shoes and put our feet in the subzero waters."

I thought about last night. The look in her eyes when I handed her the flowers, the feel of her lips against mine, and the buzzing energy between us as we spoke to each other in the moonlight stayed with me. "Yeah, that was about it. You can relax."

Forester set the thermos on the counter, his shoulders lowering a smidgen.

He nodded. "Going to the gym. You need to join me."

He handed Shawn the shake and left the room.

I turned to the dairy farmer. "Was that a threat?"

He shrugged and took a sip of the protein drink. His nose wrinkled. "This stuff is nasty."

He walked out of the kitchen, grabbed the remote, and flopped on the couch. "Want to see if there're any games on at this hour?"

I looked at the full egg carton and decided to make breakfast first, then I'd be a man and join Forester in the gym, at least to see what he wanted.

Thirty minutes later, loud grunts and banging noises echoed from the basement. No question Forester could flatten me like a pancake if he wanted to. I had hopes that weren't his intention, especially since cameras followed us everywhere.

I opened the exercise room door but left my hand on the doorknob. "What do you want?"

Forester gave a side smirk. "Your arms are flabby. How often do you lift weights?"

Hmm. "Does bringing in groceries count?"

He shook his head. "The older you get, the more muscle mass you lose. If you don't constantly workout, your body will take it as a signal that you don't need that muscle group anymore, and you'll start atrophying."

The man wanted to remake my body. His way of calling a truce, or maybe to make me so sore I'd drop out of the competition. Either way, I was up for it.

CHAPTER 15

Charissa

*V*oices outside my hotel room penetrated my sleep. I buried myself deeper into my fluffy pillows. Black coffee aromas tickled my nose. I breathed deep to allow sleep to encompass me once more but, before it could overtake me, the noise outside my room grew louder. Then came the click of a key inserted into my hotel door.

Before my eyes completely opened, I made out a long stream of film crew members dressed in jeans, or shorts, T-shirts, and jackets. They circled my bed with their booms, cameras, and cords. I hid under the sheets. It was too early for this. I closed my eyes, wishing every one of them away. The schedule hadn't said anything about a dawn start. I squinted at the clock: 5:46 a.m.

"Seriously," I snapped, putting a pillow over my still-damp hair from my bath last night. "Get out."

My head hurt from lack of sleep, and the light someone had flicked on was too bright, forcing me to squint to see anything clearly.

Dee's voice broke through the rest of the mumblings. "A boat with more men is coming in less than an hour to meet you. Time to get up."

"It's too early to function," I spoke from under the pillow that dampened my voice, hopefully making it hard for the camera to pick up. I grabbed onto the sheets and shoved them between my legs, not wanting to risk exposure to the cameras.

Every exhale warmed my face as I breathed into the pillow. I closed my eyes in an attempt to settle into enough darkness to make everyone disappear.

Instead of finding much-desired sleep, a harsh tug on my blankets startled me.

"Get up. They're coming, and you're going to greet them."

Dee, again.

I grabbed my sheets and pulled them over my head. I wasn't going to be exposed on national TV looking like a Lost Nest Monster. "No cameras," I growled.

I pulled the white sheet higher over my head, wrapped it around my skull then peeked out from under it like a little kid hiding from Mommy. I blinked at the too-bright lamp and noticed Dee looked too wide awake for this hour. She stood there with coffee in her hand, steam swirling up from the styrofoam, and her narrow, intense gaze locked onto mine.

I don't think, if the roles were reversed, she'd like going on national TV looking like she did now with her greasy hair pulled back into a baseball cap.

"Dee, get them out of my room. You got a lot of great footage of me breaking the rules with Andrew last night, running into the ocean, no less. You don't need boring footage of me washed out."

Her shoulders lowered as she took me in. Her face was full of confusion, which I don't think I'd ever seen before. In her mind, she probably weighed the pros and cons of how to create the best TV.

As she stewed, I tried to assess if there was anything human in her. Last year, she had been ruthless to some of the women just to capture good footage, and I wasn't sure if she rode the same pony this year. The fact that she could be so cold and calculating was hard to understand.

She suddenly spoke up, loud, and shattered any remaining quiet in the morning. "All right, you heard the lady. Everyone out of the room." She slapped her hands together. "Now."

Immediate scurrying and rumbling sounds filled the room. Someone banged into the shutters, rattling them and making them hang ajar, which allowed in another inch of early morning light.

Once the hotel door slammed shut, Dee snapped around to face me. "No more pissant excuses. Get up and get going."

I popped my head out from under the sheets and blinked at her. "What is wrong with you?"

"What do you mean?" She planted her feet firmly on the floor, preparing for a fight.

"Why are you so rude? When I broke the rules last night, you shot some good TV, so it can't be that. Plus, I have complied with the schedule so far and don't plan on varying from it... as long as I know what it is." I stared at her to emphasize how ridiculous she was acting and climbed out of bed. "You might actually find, someday, you could use a friend. I hope you haven't snapped everyone's head off or glared at them until they went away by the time that day comes."

In response to my lecture, Dee took a long chug of coffee and wiped her lips with her forearm. "Let's go to make-up and wardrobe. Your breakfast will be waiting there."

After I dressed, we left the hotel. Once bucketed in our seats in a tiny, royal-blue smart car, some people passed by us. They wore tee-shirts and shorts, cameras draped around their necks and held a map spread open in their hands.

Dee pulled the car out in front, nearly clipping them. They cussed at her and punched their arms out in anger.

Grabbing hold of the armrest, I laughed to release nervous tension.

"Don't complain about this wimpy car," Dee shot out, apparently oblivious to almost hitting the tourists. "We were lucky even to secure this. We were almost unable to find any cars at all. There's a major car shortage on the island. It even takes fourteen years to get a permit to own one."

She continued to drive haphazardly as she lectured, her eyes mostly on me instead of the cobblestone road she drove on.

I decided to appease Dee and keep her from getting more agitated. "Wow, that sounds crazy. So, when I bolt from the show, I won't be able to do it with a vehicle."

My comment referred to last season when Maggie bolted after deciding she was too good for camping.

"Not funny," Dee said with a heavy sigh.

She wove us through crowds of people lining up at restaurants. Fortunately, at least for the tourists, she slowed to give them time to move out of the way.

Dee stopped talking, I thought, to focus on not hitting people. But, after a moment, she asked, "How do we do this friend thing?" Her face flushed in patches of red. "With me being the boss and all. How would that work? I still need you to mind me."

I had really hit a nerve. "We talk like we are doing now," I said. "Haven't you ever had a friend you worked with?"

Dee's hands on the steering wheel tightened, and her knuckles whitened.

Wow. She hadn't. Okay.

"We just talk and stay on each other's team. That's it," I said. "It's not that hard." The moment those last few words left my mouth, I knew they were stupid to say. I had insulted her.

The thick silence of the car almost choked me. My heart rate double-timed as I wondered how Dee would deal with this. Clearly, I had caught her off-guard.

She parked the car, climbed out, and locked the doors behind us. "Marilyn Monroe lived here for a year. Fifteen. Married. Husband in the war, stationed as a merchant sailor."

Why was she telling me this? She flipped from wanting

to be friends to talk about Marilyn Monroe. That was a big leap.

"Today it's your turn to be Marilyn."

"What?"

"You'll find out later after you meet the new guys."

I stared at this woman. She was really hard to befriend. She liked to pile worrying things on top of me. I would not give her the satisfaction of asking any more questions about the day's plans because I certainly wasn't like Marilyn Monroe. Nor would I ever be like her. I would pretend Dee hadn't said it, and consider it a tease, because it was ridiculous.

Dee escorted me to the same shaded gazebo with fresh flowers. The same set-up for meeting the guys. The same rules applied. The only real differences this time included me knowing enough to insist on flat shoes and having a general idea of how this would go so I could be even more nervous.

This time I wore designer jeans and a long drapey cream shirt with my flats.

When I heard, "Quiet on the set," I wiped the sweat from my hand onto my pants, inhaled, and looked to see an extremely short man approaching me in the morning glow.

This wasn't going to go well. I tried real hard not to be judgmental and be open to all the types sent my way, but having someone shorter than me made me extremely uncomfortable. Hardly anyone, ever, was shorter than me. I kept trying to make myself smaller by hunching down and sucking in my stomach, knowing the cameras would make me look like an Amazon woman next to him.

The second guy wore too many chains and used too

much southern slang. I kept repeating over and over again, "I don't know what you're saying."

At that point, I wouldn't have been disappointed if no other men waited to meet me on the porch. I started seeing the real value in giving the guys the power to say no. That saved me from having to do it over and over again.

After Mr. Slang left, I yawned. "Do I have to meet more?" I asked Dee. "I like the men we have now. I'm sure they will provide the show with its much-needed drama."

From across the way, standing next to a camera, Dee's jaw tightened. She yelled back, "Straighten up! Here comes another one."

She had just scolded me like a child, but I deserved it this time for whining and being a pain. I would stop that. No use in making a fuss. That wasn't like me anyway.

A really tall and slender man headed my way. The closer he came, the more I could see his dark, slightly balding hair and a lot of dark arm hair. He wore a goofy grin under a Roman nose and dark eyebrows. Overall, he looked like an attractive Italian.

"Hello, there beautiful lady."

"You have an accent." I raised my eyebrows and cranked my head all the way back to see his face. "Where are you from?"

A smile lit his face, making him even more handsome. "Rhode Island, and it's you with the accent."

I nodded, liking his comeback. "What's your big dream?" I asked.

"I'm a professional speaker, currently. I put on seminars all over the world encouraging people to live healthier."

That statement woke me. "Really? What do you think will make people healthy?"

His chest puffed up. "Lifestyle, and what you choose to put in your mouth."

I had a feeling Mr. Tall and I would get along nicely. "Good answer."

His dark brown eyes clearly drank me in. My heart rate picked up, but I tried to minimize my reaction so he wouldn't notice. I needed to play this cool.

"By the way, I didn't catch your name." My voice actually sounded free of the nerves wracking me.

"Rocco."

Rocco. That fitted him perfectly. His angular face and stern nose hinted at stubborn traits, yet a lot of energy and positivity oozed from him.

He leaned closer to me, and my heart picked up even more speed.

"I'm a big believer in playing full out. Do you want to live your life fully?"

"Time!" a producer called out.

That jolted me. We had just started talking. I wanted to know what he meant by living full out and more about what he did. It sounded fascinating. He looked at me with startled eyes matching how I felt.

"That was fast." He stood and held out his hands. I took them, and he lifted me to my feet and pulled me to him. His firm arms wrapped around me as he pressed me close. My head reached his stomach but, despite our height difference, I could feel the hardness of his body. He was toned and buff.

"See you soon," he whispered.

That was against the rules to hint at what he chooses, but I appreciated it. He also sent a warmth through me. Another strong possibility.

After Rocco, two more unattractive millionaires stumbled through.

One was an international surfboarding champion who wasn't much of a conversationalist. He muttered and mumbled. He did manage to ask if I could live on the ocean.

When I shook my head, he smiled, stood up, and left.

That was really small-minded and limiting, but... to each their own.

The last man to stroll onto the stage sported the perfect tan, blondish-brown hair gelled to perfection, and chiseled facial features. Though on the short side, he stood maybe a few inches above me.

"You look like a movie star," I told him as he settled on the bench.

"Funny," he said, "that's what I am. Currently only starring in commercials and this TV show, but soon my name will be in the spotlight."

He was an immediate "no." I couldn't live with a fame-seeking individual. He must be a trust-fund millionaire. I had to have a way to sort through all these men, so I needed to rely on my instincts.

The sun had moved higher in the sky, and it grew hot. I wanted desperately to make it to the group date cocktail part of the day, in the late evening... How I would love to skip the shells and goodbyes to certain suitors. No matter if they weren't for me, they had tried and still had feelings. I wanted to jump over that and go right on to kissing

Forester. I craved those kisses. I wanted to know if kissing him was as good today as it had been last night. They had been so seductive, as opposed to Andrew's tender kisses.

Dee joined me, looking stern. "Time for you to pick who'll go to the next round. You only get three."

My heart skipped beats in my chest. "I'm not sure how this works. Do I pick three from the five I just met or three including the three guys from last night?" This all seemed overwhelming. The guys seemed nice and all, but the only way I could handle it was not to have so many of them.

"Three from the group you just met." Dee walked the boardwalk. "After that, you'll go on an immediate group date. We're going to do the Marilyn Monroe photoshoot."

She was really going to make me do this stupid Marilyn thing. I sighed.

"Can we have all six remaining guys there on the shoot?" I asked.

If I were going to have a nice time on this show, I'd have to make the rules work for me.

Dee stopped walking. Her hat was low on her head, hiding her eyes until she looked at me, chomping on her gum. "Why?"

"Well, I miss them already."

"You just met them yesterday."

I pressed my lips together and stared at her. She wanted to keep Shawn, Andrew, and Forester away from me.

"How am I supposed to make a decision as serious as who I want to marry at the end of this if I don't have as much time as possible with them? I need to get to know them, understand them, see how they respond to different situations, and how I feel and connect with them."

She rolled her hands. "Yeah, yeah. I heard it all before. Tell me the truth. Why do you want them there?"

My jaw dropped. "Because I like them and miss them."

"How about these new guys?"

"Only Rocco is interesting."

She tapped her fingers against her lips. "Rocco against Forester. Yeah, I can see immediate tension there. They both have good bodies... a jock theme. Okay, yes, you can have them there, but this is how we're going to play it out..."

NANCY and I strolled down the ocean dock toward the makeshift bar, and I thought about how much it sucked to say no and goodbye to people. Especially good-looking ones who made me nervous in the first place. My stomach felt like a decaying apple nestled in the bottom of it. I thought about the five new men, and my chest tightened. Hopefully, most of them had already opted out. Even though that would serve as a slight blow to my ego on national TV, it'd be much easier than the coerced, awkward goodbyes with strained explanations.

The air remained still. Slivers of light managed to squeeze through recent cloud cover, suggesting hope. Before taking in who had chosen me, I forced a smile and pranced up to the bar. Some of the suitors already held drinks and stood at a tall lounge table.

"It's so early to be drinking." The statement sounded like a nagging mom, not a love interest.

From the guarded facial expressions the men returned,

I could tell my comment didn't land well on any of the three guys who had opted to stay.

Nerves bubbled in my stomach. "Good to see all of you."

I unfolded the same spiel about the conch since they were new guys. If I did this enough times, I'd have it down pat.

The men continued to drink and showed their own nerves in pale faces and twitching fingers. How could they not be nervous? This whole set-up guaranteed the "pick me" syndrome. Within the rules, I could keep all three of them, but it would be unfair to knowingly detain them from their lives, families, and careers, if I already saw them as a "no."

Only Rocco gave me a buzz with his charm and the way his eyes took me in. The other two, I just wasn't into. I looked over at the crew and the cameras on me... waiting. Dee had instructed me to just pick three, and we'd take them on the photoshoot.

All the men watched me, too—some with straight expressions, others wan and looking sick. If I gave them the shells, they'd experience relief and hope. They would believe they had a chance and it was worth putting their lives on hold. Or, they would move closer to fame: talked about, gossiped about, and mean jabs would head their way, like in my experience. My stomach seized. It didn't feel right to hand out the shells. I needed to talk with Nancy.

I put the conch shell down and faced to the beauty queen. "Can I talk to you?"

She agreed, and we paced down the boardwalk. The

sun glowed behind her, making her look even more stunning, if that was possible. The cameras zeroed in on us. In the distance, I saw Dee plowing toward us.

"I can't do it," I said.

I needed to hurry before Dee arrived and worked her manipulation on me. She had some sick radar whenever anything unusual occurred. I wasn't up for using people, no matter how much pressure they put on me to make a show. If I were the editor, I'd have cut the scene right there, after I admitted I couldn't go on, then pick up the drama later. But, I wasn't the editor, and I'd have to wait weeks to see what they did with all this footage.

"What?" Nancy asked.

"I only want to give out one shell. The other men aren't cutting it for me compared to the men I already chose."

Dee had joined us by this point, her hands on her walkie-talkie and looking prepared for war.

Ignoring Dee's stare seemed the only thing to do. So, I stammered on. Nancy's delicate mouth fell open, apparently shocked into speechlessness. Red spots popped on her thin neck. I waited for her answer. Dee shifted her weight, waiting, too. Nancy's lip quivered. She nodded her approval. I flicked my eyes to Dee to see if she'd block the decision, but she didn't. She continued to stand in her front-row seat between Nancy and me.

Taking that as approval, I went back down the boardwalk. Nancy trotted after me. By the time I reached my spot, facing the men and the ocean, one shell remained to hand out. The men shifted their weight apprehensively, causing the deck to creak. I could almost eat their anxiety. It was so palatable.

It was impossible to look at them. Instead, I stared at my feet to gather confidence. Funny what you notice in high-pressure moments. A distant motorboat roared a dull hum. My stomach cringed like I was about to dive off a high dive. My toes had turned pink, and I needed a pedicure if I was going to wear sandals on national TV.

I peered up from my feet, hearing Monique's haunting words about needing to be confident, or there would be chaos. Rocco gazed at me head-on with intense confidence that weakened my knees. The other gentlemen avoided eye contact. My delay was hard on them. Maybe I should invite them to stay, too, change my mind again. Dee would want to hang me if I did that, but I'd survive it.

One of the cameramen faked a cough. A bird overhead squawked. The sun had broken through another layer. I'd done this once before. I could do this again. My heart pounded in my ears, knowing I was seconds away from taking the plunge.

The bird overhead caught my attention—flying south alone. Taking a long deep breath like a sip through a straw, I picked up the one shell and on the table, signaling I'd only pick one person.

"Rocco, will you accept this shell?"

He puffed up as he strolled up to me. The other men withered, appearing shocked, hurt, and upset. I was doing to them what JT had done to me. That didn't make it any better. It simply reinforced that I should've known better. There was something wrong with turning romance into a competition for the world to watch. Sometimes I hated this show and who it made me become.

* * *

Now, it was time to do the staged performance I had briefly worked out with Dee.

Maybe it would be fun to share a group date there in the sunshine, now peeking through the gray clouds. The sun's rays created a golden promise for the event and came out in perfect timing to help me flirt and come to know the guys better. Granted, though, I felt old to be doing all these things. It all seemed very high-schoolish.

After the other men had said their goodbyes, I peered at Rocco. I have always had a weakness for Italians and their zest for life. Rocco stood to the side of the set with a crooked smile, waiting for his time to talk to me. He was strolling around the small porch with that cheesy grin when the last dumped guy hurried by him and said good-bye. Rocco waved a hand at him in a big gesture. "Have a good one."

I loved his super sexy accent, though it was hard to hear over the roll of the sea and the distant whine of the motor-boats. He was one of those guys who liked to stay in the cool category. That wasn't bad, but it certainly wasn't any category I had ever existed in. He strolled up toward me.

"Hey." He smiled, but it seemed forced.

This easy-going approach didn't fit him. It hung on him like the wrong outfit.

"Hey," I said.

"Thanks for deciding to play one-hundred percent, full out. You aren't going to regret it."

I didn't understand that. One-hundred percent of what? Behind him, one of the stage crew signaled to me we needed to go. There was still plenty more to shoot. I paused, frozen, not sure what to do.

"Am I supposed to take Rocco with me for the next part? Meet him there? How's this supposed to work?"

One of the crew members looked at me with a questioning expression. "Hold on just a second. Let me get back to you."

He didn't know either. Rocco still smiled down at me. I switched my weight back and forth on my feet.

"So," I said, hoping to shift the conversation's energy, too, "did you work out today?"

His warm hand wrapped around mine, and he brought it to his stomach. He placed my palm firmly on his abs. "Feel those muscles? I make sure other people get some, too."

Erupting in a nervous laugh, I pulled my hand away. I didn't I liked how aggressive he was being, making me touch his stomach. It was like he was trying to force intimacy between us. Like I was supposed to want to touch his stomach, which I didn't. Not yet, anyway.

In an attempt to keep this situation from becoming too awkward, I kept the conversation going. "At the gym?"

He nodded. "Yeah. I did today, but I do it mostly on TV. I'm a professional speaker on health and personal training."

That was the second time he mentioned that. He seemed proud of it. It sounded intense. I wasn't sure why anyone would want to stand in front of a crowd and talk but to each their own.

"Travel a lot with that?"

He shrugged. "Not as much as I'd like, but it's picking up."

Teaching people how to eat right and work out at the gym, and doing TV work didn't sound like a million-dollar job. Maybe he was the owner or something, or *Millionaire Engagement's* vetting process wasn't very good. Unless he was extremely successful, I wasn't sure if I should say something about that or not. He talked of his work as more of a start-up, not like he had accomplished his dream like the other men had.

"Got word!" one of the crew members yelled. "You're to take Rocco to the next meeting place since it was a get-to-know-you date for all the new guys."

Rocco grabbed my hand. My chest tightened like a trash compactor flipped on inside. We strolled over to one of the crew members, a young girl in her early twenties with short blonde hair and jittery eyes.

"Here's the map of where you're going," she said. "By the way, my name is Destiny."

She looked a little like Ava. Well, at least what my niece would look like if she hadn't gotten sick. Ava's life required more courage and growing up than other girls' experienced. She never complained about it. She just showed up to the hospital, doctor, or treatment center, and did what she had to do without a whimper. I needed to be more like her. She must have disliked a lot of things she had to do, but she never showed it. Just did what she had to, like I needed to do, even if I hurt feelings.

"How are the guys doing today? Everyone keeping up well?" I asked Destiny.

Rocco's grip tightened on my hand like he was telling me I shouldn't have asked that. Before I could say or do anything, he let go of my hand and wandered off over to the bar to secure another drink.

I blinked, surprised and annoyed that he would act like that.

Destiny darted after Rocco, and I whispered under my breath, "I think I just made him mad."

A male crew member whispered back, "I think you did."

I couldn't make them all happy all the time. He was going to have to live with the fact that there were other men. We all did.

"If I was going to find the hotel room where the men are staying, how would I do that?" I continued to whisper.

"Room 210," he said.

"Thanks," I whispered.

"Good luck."

"Going to need it," I replied under my breath.

I approached Rocco with a broad smile and the pretense that nothing had happened. "Ready to go?"

He put down the drink in his hand and nodded.

We walked in utter silence, except for the noise of our shoes shuffling against the ground—first, the muffled wood of the pier, and then a gravely sound when our path changed to brick.

I wished I could call my sister for advice. I didn't know what to do with this. The camera crew followed us. I could tell they waited and hoped for something more exciting to happen.

We passed the third store I had seen with Andrew last night, and I remembered the fun we'd shared. Finally, I squared my shoulders, "I hope you're up to meeting the other guys."

Rocco looked at me with a pout. "I didn't come here for them. I came here to spend time with you."

"I understand that," I said, "but you have to know this next event is better with more people. The show promised the men they'd set it up for a group." I almost explained that I really needed a chance to get to know every one of the guys and, just because I had met the others last night, it didn't mean I had enough information on any of them. I stopped myself.

"You got to love this," he said, "all these guys wooing you, and you get to string everyone along."

Irritation bubbled in me. That wasn't a fair thing for him to say. My eyes moved to a couple we passed. They were older, gray-haired, and dressed well. The woman wore breezy white loose pants with a flowy pale-blue top. The man was in plaid shorts and a dress top. They held each other's hands and talked animatedly. That was the dream. That was what I wanted and what the guys wanted. This wasn't going to be easy for any of us.

"Rocco, I picked you 'cause I feel a connection with you, but now I'm starting to feel a lot of frustration. I'm sorry the game is set up this way. I know it doesn't feel good. I didn't like it last year when I was on JT's show."

He stopped and took my hand in his. "Sorry if that came across snappy. Let me get you an ice cream."

I glanced back at the camera people, my stomach unsettled. I pushed my luck. "I don't know if we have time. They're waiting for us for the group date."

"Come on, it won't take long," Rocco said. He looked at me in that alluring way I liked so much a couple of hours earlier. "My treat," he whispered.

CHAPTER 16

Andrew

*I*t reached the point if I didn't leave the small, smelly makeshift gym immediately, I'd be forced to crawl out. My lower back radiated pain up my spine and down my legs. My arms wanted to fall off but pulsed instead. My hips balked, protesting movement, along with my knees.

"I'm done," I said to Forester, who was still going strong, curling seventy-five-pound dumbbell weights.

He glanced up, startled like I had broken his concentration. He stared, then nodded.

The cameraman decided to follow me. I opened the door and looked at him coming after me. I held the door open for him. "There's an entire island to see. I'm ready to go explore."

"Can't," he said.

Oh yeah. That would violate the contract they had us to sign. Fine. After swallowing a handful of aspirin, I'd violate a lesser rule. The lobby harbored a shelf of classical books —time to snatch one and read.

I stumbled up the stairs like a four-hundred-pound football player finding it hard to move. Each step hurt. Forester had been ruthless in his instructions and coaching, but there was no way I'd let him know that. I used the aid of the handrail to heft me up as my lower back and hip screamed.

I heard someone come in the hotel upstairs.

I stopped to listen to the footsteps and murmurs until Charissa's voice broke above the noise. My heart picked up speed. Last night had been so great, and she had been so easy to talk to. It had been hard to not be distracted with thoughts of her all morning long. I couldn't wait to talk to her again.

It didn't take me long to make it to the main landing. Down the hallway, Charissa stood in the lobby holding hands with a tall dude... Italian or Greek, perhaps. They hovered over a paper clenched in Charissa's hands.

My body refused to move as I stared at the lady who had captured my thoughts since last night. She had intruded upon my dreams, flooding me with tingling sensations when I thought of being near her, smelling her soft floral scent. Emotion swept through me as I remembered gazing into those large eyes, with their texture and complexity.

This woman, who had captured me, stood there holding someone else's hand. The old familiar tinge jabbed the center of my heart. Did my kisses mean nothing? Had she so casually forgotten me?

Her gaze caught mine. She immediately dropped his hand, and her lips parted slightly, forming an "O." She paused, collected herself, and smiled at me, piercing me with her attention.

Her beauty took my breath. I gulped. Other guys were part of the game, I reminded myself, but her response showed she cared what I thought. That was a good sign.

"Charissa." I approached much more slowly than normal. I smiled, hoping to hide my stiffness and awkwardness. I spotted a cameraman in the far corner of the hotel entryway. Our interaction was more than likely going to be captured on video.

"Andrew," she said. "What are you doing here?" Tiny dots of red sprouted on her face. She swallowed awkwardly, apparently afflicted with guilt.

"I was working out with Forester downstairs. The man's a monster with weights." There I went again, saying stupid things like pointing out the strengths of my competition. "I'd hug you, but I'm all sweaty."

Her nose tweaked, but she smiled. "I'd rather you didn't either."

The guy stood there taking in our conversation.

"This is Rocco," she said, gesturing her thumb toward him. "Another contestant."

I nodded.

"Hey." He gave me a slight acknowledgment and looked around.

"Where you are from?" I asked to be polite.

He shifted weight from foot to foot. "Love to chat, but

I've had to go the bathroom for the past hour. The coffee went right through me. They seriously don't give us many bathroom breaks. Is there one around?"

"There's a small one right over there." I pointed to my right.

He reached out and squeezed Charissa on the forearm. "Be right back. Wait here," he said before brushing past us.

I didn't like how he just ordered Charissa to wait. He shouldn't be doing that. Brushing off my irritation, I stepped up close to Charissa and whispered, "I enjoyed last night."

She peered up at me shyly, her eyes taking me in, then glanced away.

"I did, too."

"I've been thinking about it all night and today."

"Really?" She seemed to perk up. "What were you thinking?"

I stared at her, tongue-tied, struggling as always to put words to ideas. I shrugged my shoulders. "Just how nice it was to be with you and how natural it felt."

She smiled at me shyly with her head tipped toward her chest. "It is comfortable between us."

"It is." I wanted to reach out and hug her, but Rocco would be back any time, and I figured I better not. "I really enjoyed our kiss, so tender... nice."

Her face bloomed into a pink flush. Behind me, a door opened. Probably Rocco returning.

"I look forward to kissing you again."

Her face deepened into red just as Rocco stepped up to us. I loved how easy she was to embarrass, so different from many other women.

Charissa swallowed, trying to regain composure. "I've come to steal away any of the guys who want to come on a group date."

I did a double-take. "What?"

"I'm breaking the rules… like someone recently said I needed to do. I'm here to tell you guys you can come, too, but it needs to be soon."

The cameramen scurried around us, shooting all of our expressions. They lived for moments like this on the show. We were gathering attention as the other hotel guests were returning at the noon hour. Curiosity filled their faces, and many pulled out cell phone cameras. Charissa looked at them, the cameramen from production, and then glanced back to me.

A rule breaker. That was sexy. "I'm in. Let me take a two-minute shower, and I'll be down. I'll tell Shawn. I'm sure he wouldn't mind walking away from playing solitaire."

She took a deep breath and clasped her hands low in front of her. "Great, I'll see you soon. Oh, here's an idea, do you want to introduce Rocco to Shawn and show him the living quarters? I'll ask Forester if he wants to come."

I shrugged, not liking the fact she was headed straight to the workout room where she would see a well-built, shirtless, Forester.

CHAPTER 17

Charissa

*A*fter eating ice cream with Rocco, I had hurried with him to the small old hotel where the men were staying. In the foyer, I ran into Andrew briefly but, during our conversation, he acted jumpy, practically dancing on his feet and not knowing which way to look. I did see him eye Rocco with a deep pout. I don't think he liked seeing me hold another man's hand, and I didn't blame him. This whole show was designed to create insecurities. In the real world, if I kissed him last night, today I'd be thinking about no one else but him.

I closed my eyes, offering a wish that Andrew would soon move on from his irritation. That done, I opened my eyes and hustled down the creaking stairs. In Catalina, all the hotels were small, narrow, and historic.

Loud clanking noises and grunting greeted me before

I entered the gym. Forester lifted a barbell in the otherwise empty workout room. His biceps bulged. Large veins popped out, looking more like ropes than normal veins.

I gulped, holding back the heat he stirred in me. His loud breathing and continued grunts echoed forcefully in the room. I strolled over to the spotter position and peered at his toned, gleaming, and shirtless body. He rippled in every place a male body could.

His closed eyes flickered open. "Charissa." He set down the barbell in its cradles. "What are you doing here?"

I smiled, trying not to notice the streams of sweat rolling down his stomach. "Surprising you."

"Well, you have certainly done that. Want to work out with me?" He sat up, grabbed a towel, and dabbed at the sweat.

The cameramen showed up in the reflections of all the glass mirrors. "From the way Andrew looked, and how slowly he walked, apparently you two have been going at it for quite a long time."

Forester grinned. "He gave out. I started before him and am still here."

Thinking about what it would be like to be married to a man like this, I asked the obvious question, "So, how long do you work out every day?"

He chugged down water from a paper cup. "Four or five hours if I can. Often, I rise early. Then, I go immediately to the gym after work, too."

An addiction.

I could smell all the manliness he had been sweating out for the past hours. I flared my nose and stepped backward.

"What?" he asked. "Don't I get a hug?" He smiled broadly, showing his perfect white and straight teeth.

I put my hand up like a stop sign. "Uh, no."

He laughed. "Can't say that I didn't try."

A crew member's walkie-talkie lit up with Dee's voice demanding to know where everyone was. I needed to get this group to the set before she exploded.

"Well, I'm inviting the first-round guys—which includes you, of course—on a group date. Want to come? You'd have to hurry, though. They expected us over an hour ago."

He tossed the paper cup in the trash. "Be ready in five." He dashed out of the room, determined. Soon, a pounding noise, like a herd of buffalo, erupted from the stairs overhead.

"That's a big man," I said to the camera crew. "A really big man."

* * *

THE FIRST HORROR I found out at the photoshoot was the production company wanted me to dress up like Marilyn Monroe.

As Monique prepped me, I asked, "How am I supposed to do this? I don't have any features like her. I will look awful as a blonde. I have the wrong skin tone for that."

"Oh, sweetie, you worry too much. You'd look great with a sack of potatoes for hair."

That was a statement I knew wasn't true. The short blonde wig Monique plopped on my head proved it, and no amount of cherry-red lipstick was going to make up for it. The one small saving grace was the dress selected for me... a sleeveless black dress that ruffled and flowed. It was flattering.

I eventually shook off how horrible I looked and walked into the room with the men.

"Photoshoot time." I spread my arms out and acted like I was excited as I looked at the 1950s backgrounds and furniture decorating the warehouse.

A photographer called out from the side of the room, "If I could please have all the tall men first, come line up along the backdrop."

The men started gathering, most making sure they smiled at me. I stood at the side of the set, feeling cold from the air conditioning. I crossed my arms over my chest.

"What's the matter?"

Andrew suddenly stood next to me.

I blinked. "Nothing."

"Come on," he said, bumping into me. "I can tell you are upset. What is it?" He turned and grabbed hold of both my elbows. "Tell me. I want you happy."

I shifted. "It's stupid really." He nodded for me to go on. "It's the hair. I look horrible in blonde."

He grabbed my wig, carefully unsecured it from my head, and tossed it behind a chair. "Problem solved." He waved Monique over. "Can you help Charissa out? She somehow lost her blonde wig, and I know that will keep happening. Do you think you can find a brown one for her? I know Marilyn was dark sometimes."

Monique looked at me, pressed her lips together, and nodded. "Fine. You win."

I looked up at Andrew and whispered, "Thank you," as the photographer called for him to get into the first screenshot.

It didn't take long for a new brown wig to be found and for me to pose in many different shoots with the men. Managing so many men and their needs and wants to exhaust me. I wasn't sure if it was a coincidence, but Andrew always managed to stay close to me, emitting protective energy, plus a lot of concern for me went on in that head of his. It was cute.

Shawn was easygoing and seemed to be up for whatever we threw at him, but that didn't stop him from being competitive to spend time with me. It surprised me when he would pop up next to me out of nowhere.

Rocco told jokes and created fun, although sometimes it seemed like he wanted things to be a certain way—like that I shouldn't ask about the other guys, and it was okay to order me to wait for him.

Forester liked to be in front, always talking and seeing we had a good time. Each man was so different. No chance of pegging someone with a "type."

Dressing up as Marilyn Monroe for the afternoon seemed trivial—actually, ridiculous—but I covered those thoughts with a smile.

I thought it hid my true feelings, but Andrew whispered once, "Do you want me to hurry this along?"

The other men would reach out and touch my shoulder or squeeze my arm, hoping for my attention in-between takes. I graced each with a smile, which apparently appeased them, but my responses felt shallow and insincere in that silly costume. Only Andrew realized something was way off.

The evening weather remained calm, and I let its peace absorb me as I wandered toward my hotel after the group date. The stairs creaked as I climbed them into the hotel. Once inside the lobby, I couldn't help but grab a book to read later. I didn't care what the rules were. It was crazy they didn't want us to read. How I longed to be back in my room to rest on my bed, order room service, watch a little TV, and curl in a ball and sleep deeply.

Just off the lobby, however, I found Edward, the pilot, flushed and scrubbing his hands together. "Can I walk with you? I have some questions on how to eat cancer-free."

"Of course," I said. "Anytime." Edward and I ended up standing in the hallway for at least twenty minutes as I answered his questions.

Once I made it inside my hotel room, I ordered room service and hunted for my hidden phone, feeling the need for connection to something familiar. Finally, I found it in the secret pocket of my suitcase. I sat on my soft bed, plopped on the pillow behind my back, and called my sister. I still did not know the actual time in Mexico.

The phone answered after the second ring.

"Hi," Chelsey said, whispering. "Ava's sleeping. Let me go to the porch." Two seconds later, she said, "Thank you so much for this. This place is amazing. I have met people from all over the world, and they have nothing but positive things to say. There're so many success stories it's actually giving me hope."

I released a big breath I hadn't realized I was holding onto. "I'm so glad."

"I know I might be foolish for believing."

"Don't say that. You have to believe. You have to." My sister didn't understand how much thoughts affected things.

"The more important thing is Ava's smiling, and she's enjoying it here," Chelsey said, ignoring my lecture. "Everyone loves her... she makes even the saddest people grin, and that's saying something."

That was Ava. "I'm missing her smile. Maybe we can FaceTime when she wakes."

"Sure, I'll have her give you a ring. It might be in the middle of the night."

I sunk into the pillow, letting it relieve the pressure in my neck. "I don't care. I long to see her."

Chelsey sighed. "I know. So, how's the TV show going? You're worn down. I hear it in your voice."

No use trying to hide anything from her. "I just miss being with you, seeing Ava."

She laughed. "You never were much of a traveler. The guy you hook up with better be like that."

Never thought of that. I would have to put "settler" on my list.

"This sounds awful, but I want to curl in a hole. I'm so tired, and there's so much demand. I can't wait until this is done and I'm with you guys again."

A rustling sound came from her end of the line. "Don't ruin this experience. Go to bed. Tomorrow will be better."

"They're playing the guys off of each other. I don't like it. I'm the prize. How am I supposed to know who's real and who's doing it to win?"

"You'll know," Chelsey said. "You'll know. And, if you

don't, when you bring them to 'meet the family night,' I'll sniff them out."

That, I had no doubt.

* * *

I FELL asleep in the middle of eating and woke up the next morning to salad dressing on my arm, on my hair, and all over the bed. What would the maids think? I looked at the half-eaten chicken and sighed.

I remembered Ava was going to call, so I snapped up my phone. I had missed six calls from her. She had wanted to talk. She left me a message.

"Charissa, this is Ava. I was hoping you'd be up for a live chat, but apparently not. I hope you are having fun with all those muscley men. Remember, they have to be cute. There's no excuse. You need to show me pictures of them and tell me about them, so I can tell you who to stay away from. I have the final say. Talk to you soon, and don't kiss too many guys. Remember, I'm going to be watching the show along with the rest of America."

She did sound like her spirits were up, and that was good. The doctors had to be wrong about their prognosis. They had to be. I flicked at a tear and stood. There would be no thinking about anything but her getting better and which guy I would kiss today.

A loud banging sounded on my door and, before I could even move, Dee marched in with cameras following.

I put up my hand. "No cameras!"

Dee snapped her finger, and the camera people scurried away.

"There's not enough sexual tension. We need connections between you and the men. All the men. I want a kiss like you had with Forester on the first day. You need to have the men to do more things like that."

Once again, I was getting smacked with the reality that this was a show manipulated for the effect of drama. Yet, somehow, in the end, it would affect my life. That gave me the creepy crawlies.

Yes, it was disappointing Forester hadn't found an opportunity to lock lips again with me yesterday. I expected he would somehow manage to find us alone together after his shower and give me another one of those spine-tingling kisses. In the gym with him, he had stood there without a shirt on, teasing me with his thick muscles piled on each other—muscles chiseled in the way Leonardo da Vinci had intended a man's body to look. But, sweat had dripped off of him like a dousing from a garden hose, and the smell was extreme. All he needed was a quick shower, then he would have been good for kissing. After he cleaned up, though, I had little communication with him, other than short friendly exchanges.

Dee interrupted my thoughts. "Today we film your idea for the group date. You picked this one during our planning meeting, remember?" She had bags under her eyes and no sparkle about her whatsoever. "It'll be interesting to see what kind of drama will happen."

Seriously, she had a warped sense of what was important.

"You think there'll be drama, Dee?"

"You're going to see who you're compatible with and who you aren't. How does that not equate to high drama?"

Perfect.

* * *

THE MEN HAD GATHERED around in the hotel meeting room, looking refreshed and clean against the dull backdrop of the bland room. I waved at them as I came in. Nobody looked stressed like before. Andrew winked, and Forester flashed a brilliant smile. Rocco was busy looking at something over near the cameras, and Shawn stood calmly by, hands in his pockets and watching me with soft eyes.

I cleared my throat. "Guys, are you ready to be put to the test?"

They all yelled, "Yes!"

"I'm going to give you a compatibility test. Compatibility is important for a relationship, and I want to see who I'm most likely to get along with, and who I'll work well with, based on scientific evidence."

Everyone shifted and moved around as I spoke. Shawn and Andrew paled. Forester stayed straight-faced.

"You want us to take a test?" Shawn asked. "What? You don't trust your own senses? You don't want to think for yourself?"

Those were biting words. I hadn't expected that from him. "It's not that," I stammered. "Relationships are tricky. The more you know about a person, the better off everyone is."

"That's sheep behavior," he challenged, taking a step toward me. "Really, what does science know about it, anyway?"

The tests were all set up. I wasn't about to change it.

"Do you have something you want to hide? Is that why you're resistant?"

"No," he said. "I have nothing to hide. I took all the damn tests required to make it on this show, to prove I was a fit man for you to date. Now, you want me to take more tests. This is getting ridiculous."

He walked out of the room, and the door slammed shut behind him.

I gulped, feeling like he had just slapped me across the face. Shaking, I turned to the other men who watched me closely. "Anyone else want to leave?"

They shook their heads.

Shawn's reaction was completely unexpected. I thought he'd be happy with this, as we had the most in common. These tests would more than likely prove it. Clearing my throat, I faced the group. "If you don't mind, I'll be back in a second."

With that, I took off in Shawn's wake, only to be blocked at the door by Dee. "Where do you think you're going?"

"After Shawn."

"You'll do no such thing."

Something wasn't adding up with Shawn, and I would find out what. I took a side step to move around her.

"We don't have time for all the drama right now. We need this type of drama to unfold tonight when we have it on the schedule."

I stared at this woman, mouth gaping. "You've got to be kidding me."

She came closer to me. "This is what I'm not kidding about. If you go chasing him, after he made a stink like that, you'll look like one of those weak co-dependent women who'll do anything to make the man feel better. There's enough of that type of immature behavior on other shows like this. The whole premise of this show is to demonstrate that when people become older and more mature, they make more mature decisions when trying to find love." Her voice grew louder as she spoke. "That they handle things more respectfully. We, as women, have worked hard to gain respect in the media. I'm not going to have you put another nail in our coffin. You'll not go chasing after him like a weak woman."

The other men had scattered across the room, finding chairs to sit in. From their various perches, everyone watched us. I wasn't sure if they could hear us or not.

"You will not be weak. I'm okay if you're confused. I'm okay if you're horny and break the rules to hang out with some of the guys until early in the morning. I'm okay if you show up on set completely exhausted and out of it for not getting enough sleep. But," her voice had moved to a shouting pitch, "I will not see you run after that drunken bastard because you're worried you hurt his feelings!"

The room went dead quiet as Dee panted to catch her breath. She struggled for air, and suddenly I understood that hardened shell so much better.

I extended my arms out to her. "Dee," I said. "Shawn hasn't been drinking."

"What?" her eyes snapped at me.

She ignored my outstretched arms, so I dropped them. "Shawn is not your dad or your mom's boyfriends."

She looked at me, dazed. "Take five," she yelled into the room and stormed out.

CHAPTER 18

Charissa

After taking a few moments to compose myself, I slipped out of the room to find Dee with her hands on her hips, chin drawn tight, talking emphatically to Shawn.

He stood close to her with his head hanging in apparent shame. When the door behind me clicked shut, both peered over at me.

Shawn glanced at Dee, nodded his head, and hustled over to me. "Uh, I decided to do the test, after all."

He avoided eye contact, and his face flushed a crimson red.

Something was wrong. This wasn't good. Did Shawn have a big, dark, ugly secret he wanted to keep hidden from me?

"What's going on?" I extended my hand, touching his shoulder.

Unflinching, he said nothing.

Dee cleared her throat like a signal to Shawn.

He glanced at her. "I need to go back in there." He didn't look at me, even though my eyes burrowed into him.

"Dee, what are you up to?"

"Trying to run a show," she said, face blank.

She had threatened Shawn somehow. I caught his arm. "Shawn?"

His face was on fire with pink.

"Shawn, tell me, why are you out here? What upset you? How's Dee threatening you, and why?"

His eyes flicked down to me. He extended out his arms asking me to come to him. The next moment, I felt myself engulfed in his embrace. His cologne, smelling like midnight mist, engulfed me. His heart thudded against my cheek, confirming what I already knew, he felt deep emotions.

"Later," he covered his lips and whispered in my ear, "when there're no cameras."

* * *

THE TESTING ROOM remained completely quiet until Nancy's shoes clicked against the tile as she sauntered in front of us. She faced us holding a paper, which we all assumed held the test results.

Chelsey and I used to take personality tests growing up. We'd laugh and make fun of the tests because a lot of the time, the results were ridiculous. But, now it was serious. It meant something. The results would be broadcast across America. What if it turned out I wasn't compatible with any of the guys? What if the results were completely wrong? What if I could have had a good happy relationship with someone and sabotaged myself because I put too much reliance on a stupid test for a reality TV show?

I sat in the middle of the group: Andrew to my right, Shawn to my left, and Forester behind me. Rocco managed to squeeze in-between Andrew and Forester. I struggled to breathe. "You guys are making me nervous. I could eat your anxiety."

The guys laughed, and Nancy cleared her throat. "Charissa doesn't know this, but we aren't going to say who she's most compatible with. We're only going to reveal the top three men, who will go on a group date after this."

More tension. Why weren't they going to tell me who was on top? Didn't they think that would be important for me to know? Not that I'd base my decision on it.

"If all goes well... Charissa, and whoever she ends up with, will have the option to see the test results."

The camera flipped on me. I could feel myself frowning. "What was the use of having them take the test? It was supposed to give guidance through the process."

Someone patted me on my shoulder. I looked back and saw a dark hand. Must be Forester. It was nice of him to comfort me like that.

Nancy continued. "We are going to give you hints."

I rested back in my chair. At least that was something.

"What we're going to do is tell you, in no certain order, who the top three guys are. They will proceed with you to go zip-lining, followed by drinks."

That caused a lot of varied noise from the men.

"Cool." Rocco nodded, giving his approval.

"You've got to be kidding." Shawn's response made me wonder what he was thinking.

"Should be interesting." That was my thinker, Andrew.

Nancy waited until everyone settled. "Are you ready to find out who the top three are?"

Sometimes I really hated how dramatic these show people made everything. Why did there have to be winners and losers?

"How about all of them can come because everyone was willing to play the game?" I asked. I wanted to be with every single one of them.

Nancy glared at me as the men rallied in applause.

Cameras rotated to me, but I ignored them. "If I'm not going to be told the exact results, or what areas we're compatible in, then let me have more time with all of them. I'll figure it out myself."

Nancy smirked and completely ignored everything I said. She looked in the camera with a serious expression. "The first man most compatible with you is..." She held out her breath for dramatic effect. "Rocco."

Rocco jumped to his feet and did a football dance. "Yes!" he said, then he hustled over to where I sat and bent down to give me a big hug.

Shock must have taken over because I felt out of my body hugging him. All I could think was... Rocco?

"What do you think makes us compatible?" I asked him.

He smiled. "We're both into health. We both like to have

fun. I like to create it, and you like to laugh. That makes us perfect."

That response piqued my interest.

Nancy cleared her throat.

One of the crew members instructed both Rocco and me to stand on the winning line. We hurried over to it. Rocco squeezed my hand, and it sent shivers up my arm. I looked across the room to Shawn, Andrew, and Forester, and wondered who would be the odd guy out. A pain pierced my heart. On paper, this seemed like such a logical next step. I had thought about protecting myself, not about what this would do to the guys... or me, for that matter.

Maybe it had been a mistake not to have two more guys stay, as the production company had planned. The guy who hadn't been picked or scored as well was going to feel awful and rejected.

During drinks after the zip lining event, I'd have production send for the remaining man so he wouldn't feel so bad. I'd make sure he was first to share time with me. That solution sounded arrogant like it was some big grand prize to be with me, but it did mean more airtime on national TV, so maybe that would be a perk. I shook my head. I was as bad as a mother trying to ease the pain of neglecting her child.

"And, the bachelor next most compatible..." Nancy interrupted my internal lecture.

The men shifted in their seats. At least this time the production crew wasn't making them stand, like at the shell ceremony. Torturing the contestants, I liked to call it.

Forester had taken a military stance. Shawn clenched and unclenched his fingers. Andrew stood still, as close to me as he could be, looking ready to spring into action if I needed anything. That protective nature was endearing but also worrisome. I wasn't sure if he acted like that because I was a reality TV show star and more of a target, or if he naturally was more possessive.

Nancy spoke again. Her expression showed she didn't care if I was ready for this additional information. She gave it anyway. "According to test results, the second compatible millionaire is..." She raised her eyebrows, like that would enhance the suspense.

Maybe it did. Who knew?

"Shawn."

I burst out laughing even though that was unprofessional. I couldn't help it. The man who threw such a fit about taking the test, and he end up rewarded.

Shawn came up to me, arms extended for a big hug. I slipped into his arms. His embrace was warm and tender like he didn't want to break me.

When he pulled away, I whispered, "So, my Wisconsin guy, how do you think we are compatible?"

He looked at me with eyes ready for the game. "Simple, I'm probably the person on that list who's the most compatible with you because we come from the same stock. We're both country people. We both like and want the simple lifestyle. We have grown up close to the land, and nature feeds us. With that as our foundation, we're still open to broadening our life experience by including love if it happens to us."

Our gazes connected, and I sensed him searching to see if his words resonated with me. They did. I wiped at my eyes.

Nancy was ready to go on. "Well," she said, "Shawn, are you glad you took the test now?"

His eyes snapped on Nancy, and the room turned chilly. That was the wrong thing to say, apparently. Shawn said nothing.

Nancy cleared her throat and looked back up at the camera. "We are now down to two men," she said.

I didn't want the one last guy—the guy who didn't answer his questions completely right because his personality was different from mine—to be singled out. Pinpointed as the wrong one in the game was worse than not being picked to play in the game.

I stepped forward. "I declare that both of them are compatible with me, too."

Nancy gave the camera an expression of extreme patience. "Charissa, I'm sorry. I know you'd prefer it that way, but that isn't what we're going to do. In fact, we're doing you a favor. We're giving you a tip about which one of these guys you're more likely to match with well in the long run."

I straightened my back as I took in the information, still feeling bad for the guy who wasn't going to be picked. This was one of those times Chelsey would say I was co-dependent. I put the needs of the guys over my own.

Andrew looked pasty white, head lowered, and Forester, in his military stance, appeared confident, like none of this stuff mattered.

Nancy squared herself in front of the camera again. "And, the third suitor who's most compatible with Charissa is…"

She gave another dramatic pause, which, if you asked me, was becoming predictable. "Andrew."

When Andrew heard his name, he jumped into the air, shouting like he just won a fancy car. "Yes!"

Forester shook his head and walked away.

I looked at Andrew approaching and ready to be congratulated and talked to like the other guys in the exclusive club. Beyond him, I glimpsed Forester exiting the room with his head down. I nudged back the guys and sidestepped Andrew's outstretched arms. "I'll be just a minute."

As best I could in the too-high heels they had me in again, I hobbled quickly away and tripped over a chair I didn't see.

"Forester!" I called out to him, sure at this rate. I would never be able to catch up. He had rounded the corner and headed down the hallway.

He turned and saw me struggling to run. His facial expression stayed the same, completely blank. I scurried up to him in the hall, grateful we were out of the room where the other guys were. He stood tall and expressionless, waiting for me to be near him. I came up, breathing heavy and making commitments to myself that I'd start an exercise routine once I returned home.

Anger emitted from him in massive energy waves. "Yes?"

Not sure how I should proceed, I gulped. "I wanted to see if you are alright."

His eyebrows rose, giving me the sense he was amused. "Yes, why wouldn't I be?"

I looked at him, at the camera crew that filled the hall,

and back to the room where the other guys stood. "Well, what just happened?"

He shrugged. "You learn in law you can't always win every battle. It was a silly test with silly results. I'm not going to worry about it."

With that, he stepped closer to me, took me in his arms, and landed another passionate kiss. This time he leaned me back and ran his hands through my hair. He kissed and nibbled my lips and, just as quickly, planted me back on my feet.

"I will have my time with you," he said.

CHAPTER 19

Andrew

The flush on Charissa's face was impossible to ignore. As she slowly approached us, she kept glancing back toward the door. I had won. I wanted to talk with her and answer the question she asked the other two guys. Instead of coming up to me and picking up where she had left off, though, she stumbled into the room with a flush that lasted too long. It made her face pink like she had been in the sun too long.

A crew member greeted her with a bag and tennis shoes in her hand.

"Time for zip lining!" Dee called out.

The room grew noisy immediately. The crew members scurried around. Shawn and Rocco beelined to talk to one of the crew members.

"Don't I get to talk to Charissa?" I yelled at Dee.

She gave me a blank look. "What are you asking me? You're going on a zip-lining date with her in a few minutes."

Pressure built in my chest. My reaction was silly. I had a good relationship with Charissa. I didn't need to worry about that, or the things the other men had said to her, nor the way she looked up at them dreamily, or the fact she had returned from Forester blushing. None of that mattered. I'd have fun with her zip-lining, and she would feel supported. That mattered. If I trusted my feeling that we were meant to be together, I didn't need to be concerned about those other things. They were distractions.

In sales, it only worked if I believed I would make the sale. I was going to stop sabotaging myself by making a big deal over nothing with Charissa's slight. I was, instead, going to close the most important deal in my life.

Nancy rushed over to me and said I needed to follow her. A crew member took us guys to the base camp for the zip lining. We needed to be weighed and strapped up. I wandered over to the edge of the room to join Shawn and Rocco.

"I thought you weren't coming." Rocco shifted his weight, taking me in.

I slapped him on the back. "Don't you wish? No worries, boys, your chief competition is here."

"Not happening," Rocco said. "Charissa is all mine. When I get her home alone, away from all of you, I'm going to get her on an exercise program to lose those extra pounds on her backside. When those pounds are gone, and she has proven she can do it, I'll schedule the wedding."

All the air left my chest as blood raced through me. This guy was one piece of work. My hands curled into fists. A flicker of the light from the camera caught my attention. The world watched.

"She's great the way she is." Shawn's tone sounded thick with anger.

Rocco laughed, not seeming to notice our reactions. "I'm a professional speaker. Average might be alright for you boys, but I have an image. A reputation. I make money based on how I look. I can't have my woman looking anything but perfect. Charissa is close, but with a month of hardcore training, she'll get there."

I stepped in front of Rocco. "That's the biggest load of crap I've ever heard! You shouldn't have plans to change Charissa. Either love her for the way she is or get off the show."

"Whoa, step back, dude!" Rocco put up a hand to create space between us.

I wouldn't back down. "No. I won't tolerate the way you're speaking about a woman I care about." I planted my feet more firmly with a slight bend in my knees. I felt the stiffness from my earlier workout with Forester but ignored it.

Rocco laughed, then spit a huge wad of liquid in my face.

I didn't move. I wouldn't back down to him. I stood there silent, glaring at him.

"You barely know her," he added. "You might be infatuated with her, but she'll eventually become annoying. You'll see her flaws."

He took a step closer, trying to intimidate me. "It's not

my fault you're so hoodwinked right now and don't have any wisdom. I have guts enough to speak the truth. No man finds a woman he doesn't want to change, at least a few things. That's honest."

CHAPTER 20

Charissa

The afternoon light shone on the green vegetation. Ziplining sounded nerve-racking. My heartbeat had picked up with the thought of stepping into a harness and flying across the island high in the air. What had I been thinking of, agreeing to this? I guess I thought the guys would love it after the Marilyn Monroe event. I had only thought about making them happy, not how it would affect me.

Maybe they could do it, and I would stand by on the sidelines and cheer them on. No, I'd never get away with bailing out.

Eating crackers, I strolled past a long line of tall palm trees bordering the black asphalt sidewalk as it curved along the ocean. Large fabric signs flapped in the wind announcing events on the island. About half the sailboats remained docked in the watery slips. The sky had, once again, gone gray, with a smattering of white hinting that the sun might poke through again.

We headed toward the large casino building. I asked the crew member next to me, the young girl who looked a bit like Ava, "Have you gone gambling yet, Destiny?"

She shook her head. "It isn't a real casino. They call it that, using the broad meaning of 'entertainment.' It's a movie house with a dance floor on the top."

It was a movie house with a dance floor, not a gambling joint. I had completely misread that building. Maybe I did the same thing with the guys. I looked out onto the ocean-front and across the spread of water. Its massiveness settled my stirring heart. Three men waited to volley for time with me. Huge waves of uneasiness washed up against my chest, stirring and whirling.

My legs grew heavier to lift as I lumbered around the island. I stifled a yawn. I needed a nap. These men each wanted constant attention. They wanted time to woo me and connect. Had I been like that? If I had, that was embar-rassing.

The silence I could have enjoyed by staying at my cabin taunted me. It teased me with what could have been if only Ava would've stayed in remission. The poor girl had suffered enough and didn't deserve to be afflicted with more pain, more procedures, and more worry.

She was innocent. She had done nothing in this world except arriving at birth with a will to live. Maybe I could come to terms with it if I had been at the cabin and experi-enced the type of healing that only came from the silent witnessing of oneself.

I fed myself lies. It'd never be okay with Ava's illness and suffering. The only thing that made it tolerable was the fact that she was getting help. I needed to stay strong with her. This could save her life. So what if I felt weird with everyone's attention on me, including the camera's? Soon, all this would be over, and I'd be reflecting on it, wishing I had better appreciated the attention from these good men.

At least they wanted to take the time to get to know me and wanted to talk with me. They appreciated my home-spun background. They enjoyed my quiet nature and didn't cause a lot of drama. They had all said in their own way. That was why they came on the show. Well, everyone except Rocco and Forester. Neither made their intentions clear, but both seemed to be in it for the right reasons. I had a great connection with both of them.

As I thought about Forester's kisses one more time, I flushed.

The crew noticed how I dallied behind. Destiny sidled up to me again. "We need to hurry. The zip line is going to take a while, and we need to be there before the sun goes down."

I picked up my pace. We approached some short green grass and walked around a hotel and up to a station. It included a shed, a bathroom building a short distance away, and a young smiling youth ready to scare me.

Several minutes later, after a pee stop, because the nerves were getting to me, I strolled up to the shed where more official-looking young people, wearing company shirts, greeted me.

"We need to weigh you," said the girl behind a make-shift podium.

"This," I turned toward the camera, "better not go on TV. My weight is my own business."

The camera people scampered back, turning their heads away. The lady who wanted my weight smiled, probably more for the cameras.

"Don't worry. No one will know your weight. Believe me, the only reason I'm asking is for your safety. We need to make sure we fit you with the right harness. We take extreme measures to ensure our customers are safe."

I glared at her as though she had already revealed that information to the tabloids. I closed my eyes. I was paranoid. Taking a breath, I stepped on the scale and looked around carefully for the cameras to see if anyone of them was close enough for the zoom. I saw nothing but Shawn coming up to me.

He stopped several feet away to my right. They had geared him up with a construction helmet and thick strapped harness, and he carried heavy metal hooks. The equipment made all of this look serious.

The blood drained out of my face, and my fingers tingled. My stomach felt empty even though I had nibbled on crackers while heading over here.

"Hey," Shawn said. "You ready for this?" He spoke like he didn't have a care in the world.

My legs were jittery. I shrugged. "Don't know." I needed to shift the attention from me fast. "This your first time at this?"

Shawn shook his head. "Heck, no. Remember, I come from farm country. We do this kind of thing all the time in the summer. In the winter, it's more snowmobiling, skiing, and snowboarding. Have you ever gone cross-country skiing?"

The employees of the zip line interrupted and handed me an iPad to sign away my rights to sue. That didn't help. Zip lining across the Island of Romance had sounded so romantic and ideal when the show pitched the idea in their nice safe production office.

They didn't mention the harness or the hooks and weigh-ins. "This is just one zip line, right?" I asked.

The worker laughed. "No, there are five and will take you to the beach area of the island. The longest line will be over a quarter-mile long. You can take in the ocean and a lot of the different vegetation. It's quite a view."

I hadn't asked for the infomercial, and I didn't like what she said. "Five?"

She smiled. "It's not bad. It gets easier."

The crew told us to sit in the waiting dock where they would give us instructions. They would then drive us up to the first line.

My jittery legs became worse. I slumped over to the bench where a demo area had been set up for our training. I closed my eyes to stop the swirling in my head.

I turned to Shawn to focus on something other than the fact I was about to dangle and rush through the air attached to a small hook. "What did you say about Wisconsin and winter?"

"I had asked if you have ever gone cross-country skiing?" Shawn asked.

I shook my head. "I haven't. Why?"

"Oh, I have to take you. I want to do that the first time it snows." He slipped his hand down against my leg. "You're going to love it. It's peaceful out in the wilderness with just you and the snow. Sometimes I listen to inspiring music on headphones."

We were a lot alike. We did the same things.

I touched him back on his thigh, and his face blushed with my touch. My hand lingered. "So, where are the other two guys? Did they chicken out?"

He stroked my fingers. "I wish. They went for a restroom break."

"That's odd." I strained to look in the area of the restrooms. "They are taking a long time."

He withdrew his hand and slipped into silence.

Something was wrong. "Did I say something wrong, Shawn?"

He looked at our hands and flushed. "Charissa, some things are going on in the house with the guys. I'm not sure you want to know about it."

My heart picked up speed. The show had this scene every year. One of the housemates starting to talk to the love interest about what happening in the house. Never a good thing.

What the person said was often the truth. Most of the time, the love interest failed to believe it and ended up looking like a fool for not listening to the warning. I thought with fewer men, and all of them rich and older, we would've skipped this part. I blew out a sigh, glancing toward the restrooms to see if the guys were returning. They weren't.

"Tell me." I looked directly into Shawn's eyes. His gaze lacked his usual confidence. This must not be good if he was acting this way. "Come on." I tugged his knee. "Out with it."

He flicked his gaze at me, then it moved away. "I don't want to cause anyone trouble, and I don't want you to think I don't trust your judgment in figuring out who's good for you. You have a smart head on your shoulders, and you'll eventually figure things out."

Shawn wasn't one of those guys to make a big deal about nothing. He didn't have that in him. If he thought it was a problem big enough to talk with me about, it must be an issue.

"Shawn, I trust if you're bringing this up it's something you need to tell me. I'm glad you trust me and believe I'll eventually figure things out... The truth is that I'm not a mind reader, and I can use all the help I can find."

The sun tucked under a cloud as his face flushed a ripe raspberry color. He bent closer to keep his voice down. "There's a guy in the group who's saying things I don't believe any gentleman would say, and it's causing alarm in the house."

My stomach had decided to join my legs in being jittery. "What's he saying?"

"Things that aren't appropriate."

He was struggling to tell me. He didn't want to break his brother's code and speak ill of someone else. I could see that. I could appreciate that... a lot. It was one of the reasons I liked him so much. He was a good guy, and he had good intentions. I put my hand on his shoulder. "Who is it?"

"What are you talking about?" Rocco asked.

My eyes darted up. Andrew and Rocco stood behind

Shawn in the graying afternoon, both harnessed up. I hadn't heard them or seen them coming, and from the way Shawn jumped, he hadn't either.

I tipped my chin back, taking them in. The guides flanked them, ready to go. My chest pounded against my harness. The expected thing would be to drop what Shawn said and come back to it later and go on with the date. Sweat rose on the back of my neck. I lifted my hair and brushed at it. I had promised Ava I'd stand up for myself. Butterflies fluttered in my stomach. All wasn't as it appeared to be, and I really didn't like it.

I held up one finger toward the guide. "Would you mind giving us one minute?" My voice sounded as weak and as unsure as I felt.

I widened my eyes to wait for the verdict. The guide's startled gaze flicked over to the cameras, and he swallowed. "No, I don't mind at all. Take all the time you need." He stepped away. "I'll be over here when you're ready." He pointed off set.

With that, I picked up my metal hooks for the zip line and stared at the guys. "Shawn here has been telling me he thinks someone in the house isn't here for the right reason." My voice broke, but I kept talking anyway. "Who will tell me what he's talking about?"

Rocco clenched his jaw and peered over my head. Shawn looked down and flushed again, and Andrew's fingers twitched against the harness he held. Every one of them remained quiet.

I folded my arms across my chest. "I wanted to go on this fun adventure with you guys, but I can't unless someone tells me what's going on."

CHAPTER 21

Andrew

*A*ll the color had drained out of Charissa's face. Her eyes were wild with helplessness, appearing like a fragile girl. One of us needed to speak up for her, even if it might make her mad. If we didn't do it soon, she'd be in tears, and I certainly didn't want to see her cry.

"I know what he's talking about," I said.

Everyone's head pivoted to me, and I could feel the tension of the cameramen hurrying to capture what I'd say. To give those guys a chance, and to give myself a moment, I waited. "Shawn and I heard some disturbing comments from Rocco earlier."

Her eyes snapped onto him. "Rocco?" Shock sounded thick in her voice. "What did you say?"

Rocco's eyes narrowed. "Andrew set me up because he's possessive. He'd do anything to get you to himself."

That creep was trying to take me down. Time to get to the point.

"Rocco said when you pick him, he'll take you to the gym and whip you in better shape. Then he'd be willing to marry you."

My words came out loud and crisp and seemed to punch her in the gut. She paled and tipped her head down as if all her energy slipped out of her. What I said hurt her. Maybe I shouldn't have been so blunt.

"Personally, Charissa," I added, "I find you perfect the way you are. There isn't anything that needs to be changed."

She didn't seem to listen. Instead, she moved her focus to Shawn. Her eyes became even larger. "Shawn, is this true?"

He glanced at her, then me, then over to Rocco, who clenched his hands into fists. Shawn gave a barely detectable nod and whispered, "It is."

Charissa gasped, tears swelled in her eyes, hand on her lips, she turned to Rocco. "You can go home now."

He jumped in front of her, his face a violent red. "You can't do that to me!" He moved in on her, arm swinging back like he was preparing to hit her.

In a split second, I found myself standing in front of Charissa, protecting her from Rocco. "Back down!" I growled.

"That's a bunch of crap. Do you want to be coddled by these piss ants?" He tried to look around me to Charissa.

Shawn leaped to Charissa's other side. We looked like the FBI, working together to fight a terrorist.

"That's enough," I said. "You heard the lady. It's over."

Rocco looked to the staff. "She can't do that, can she? She can only do that when it is the shell ceremony, and that isn't until tomorrow. We have a group date to go on. I have zip lines to conquer."

I folded my arms across my chest. "Not happening. You two aren't a match, and it's time for you to go home. Security!" I yelled out. "If you don't escort this man away, I will."

Rocco tipped his chin up toward me. "Nice one. Not going to happen. You don't have the authority."

By the time he finished his sentence, security had surrounded him. Apparently, it *was* going to happen, and fast. They escorted Rocco away, pushing and cussing.

Charissa burst into tears. "I didn't see that coming. I thought he was a good guy. I had no idea he was like that."

I sat next to her with Shawn on her other side. I reached out to comfort her by stroking her back. The moment my hand touched her, she stiffened and jumped to her feet. The metal hooks of the zip line slumped to the ground.

"Don't touch me!" she yelled. "Don't anyone touch me."

She bent down, picked up her metal attachments, and hurried off toward the bathroom in tears.

* * *

Charissa

DEE WAS at my side by the time I found a patchy spot of grass to sink onto.

"Charissa, what's going on?"

"Rocco lied to me."

She yawned. "Yeah, I know. That kind of shit happens every season."

"Well, I'm not every girl." I looked up and saw the cameras on me. "Get those cameras off." The cameramen stood there, continuing to shoot. "Get them off me now!"

I had enough of this. I wasn't doing this anymore. Not every moment in my life needed to be filmed, especially not when I was having a breakdown. My crying scenes would make the commercial outtakes that would play over and over. I knew how they played this game from last time. I covered my eyes with my hands and hung my head.

"I mean it, Dee. Get them off me, or I'm not doing this anymore."

"Okay, guys, go." I could sense she gave them some signal. There were shuffling noises as she turned to me. "Okay, they're gone. Why are you so upset?"

Tears flowed down my face. I didn't know why the situation freaked me out so much. Yes, I had liked Rocco, but I liked some of the other guys better, like Forester and Shawn and, of course, Andrew. They were all nice men, and I'd be lucky if I ended up with any of them. I shrugged.

"It's stressful being the object of desire and having to juggle so many males' attentions," Dee said, uncharacteristically sympathetic. "Rocco isn't worth all this. He was a creep. Don't let a stupid man steal your happiness," she said.

I raised my eyes to her brown ones, and they bored into me, communicating a far deeper message than her words.

I snuffled. "Someone hurt you. That's why you are the way you are."

She bristled. "This isn't about me. This is about you not

giving your power away. You're here to shoot a show. You have a niece to return to. You need to make sure that little girl has all the healing and loving she deserves. Don't let some stupid player, who wasn't that smart or good at playing, bother you. You caught him. You stood up to him in a strong, powerful way. I'm going to love it when that scene airs on TV. You made women's power proud. I couldn't have coached you to do better myself."

I wiped at my eyes. "Really?" That was a *compliment* coming from Ms. Critical, Dee.

"Really." She smiled and patted me on the back. "Now we need you to shoot a take where you tell the cameras how nervous standing up to him made you feel. We need it for dramatic effect. Then, we should see if we still have time to shoot the zip-lining date before dark. I hope we do because we have more great eligible guys scheduled to fly in tomorrow."

More guys! I felt sick. They weren't giving me a break from the consistent onslaught. Other shows gave the main lead a week to make the next choice. They had me on super speed, and I couldn't keep up. I didn't like it. Three was more than enough. I needed time to ground and connect with them, not have new ones thrown at me in a constant barrage of chaos.

* * *

The zip line company was more than understanding in working with us on our much-delayed schedule. They agreed to let us still go. Two instructors eagerly gave us the guidelines about what we needed to do while on the lines and how to keep safe. They hurried through the presentation and even demonstrated on the practice zip line cords.

As they talked, my temples throbbed, making my sight blurry. I didn't know if it was from standing up to Rocco or from the prospect of dangling hundreds of feet in the air suspended by a few clips and cords. I grabbed both Shawn and Andrew's hands as we watched the demo and squeezed them.

"This is going to be scary."

Both men squeezed me back.

"It's okay. I'm here for you," Andrew said.

I felt the warmth of his heart. He'd do anything he needed to do to keep me safe. He had actually just proven with Rocco that he'd put my interest before anyone. I leaned into him and rested my head on his chest. After a moment, I lifted my head to smile at him.

He smiled back, watching me intently as if determining what I felt toward him.

Shawn watched us, flushing but not saying anything.

Feeling guilty, and not wanting to hurt Shawn's feelings either, I bolted up, my back straight. I hated double dates for this reason. Too many feelings to constantly juggle.

One of our guides was a young man in his late twenties with unruly curly hair that gave him an Einstein look. He was friendly and asked us each a lot of questions.

"Ever zip line before? Where are you all from? How's the show going?"

He listened intently to our answers. "Sounds great. The Island of Romance is definitely the place to come if you want romance. You guys need to make sure you check out the back part of the island. Did you know it's home to some endangered animals? It's amazing. They have a wonderful conservatory here. The island's lack of predators allows the buffalo, deer, and small foxes to flourish. They take the eggs from the mother birds threatened with extinction and put the eggs in an incubator. After the eggs hatch and are stable, they reintroduce the baby animals into the environment."

I leaned in to hear the guide more clearly. This was interesting. "Don't the moms know their egg is missing?"

"They give them a fake egg, and they don't detect it. This new project really increased the survival rate."

"Wow."

The guys and I walked over in the late afternoon sun to the open Hummer. The vehicle didn't have windows, except for the windshield, and its tires loomed higher than me. I grabbed onto the handlebar to leverage myself up and crawled into the back seat. It would only be right if I sat in the middle, so I did. I should've let one of the guys go first. Shawn followed had to crawl over me. Andrew sat on my other side. Both men grabbed hold of my arm—one for each of them.

Things could've been worse. A lot worse.

* * *

THE OVERCAST SKY matched my mood… melancholy. The tour staff was friendly and talkative. They asked us questions and told us about the place, but I struggled to listen. I couldn't shake off the longing of wanting to be with Ava. I needed to see her myself and know she was alright. But, all this was for her. I needed to remember that.

Both Shawn and Andrew repeatedly bumped into me as we drove over the various pits on the road. I liked being near both of them, and I let my legs accidentally fall against theirs'. Heat exchanged from touching them as I watched the rough terrain in front of us.

Our zip-lining tour guide had encouraged us to take the bus ride around the island and to see more of the wild. That was all part of the schedule, and I'd be doing that in a day or two, but I couldn't say anything. The dates I planned were kept secret, and I hadn't picked who I'd be going with yet. I needed to keep my thoughts away from what was coming and focus on what was in front of me.

The landscape had definitely transformed into something more rugged. It looked desolate. Shawn and Andrew appreciated it more than I did. Maybe that was a guy thing.

When the Hummer jerked to a stop, my jello legs returned. It soon would be time for me to jump out into the air with only little hooks holding me as I flew across the terrain.

There was absolutely no way I'd go first. I wasn't even sure if I *would* go. I needed to. There were cameras on me, and the world watched. The men expected me to go. I didn't want to take away from their fun. They had already put up with enough crap with that whole Rocco deal.

We all climbed out of the Hummer, and our guides walked over to a short wooden staircase. We needed to climb it to reach the platform. I breathed deeply, not thinking, taking one step at a time.

Einstein stopped and pointed out a white-flowering plant. He told us its name and how rare and hardy it was. He said plants like it kept the animals fed on the island.

The tiny white flower, in all its small beauty, shone only in that little spot in the world. It had to be strong to live there and was a blessing for the animals. The bloom needed a minimum amount of rain. It also harvested moisture from the fog. The plant took the love it was given and made the most of it.

I admired that.

I didn't notice the height we were climbing to. This platform had been built onto a cliff overlooking an extremely deep ravine. Three hundred feet down, I was told. A tremble started deep within me, telling me to get away from there.

"Still going?" Shawn asked as he crept up behind me.

I looked up the couple of feet to where Andrew and the tour guides stood on the platform.

"Oh, sorry. I guess I spaced."

Shawn laughed. "That's a normal thing to do when you're nervous."

"I'm not nervous." I rubbed my lips together, wondering if the guys were scared, too, but just hiding it.

"Then you're going first?" He asked, calling me on my crap.

"Okay, you caught me," I said. "I lied. You or Andrew need to go. If you survive the trip, then I'll think about taking it myself."

He laughed again as I joined the others at the platform. Why hadn't he acted the gentleman and volunteered to go first? Why was he giving me a bad time instead? I didn't like it.

I looked out over the terrain they expected us to zip line over and gulped. We stood hundreds of feet above the trees. Trees! This was no baby zip line. This was hardcore.

* * *

Andrew

THE JEEP PULLED over and stopped. Time to jump. Poor Charissa trembled. I wanted to wrap my arms around her and hold her until she calmed, but that would make this situation worse. There was absolutely no color in her face. I would make sure I went last. I wanted to root her to the ledge and help her find her courage to take that leap. She'd need all the encouragement I could give her.

The curly headed guide gave us more instructions and then charged through the drill of the safety checks. He talked about how we needed to raise our legs to our chest at the end so we wouldn't get hurt in the landing. The terrain we would fly over was a mixture of trees with various shades of green and brown shrubbery, all of which looked snarly and angry. If we twisted sideways on our flight, we'd see this wild land spread all the way to the ocean with its choppy gray waters and the rolling, white, dingy sky.

I edged over to Charissa, noticing her shaking hands as she gripped the metal bar and harness. She eventually glanced at me, color still gone.

"You'll be fine," I whispered.

Curly locks asked her if she wanted to go first. Unable to find words, she shook her head. The guy nodded at me. "I'm going after Charissa for moral support," I said.

Charissa gave me a funny expression I wasn't able to read.

Shawn stepped up. "That leaves me. I'll go." He winked at us.

"Great," curly locks said, "I'm going to zip over there and set up to be ready to receive you." With that, he opened the little wooden gate that held us in, did a few snaps of links, and jumped to the other platform at least five feet away. He flew across the land, harness attached, arms spread wide, showing off.

"Sweet," I said.

Even though that was a cool feat, Charissa's strength seemed to seep out of her.

"You have to jump out in the middle of nothing," she said.

"You're secure," the other helper said, flipping her ponytail over her shoulder. "Think about jumping for the perfect future you want to create, speaking metaphorically, of course. You have to leap."

Charissa sat on the wooden bench as Shawn prepared to take off. He stood on the top stair to have his harness and hooks double-checked. Charissa's rugged breath increased.

"Going to do any tricks?" I asked Shawn.

He laughed. "I think so."

He strolled to the ledge. The escort opened the gate, and Shawn jumped without a sound. Within five seconds, he let go with his hands and flipped his whole body toward us, whooping.

Charissa had stepped up to the rail to watch. She trembled more as she grabbed the guardrail, apparently for strength. "That first step is into thin air. The ground isn't there," she said.

I nodded. "But you can do it. You'll be attached. You're safe."

"Are you ready?" the ponytailed attendant asked.

"No," she said, but she did step up to the plank for a safety check.

"Charissa?" I asked. She looked straight ahead, pale. Her eyes swiveled to me, and I winked. "What is it that you most want in your future?"

She held out her hands and let the gal do her safety check. "Um, for my niece to… get well, and for me… to be the best aunt possible."

Her voice struggled to say it through all the emotion. There was an untold story there.

"That sounds like a great thing to bring to your future."

She didn't say anything as she received the signal it was time to go. She stepped to the small open gate and peered down and across the land. A flutter of swear words spilled out of her mouth.

That made me laugh. "Jump for your niece!" I called out. "Jump for your time with her and for lots of laughs."

Charissa gave a grunt that became a yell. She crept off the ledge with a scream that followed her. The noise grew into an ear-piercing sound. She continued screaming until she reached about halfway across. When she stopped yelling, she continued to clench the handles. Another short scream escaped her, but it was the last until she zoomed in the remaining hundred feet. She raised her legs, and curly locks caught her on the other side.

She had done it.

"Did you see that?" I asked the zip-line gal. "That was awesome. She was totally scared, and she jumped anyway. That is one gutsy, focused woman."

The guide prepared the equipment for my jump. "I didn't think she'd do it. Most of the scared ones don't. I thought I'd have to take her back."

I looked across the ravine at the impressive woman. I found her quiet grit just plain sexy.

* * *

Charissa

I HAD MIXED feelings with Andrew always hanging close, but when he stepped in front of me to guard against Rocco, and made sure to stay behind on the zip line to support me, my mixed feelings changed into relief.

After I did the third zip line, he placed a hand on my arm. "You have this down, want to go first?"

Not finding the words, I shook my head. Zip lining, flying so high above everything, was intense, and I liked to gather my courage before jumping into nothing.

"You going to scream this time?" Shawn asked with a teasing grin.

"Yes." There was nothing wrong with screaming, absolutely nothing wrong, and if it got me down the hill, I'd do it. Ironically, when I stepped out into the nothingness that time, no yells came.

Shawn grinned at me when I landed. "I didn't hear any screams."

What to say? I shrugged. Sometimes I surprise myself.

When we reached the last zip line, Andrew put both hands on my shoulders. "I'd like you to go first."

If I could send hate bombs with my eyes, I'd have done so. I said nothing. Andrew hurried in front of me and talked to Shawn. Shawn faced me. "You're going first."

What use was it to have two boyfriends if they conspired against me? Without saying a word, I strutted past them, did the safety check, walked to the gate, waited for it to open, and jumped. My heart wasn't pounding in my chest, my eyesight wasn't blurred, and I realized I was rather calm. Five jumps gave my body and my mind time to adjust. Hopefully, it would do the same thing to all these men.

When each man arrived on the lowest platform after his turn, he showed his pride in me with a pleased expression and congratulatory hug. I was proud of myself, too. I'd mirrored the courage my niece showed every day.

After the zip lining, the men headed to their hotel. I stayed back to go over the last details with Dee as we made our way to my hotel room without cameras. The sun had already sunk, and the temperature grew nippy.

We needed to dress for a cocktail party where I'd spend time with the guys. I also had to prepare for who I'd keep and who I'd send home before I met the new round.

I watched the brick walkway and stepped carefully, even though I wore tennis shoes. My legs still wobbled from all the excitement. "Since I sent Rocco home already, do I have to send someone else home?" I asked Dee.

"Not if you don't want to, but you'll have three more men you'll need to choose from tomorrow, and one will have to go home."

This was getting routine like the fifth zip line had become. I bet, if I redid the zip lining, I wouldn't even be half as nervous.

I nodded as Dee waved and headed off in a different direction. I inhaled the ocean air, appreciating it.

When I turned down the street to my hotel, I found Shawn standing against the building, hands shoved into his pockets. He had one foot kicked against the building.

"I thought we should have the talk I promised."

"We should." I looked at him expectantly.

His foot thumped to the ground, and he hunched over a bit. "Uh…" He shuffled his right foot. "Jus' wanted to see if we're okay?"

His face paled, and he avoided eye contact.

Though he clearly acted uncomfortable, that didn't mean I'd grant him a pass. I had promised myself I wouldn't do things like that. I'd be strong.

"Depends," I said.

His head snapped up. "On what?"

"What you were protesting about with the compatibility test."

"It wasn't a protest."

I took a breath like I always did when Ava was young, and I hunted for patience. "Okay, what was it then?"

His lips closed. The longer I waited, the more it seemed he wouldn't answer me.

"Shawn," I said in a firm voice. He didn't budge. "Shawn," I snapped.

He glanced at me.

"Tell me. What was it?"

He paled more and worked his jaw.

"Are you going to answer?"

He shrugged. "Don't know."

"I don't get it. You already took a lot of psychological evaluations to make it on the show, so you can't be that against such tests. Not to mention we're probably the two people most alike. We have similar values and upbringing, so what could've made you flip out like that?"

He flushed. "You think we have the most in common?"

"I do." Why not tell him that? It was the truth. "What was it that upset you? Please tell me. There are no cameras."

He shoved his hands into his front pockets again. "I'm embarrassed to say."

I touched his shoulder. "Please, don't be. Trust me."

"Well," he said. "I get dirty all day. That's what I do."

"So?" I asked. "Nothing wrong with that."

His head stayed down. "I never was one much for school."

What was he saying? I stared at him. "So?"

He remained quiet.

Then it hit me. "Do you think because I have more education than you, I'd hold it against you?"

He looked up, searching. "It wouldn't be the first time."

"You're a millionaire."

"I'm not Ivy League."

"So?" I said, completely confused why that mattered.

"Really? So?" he asked.

I nodded.

He pulled me in for a gentle kiss. One that was nice but really didn't stand out compared to Forester, or Andrew for that matter.

After saying our farewells, I looked forward to a good shower, the dinner the crew would deliver to my room, and maybe even a nap. I dumped my stuff on my bed and picked up my phone.

A list of twenty calls from my sister, and another host of texts, bombarded my messages. Something had happened.

* * *

Andrew

Us GUYS: Forester, Shawn, and I were the only ones remaining now. That was doable. Forester deserved time since he was squeezed out of the zip line experience. That only seemed right. I told him so while we ate dinner and prepped for the next event.

"Thanks, man. I appreciate that."

I grabbed another heaping plate of spaghetti. Two minutes later, the crew gave us the signal to go to the hotel for cocktail hour. I wolfed down the remaining bites on my plate and headed out.

At the party, it took two seconds to see Charissa wasn't there yet, so I sat on the couch next to Shawn, wanting to talk about the events of the day.

"You were flying out there this afternoon."

He smiled. "Used to do that when I was in Boy Scouts. I forgot how much fun it could be."

Naturally, Shawn had been a Boy Scout. This guy was as squeaky clean as could be. The crew drew quiet as we waited for Charissa. "So, what did you do for your Eagle Scout project?" I asked to fill in the quiet.

Dee burst into the room, still dragging in cords and gear. She hustled over to the center of the room, with a glance at Shawn, me, then to Forester. She looked frazzled.

"Gentleman, something's come up, and Charissa regrets having to cancel the cocktail party tonight. She says she'll see you tomorrow. First thing."

I jumped to my feet, my muscles still complaining. This wasn't like Charissa. She had acted like she looked forward to having more time with all of us. She was the type who needed time to get to know us and space to process. She was clearly frustrated at how the production threw men at her so quickly.

"What happened?" I asked, ready to do what I could.

Dee shook her head, chewing her gum. "You'll find out tomorrow."

Like hell, I'd wait. I'd find out now. This wasn't like Charissa. I'd go to her room and get the scoop.

Dee chased after me, calling my name. I swiveled around to face her.

"I know you care about Charissa, and you have broken the rules a few times to see her, which is all fine and dandy, but this time you aren't. You're going to give her space."

"What's up?" I asked. "Is she hurt?"

Dee shook her head. "You'll find out tomorrow, but if you care or love her at all, you'll give her this space. I mean it."

CHAPTER 22

Charissa

The morning after zip lining, the bachelors gathered in a semi-circle around me on a small empty beach populated by sailboats in the water less than a hundred feet away. Still early, the birds hadn't bothered to flap their wings, and the sun hadn't risen in the sky. The white casino on one edge of the island shone as the only bright spotlighting the gray day. The only sound came from the camera operators whispering. No one else on the island was awake yet.

I cleared my throat, self-conscious about my red-rimmed eyes. "I'm sorry to say I must take a hiatus from the show for about a week."

Surprised expressions flashed through the group.

"Why?" Forester's deep-brown eyes grew alert and

hunted for deception. His lawyer button had triggered, and it would be hell to snap it off.

"Okay," Shawn said. He appeared to take the news in stride like he completely trusted I had a good reason and would be back to shoot our love story soon enough.

Andrew's immediate flash of concern showed in his face. True to his role as my faithful guard dog, always ready as the confidant and hero, he reached my side within seconds. "What's going on?"

"A family death," I choked. "My niece." My composure crumbled, and I succumbed to my grief.

Andrew engulfed me in his arms and rocked me like a little child. He held me like that as I cried. In the background, I heard Forester talking to the camera people. Telling them something about a class action lawsuit or something like that. Two minutes later, the camera crew packed up and left as I continued to cry.

Andrew lifted his head from mine. "Guys, I got this."

"We love you, Charissa," one of them said. It sounded like Forester.

"You going to be okay?" Shawn, I guessed through my sobs.

I nodded into Andrew's chest. "Sorry. I can't..." More tears.

"Please give her space," Andrew said. "You can comfort her later."

"Is that what you want, Charissa?" Shawn asked.

I nodded into Andrew's chest.

"She said, yes." That had to be Forester. "Let's go." Scuffling sounds quickly faded into the distance. That made me cry even harder. The guys were being so cool about this.

Finally, after I had completely dampened Andrew's shirt, I pushed away from his arms and wiped my tears. Ava was gone, and I was stuck here with guys trying to make romance happen.

"I can't do this." I struggled to my feet and tried to get away, only to trip and fall hands-first into the sand.

Andrew dropped next to me and took my hands into his. I appreciated the warmth of his fingers.

Brushing off the sand, he stared into my red eyes. "You don't have to."

"What do you mean?" I choked on my words. I couldn't look at him. I couldn't look at anyone. "My world is over. She's gone. She was everything."

His hand pressed against my back as I cried. My head hurt as grief welled up. I couldn't think. Tears poured.

Since talking with my sister last night, I had been doing huge rounds of sobbing. Subsequently, I'd be fine for twenty minutes. Well, as fine as a person could be... considering. I had been at least with it enough to call Dee.

She had hurried to my hotel room within minutes and took over. She made sure I sat in a chair, instructed a crew member to go out and find tea, then she was with me for a long time before she asked what had happened. Sometime in the middle of our talk, she managed to stream soothing background music from her phone.

She put it up against my hotel door. "To drown out any eavesdroppers," she said.

Whether that was the reason or not, it had calmed me. Dee stayed with me all night. Sometime after I drifted into a rough sleep, she organized a plane ride for me to attend the funeral.

Andrew cleared his throat, bringing me back from yesterday's events. "I'm coming with you. You're not doing this alone."

Wiping at my nose, I looked up. "What are you talking about?"

My head hurt. The other guys had left, and I didn't spot any camera crew near, but I could never trust that they weren't shooting this scene. It would be full of what they wanted. They might be lurking somewhere in the bushes where I couldn't see them. Dee told me she gave them strict instructions to respect my grieving process after I made the announcement, but that could've been a trick.

"I'm coming to the funeral with you."

I wiped at hair that the wind had blown into my face. "Don't be silly. I have to catch a flight. This is something I need to do on my own."

Andrew continued to stroke my back. My thoughts and intention drifted to his hand. It was warm, and its touch eased me. If I just focused on the movement...

"Look, I don't know if you noticed, but I've been acting like your self-appointed bodyguard."

I laughed. It was funny how he said that.

"I've noticed."

"You're a public figure. You're supposed to be shooting one of America's top reality shows right now. Everyone knows that. People will recognize you. You need someone by your side guarding you."

"I'm sure the production company is sending cameramen."

Andrew moved in front of me and sat with legs crossed. "I'm sure they will, but they wouldn't protect you like I would. Their job is to shoot video. My job is to take care of you."

I wiped at more tears. "What are you talking about? I'm not your job. Besides, they might kick you off the show if you come."

"Doesn't matter. Your wellbeing matters. While I'm here, and while you will have me, I'm standing by your side. I protect the people I care about." He reached out his finger and traced the side of my face. "I care about you."

My head spun. I cared about Ava. I would always care about Ava. I had tried to protect her, but cancer snuck up and took her. I had failed. I blinked. The sun was in my way.

"Andrew, I'm afraid I'm not good company. It'd be best if I don't see anyone. I just can't—"

He pulled me to him, burying my head in his damp chest. "You don't have to do anything. I'm coming with you, and all you have to do is whatever you are going to do. It doesn't matter if you don't talk to me the whole time. You need space and room. I understand that, but you also need safety. I'm going to provide it."

I didn't have the strength to protest any longer. "Do what you have to do, and don't let the other guys know. I'm sure they'll figure it out soon enough, but I'm not showing up to the funeral with a trail of male suitors."

* * *

THE FLIGHT to Idaho Falls happened in a blur. I cried through most of it as Andrew caressed my arm and listened to me when I did talk. He had been right in coming. At least he was there, standing guard against anyone who gawked at me, his presence and expression warning them not to interfere.

The familiarity of the airport haunted me with my dream that would never be. The last time here, I had been full of so much hope that, while I was off being courted, Ava would receive the treatment she needed. Many patients with more advanced cancers than Ava's had climbed back from the dead into full lives. So many people had recovered. Why not her? That question stayed with me as I stumbled through the airport with Andrew at my side. The cloak of death followed us, mocking my naiveté and deluded hope.

As we secured a rental car, I wondered how I could keep on living without Ava's phone calls, smiles, laughs, and her wise counsel? What else was there to live for? Blackness crowded my head.

Half-blind, I signed rental papers. I grabbed the black key from the car rental's cold hard counter and flipped its ring around in my left index finger. Around and around, I spun the key. The motion released tension, so I kept spinning it. I aimed all my anger, pain, and sadness into that spinning key. It picked up speed on my finger as we slunk to the cheap rental car. My fingers grew tired and pink, but I spun the key. Its dizzying movement matched the spinning inside of me.

I stopped only to drive to my sister's apartment. Andrew protested, but I knew the way, and I convinced him I needed the control of driving.

My thoughts continued going around and around like that key. How could she be gone? Did the doctors miss something? Is Chelsey surviving? What does Ava think of this? Oh yeah. She can't. More tears and trembling. Andrew's touch on my shoulder brought only a small relief.

He and I made it to Chelsey's. I pulled out the rental car key with its thick keychain and immediately began spinning it on my finger again. I looked at the apartment and the half-dead grass. It registered dully that we were in Idaho and heading for another winter. This year would be bleak, but not only because of the subzero temperatures forecasted.

I stumbled into my sister's home, and she fell into me, weeping. I clung to her, barely noticing Andrew as he melted unobtrusively into the background to give me a few moments with my sister.

"What happened?" I asked, feeling myself going weak. I slumped to the ground and stared at her as she joined me on the carpet.

"She was just too far gone. It's alright, Charissa. It's alright."

My eyes flashed to her. "What do you mean? It is not alright. Nothing is alright."

Her arm still around my back, Chelsey leaned her head against mine. "She wanted to go at the end. She only hung on because I wanted her to."

Chelsey pulled away and wiped at her eyes. "She was in so much pain. She never showed it. She never told me because she knew it'd upset both of us. She didn't need that pain anymore. I told her if she wanted to, she could go. She looked at me with that look, and I knew she wouldn't go if you didn't give her permission, too."

I'd never give that. Never.

"I called you. I called you many times. I just kept piling messages on your phone, and you didn't call. Charissa, the tumor took over. It was so big. It had tripled its size in a matter of weeks. It was choking her." Her fingers twisted. "The doctor said it was hurting her. At the end, they had her on so much medicine to stop the pain."

"She's dead," I said. "She died. You said she wouldn't die without my permission. But, she did."

Chelsey flushed, and her gaze froze on her twisting fingers. "Sis, please forgive me."

My heart screeched in silent pain. "What did you do?" I asked, my voice cracking. "What did you do?"

"I told her you said to tell her to go ahead and go. That you loved her, and you looked forward to connecting with her as an angel. I told her you understood, and you didn't want her in any more pain."

"You did what?" I yelled, standing. "I said no such thing. I'd never. She gave up because of *you*. How dare you speak for me? She could be alive today if it weren't for you."

Andrew stood in the shadow of the hall. Other family members looked on from adjacent rooms. Every eye on us. Not one dry.

My throat started closing. I couldn't breathe. I couldn't stand there with everyone watching or even stay with my sister, who had killed my niece.

"I have to go." A sob wracked me, and I hurried for the door.

Andrew better not try to stop me. He needed to stay out of my way. To his credit, he did.

I stumbled out onto the pavement and ran into the

crisp Idaho air. Ava. I could see her with her sweet smile, her laugh. As I ran, I pictured her in the hospital bed where I had visited her so many times. That took my strength, and my legs buckled. I collapsed onto the front lawn.

"No-o-o-o-o!" I sobbed. "No-o-o-o-o!" It was a cruel world that took my baby from me. I'd never forgive it. This wasn't right. The thought brought me to my feet, and I started walking.

* * *

Andrew

I SAT on the cement porch step, waiting for Charissa to return. As I kept watch, I thought about our trip so far. The plane ride had been stressful. Charissa cried most of it, and I sat next to her feeling stupid and very unsure what to do. A lot of people sneaked peeks at us as though it was their business. It wasn't. It wasn't even mine. Charissa deserved to grieve in privacy, and I wasn't sure she would get that. I couldn't stop thinking about how helpless I felt on the plane and now. This was something I couldn't make better.

She hadn't stopped crying for the whole trip to Idaho, except for a very few minutes here and there. She'd calm and wipe her nose and her eyes. She'd look across the airport or plane, spot someone in their teenage years, and tears started again. My heart felt ripped apart as I witnessed the devastation of this death so apparent on her face.

About a third of the away from the Idaho Falls airport,

though, she blew her nose, shifted toward me, and started talking.

"Ava was the most beautiful girl I ever saw. She loved life. She liked to dance and to sing. She'd watch reality TV shows with me and would give advice far beyond her years. She was wise. She was so wise."

Charissa smiled, envisioning something I couldn't see.

After a moment, she turned back to face me. "One of the last times I talked to her, she was a participant at a modern jazz recital. She just loved it. That girl could put emotion in her movements. It was amazing to see her go, even as the cancer was eating her up. She'd didn't let that stop her. She'd do what she could when she could. She was an amazing example of living in the present."

I had nodded, afraid to say anything to knock Charissa out of her memory. I listened to her… learning a lot about what was most important to her.

Charissa's heart was made of gold, I suspected. She saw such amazing things about her niece and truly cared. Ava was surely a special person to build such a great relationship with her aunt. I doubted I'd earn such high marks.

Finally, Charissa stopped talking.

"You sound almost like you were her mother," I said.

She said nothing to that but slipped into a thick silence where she remained for the rest of the trip.

When we arrived at the sister's, their conversation came as a jolt. It kind of shocked me to see her sister clearly handling the situation better than Charissa. Chelsey held a peace about her, which I found commendable.

Despite her composure, it didn't take long for the two to fight and for Charissa to storm away. The look on her face as she fled told me I needed to stay away, let her be, and allow her to work out her feelings on her own.

After five minutes had passed, I stepped outside in the darkening day. Cold slipped around me as I stared at the light dusting of snow and waited for her to return.

I'd been out there about fifteen minutes when Chelsey flipped on the porch light and joined me.

"Hi, I'm Chelsey, Charissa's sister. You are Andrew?"

I nodded. I went to shake her hand, but her arm had a blanket drooped over it. She held a teacup in her other hand.

"You're a good friend to be so concerned about her."

She set her teacup down by her feet then lifted the quilt from her arm and handed it to me. I wrapped the blanket around my shoulders, staring at the wooden porch, shivering in the burrowing cold. "I wish I could do more."

After reclaiming her tea, Chelsey joined me on the frozen concrete step. "You're helping her more than you know. I see how she looks at you for strength, and you know when to stay back. My sister sometimes needs space. Lots of it." Steam rose out of her mug.

That was good to know.

Though Chelsey looked worn, beat up, with thick shadows under her eyes, there was an undeniable toughness about her.

"You seem to be handling this so much better than Charissa, and it's your daughter," I said. "How is that?"

She smiled faintly as though she appreciated me noticing. She stayed quiet for a while, peering out on the dark horizon. Distant cars sounded in the background, and quiet mumbling drifted from the house out to us.

"Charissa feels things deeply. She's an emotional lady."

I had seen that.

Chelsey sipped her tea. "Don't take that for weakness. She's strong. She just feels deeply. I admire that about her. I come across colder than her. I always have. She's a dreamer. I'm the practical one, and even though I love my daughter dearly, we have been through five years of struggling and suffering. I wanted to see her out of pain." She pressed her lips together as if to gather her strength. "She's out of pain, and that's what matters."

I nodded, seeing the beauty in that and the wisdom. "What about you and Charissa? Are you two going to be okay?"

She gave a polite laugh. "Yes. Don't you worry. When she's done with her grieving, she'll come in, say hi to you, then walk up to me and give me a tight hug. That'll be our signal for all the words we don't need to say. We aren't much for talking through our fights. Tomorrow she'll rise early, help me with breakfast, and stand by my side at the funeral in her annoying protective stance."

I flinched. I did that to her, too. Did she think I was annoying? Did I remind her of her sister? If I did, even if she didn't like it, it might be a good thing. It would familiar to her in an unconscious way.

Chelsey coughed. "We are best of friends, and we'll always be. I shared my daughter with her. She's her daughter, too." With that, Chelsey stood. "Thank you, again, Andrew." She left me alone to wait for her sister's return.

Charissa eventually came back and acted just as Chelsey said she would.

Several hours later, I found myself in a hotel room that

was plain as any I have ever stayed in. Tan-striped wall-paper backed bad impressionistic mountain paintings hanging on the walls. The bed, a chest with a TV resting on it, and a cold utilitarian bathroom comprised the rest of the room.

The mood was lonely, but I stayed in it to give Charissa space. Now wasn't the time for me to meet the family and all that crazy stuff. Besides, if I was going to be honest, I was relieved to be away. I had no idea what to say, and standing there watching Charissa cry made me feel like firecrackers were exploding inside me.

Sleep eluded me. I popped sleeping pills, to little effect. Ava was just a kid with her whole life before her. She shouldn't have been taken so young. The pictures of her, set up everywhere in Chelsey's home, showed a stunning girl with bright green eyes. In every picture, she looked full of happiness.

My sincere desire to do something, anything, to make the situation better settled as an ache in my stomach. Its pressure constricted around my gut like a physical weight, but there was nothing I could do. I felt completely helpless.

* * *

Charissa

AFTER SAYING GOODBYE TO ANDREW, who left for the hotel, I stumbled into the guest bedroom where I'd be sleeping at my sister's. I had slept in that room many times, and its walls embraced me with familiarity. Its scents of lavender and rose brought back happy memories that clung to me:

staying up late chatting with Ava, and me doing her hair, or her doing mine. All I wanted was to lay down and snuggle with her, rest my chin on top of her head, and breathe her in.

My sister had laid out an elegant black dress for tomorrow. I held it up tenderly then pulled the fabric against my breaking heart. I cried another round of tears. I didn't know anyone could cry so much, and I didn't know if I'd ever stop. I hoped I wouldn't cry at the funeral... that my tear ducts would run out of production.

That hope washed away at the funeral the next morning. Before the ceremony, we greeted people who wanted to offer their condolences. Most had tears brimming in their eyes and warm hugs for me and Chelsey. We stood there greeting them and thanking them. I didn't say much other than, "Thanks so much for coming."

In respect for my family, the camera crew tried to be as unobtrusive as possible, which I appreciated. I barely remembered they were there.

The line finally was slowing down when I saw Nia walk into the room, dressed in black, diamonds, and her hair still springing everywhere. I slipped over to her, not wanting to thank anyone else for coming.

She smiled wide when I approached.

"What are you doing here?" I asked.

"Charissa! So, good to see you. Not under the circumstances, but I think about you all the time, and I'm wondering how you're making out with all those men." She winked at me.

I stared at her. We were at a funeral for my niece, and

she was smiling, winking, and talking about men. How could I get her out of here?

"What are you doing here?" I repeated.

She stopped talking, reached out, and squeezed my forearm. "I am so sorry. I was crushed when I heard. I know how much you wanted her to make a comeback." She shook her head, her hair bouncing in various directions. "I've been keeping up with Chelsey and have been doing prayer groups for you and your niece. We are keeping them up so your niece will have a nice transition up there in heaven." She pointed to the ceiling.

I thanked her, touched by her efforts, after all.

"I hate to bring this up, but I found more of your stuff at the cabin after you left. Maybe I could get it to you afterward?"

I looked at this woman with her big eyes and her intense gaze as she waited for my reply. Although she was clearly an obsessed fan, she also had proven her good heart throughout this whole situation.

"Why don't you keep it," I said.

"What?"

I reached out and touched her arm. "You have been wonderful to me at a very hard time. You have it."

"Really?" She breathed deep. "I can't wait to tell my friends. Thank you! And..." she hesitated, then winked, "good luck with all the guys."

After I finished chatting with Nia, I went to find Chelsey. It was time for us to make our way to the service. Several minutes later, I sat next to her, clutching her hand and weeping. Andrew sat, silent and solid, on my other side.

With every mention of Ava from the pulpit, with every story, I smiled or laughed, then cried. Finally, the pastor stood, quoted the Bible, and preached about the process of life. It left me feeling angry. I imagined throwing rotten tomatoes… Wouldn't that make a compelling scene for the cameras?

I froze. My thoughts were interrupted by a bright light appearing abruptly next to the pastor. The brilliant shape pulsed as light rays filtered down around it like flowing blonde hair. The light turned toward me, flashed, and disappeared. I gasped.

Ava had come to say goodbye.

* * *

Andrew

AT THE FUNERAL, sitting motionless next to Charissa, I wasn't even sure she knew I was there, but I was there as her rock if she needed it. I had a sense she'd never really recover from this. I stayed by her side throughout the day until her eyes drooped, and it looked like she wanted to cry herself to sleep in her sister's front room.

That night I hardly slept. I binge-watched murder mysteries to pass the time. In the morning, I rose for breakfast at six, then made several trips down for strong black coffee. I had made it halfway through my third cup when my hotel phone rang.

The show hadn't let me bring my cell. Their fear of leaks had been at an all-time high, so I had agreed to their rules to be able to come with Charissa. I stumbled over to the ancient, corded phone and answered.

"There you are. Good," came a terse female voice on the other end. Dee. Her voice could be recognized anywhere. "How's Charissa doing?"

"Struggling."

Dee sighed. "That's too bad. The funeral was yesterday, right?"

I squeezed my eyes shut to get the images of the smiling, bright young girl out of my mind. "Yes."

"Good. I need you to get Charissa back on the plane today. There are only two flights, so you don't have much wiggle room."

My eyes focused on the ugly impressionistic painting on the hotel wall, so reflective of the hell Dee was creating.

"You've got to be kidding. She just buried her niece."

A deep breath slipped through the phone line. "I know that, and that's sad, but the production company is losing money every day she isn't here. This might sound cruel, but we can't afford to put this off."

I couldn't believe this woman. She had a hard time even acting like she had a heart. "It doesn't *sound* cruel. It *is* cruel," I spat out.

She ignored my jab. "I need you to see she's on that plane by three this afternoon. I'm trusting you."

The dial tone greeted my ear.

There was no way I'd do what she said. Knowing Dee, though, she'd find out and plan something else.

I needed to get to Charissa's side now.

CHAPTER 23

Charissa

*T*he day after the funeral, I stayed in my room. I sat on the rocking chair with a teacup in my hand, swaying back and forth, staring out the window toward the distant mountains. I tried to ignore all the track homes and apartments between me and nature. With my eyes closed, I could smell Ava's strawberry hairspray and fruity bubble baths. I loved the light she always brought. I felt her presence wrap around me. If I kept my eyes closed, I sensed she was about to talk to me, to wake me up to go on an adventure. Maybe a walk to the park or to watch a TV show. If I kept my eyes closed real tight, her energy would seep to me from the walls, the floors, the furniture.

Chelsey tiptoed into the room, also with a steaming teacup in hand. I rocked back and watched her sit on the corner of the unmade bed. She had a little more color than she did yesterday and yet still dragged as she moved. She had managed to put on makeup, but that didn't hide the strain on her face nor the deep black lines under her eyes. She wore business casual—dressy black pants and a tailored black shirt—and looked like she was headed somewhere.

I had expected her to be in her nightgown or sweats. Or, more likely, to be in her bed, hugging something that belonged to Ava. I didn't expect her to be looking like she was ready to take on the professional world.

"Why are you all dressed up?" I asked.

"Going to work later."

She had to be kidding. That wasn't a good idea. She couldn't be functional yet. What if she broke into a big grieving fit in the middle of work? There was no way she was thinking straight.

If Mom were here, she'd know what to do and how to snap sanity back into my sister, but she wasn't here. I couldn't even lean on Dad for support. Chelsey was all the family I had left.

"That's not a good idea," I said as gently as I could.

Chelsey jumped to her feet. "What am I supposed to do? Stay cooped up? All I see is Ava. Everywhere, her image stays with me, reminding me..." Tears bubbled in her eyes. She slumped back onto the bed and plopped a pillow on her lap. "I have to keep going. I need to make money to pay the bills. Things will be worse if I let everything go. I don't have the luxury to stop and grieve. Whatever that looks like."

I slipped off my rocker and sat on the floor up against

the bed. Chelsey slid down next to me. I held out my hand, and she put her shaky hand on mine.

"I'm sorry." I squeezed her fingers.

A shadow passed in the room, and we both glanced up at the window. We stayed quiet until a loud pound on the door made Chelsey jump. She moved to answer.

"No," I said, signally her to not move. "You stay here. I'll get it."

I moved carefully, getting blood back in my bare feet. I headed into the living room, along with a sudden ray of sunlight piercing through the clouds on its way into the living room.

The glare of light jolted me. Immediately, I went into a rapid round of blinking as a piercing pain jabbed into my chest. I gasped, struggling not to lose composure. I needed to keep it together. My sister was in rough shape, soldiering through it despite her raw emotions. I recognized her usual coping mechanisms: aversion and avoidance, because thinking was a dangerous landmine, and everywhere around her lurked an emptiness threatening to devour her.

Maybe I was the weird one because what most repulsed my sister, most attracted me. Chelsey didn't sense Ava in her house like I did. Maybe I was going a little crazy. Maybe I was just more intuitive. I liked having her scent close, and her clothes, her books, her life. This was where she'd come... her place of connection to the world if she came back as a spirit.

Tearing myself from my reflection, I made it to the door and opened it. Andrew stood there, shoulders slouched, and his suitcase in his hands. I couldn't process him or any guy. Despite the fact I was rude and said nothing, he leaned down and looked into my face to catch my gaze.

"May I come in?"

I didn't know. I didn't want to talk or entertain. I wanted to go back to Ava's room and rock in the rocking chair, and hang onto what was left of her. I tried to say something, but tears rose instead.

Andrew moved in to give me a big hug with his suitcase still in his hand. His woodsy cologne washed over me. After a few seconds, he stepped into the house and shut the door against the cold sneaking in.

Chelsey came out, and Andrew greeted her as he set his suitcase on the floor.

"Going back to the show?" Chelsey asked.

Andrew shrugged. "Don't know. I'm here for Charissa. Whatever she needs... and you, too." He gestured to Chelsey. "I have no idea what you might need, but I'm here."

Chelsey took a seat and fiddled with the edge of the couch cushion next to her. "That's kind of you. I don't need anything, and I think Charissa is going to hang around today while I'm at work. Do you have any plans?"

My sister looked at me with her jaw set, telling me not to mess with her. It smacked reality into me. I had obligations and bills to pay, too. "I should check in with the show," I said in a faint voice.

"I wouldn't do that," Andrew said forcefully.

That drew my attention to him. He must know something.

He looked away. "Just don't." His voice had gone into a low tone, "Stay away from your phone for a few days."

Andrew was protecting me.

"Are they anxious to get me back?"

"You don't need to listen to them," he said. "You shouldn't do anything you're not ready for."

"Maybe you should go, Charissa," Chelsey said. The traitor was egging me on.

Andrew's fingers curled, and he turned a level gaze on my sister. "She's not ready," he said firmly.

That creepy feeling of having people talk about me like I wasn't in the room crawled over me. I had borne enough of this discussion. I stood and stumbled into the kitchen. The drapes had been pulled back, and light spilled into the room. Those drapes had never been opened since I could remember. Ava was sensitive to light, a side effect of one of her medications. This wasn't right. The drapes needed to stay closed. Chelsey was erasing Ava. I sped over to the curtains and tugged on them until they released and blocked the blaring light.

The next issue was the counters... Ava was notorious for leaving a trail of breadcrumbs on the counter along with lots and lots of papers: from school, the hospital, her friends. It didn't matter where she gathered them. They managed to make their way to the counter despite all of Chelsey's protests. Now the counter was bare. The counter needed papers and crumbs. The phone needed to be ringing. Everything was so deathly quiet and clean.

My fingers twitched at my side. My niece couldn't be erased like this. As my gaze traveled to the bread box, I thought about Ava's love of wheat bread. In the box, I found three stale slices still in the bag. Chelsey didn't eat brown bread. She said something about it not tasting good, but Ava devoured it.

I grabbed the bag... the one Ava had last touched. I pulled it up to my nose and breathed in the scent, hoping to smell Ava's innocence, her enthusiasm, her joy. Instead, it smelled like bread and mold.

"What are you doing?" Chelsey asked.

I didn't move. I didn't want to see her. She was erasing her daughter like she had never been here. She wasn't showing proper respect. "Are you planning to give away her clothes?"

"What?"

"I want all of them, even down to the last sock. Don't give away anything. I want them."

Chelsey walked around to stand in front of me. Still hugging the bread, I looked at her, knowing full well I appeared crazy. I should put the bread down and treat it like bread, but I couldn't because it was *her* bread.

"You can have that loaf. Any clothes I don't hang onto are all yours. She rested her hand on the counter as if to give herself strength.

"Please remember to give me them. I want everything of hers that you don't."

She sighed, pulled out a fork from the drawer, went to the frig, and grabbed a cold potato salad leftover from the funeral. "Do you want some?" She gestured to the plastic container.

How could she be thinking about food at a time like this? Working, dressing for business, and now eating as if nothing had happened. She loved Ava. How could she be like this?

"I don't get you sometimes."

"You're grieving," she said simply, taking a large bite of potato, but choked on it. She started coughing.

"You aren't!" I snapped.

"I am… and I have." It came out sounding strangled, and she continued to cough until she found some air. "I've been grieving for years. I knew this would come someday." Cough. "The knowledge has torn me up. I never had the faith you did that she'd pull out of it. It didn't stop me from trying to do everything I could to fix it, but I knew cancer was stronger." She cleared her throat. "I'm okay with it because my baby daughter is out of pain. The only reasons I'd want her here are selfish ones."

She blinked her eyes hard like she was trying to hold in tears.

My eyes flashed to her. Was she saying I was selfish, after everything I had done for her… for Ava?

"You handled it differently, Charissa. You always believed she'd pull through." She coughed lightly and took another bite. "You really thought nutrition and alternative methods would be the answer." Her eyes took on a distant glaze. "I admired you for all those years. While I grieved the fact I was losing her, you stood strong and firm and never wavered in your belief. You still had her during that time. I didn't. I have already cried and cried. You have not. It doesn't make me cold, and I do miss her terribly." Her voice caught, and she wiped at her eyes. She squared her shoulders. "My whole body aches for her, but I prepared for this day."

The kitchen drew quiet as I considered my sister's words. I had no response, nor did I think my sister expected one. The sun must have hidden behind a cloud because the kitchen drew darker.

"Ava wanted you to be happy, Charissa. She talked to me about it many times. She was so excited about you being on this show. She loved the idea of you finally finding a guy and love."

My sister was telling me this for a reason, but I had no clue what.

"In fact, she left a recorded message for you."

Chelsey had kept this from me. My vision blurred. "What?"

"Now is the time for you to listen if you're ready."

I stared at my sister with potato salad in her hand, dropping important news like it wasn't anything. I didn't understand her today. The need grew to be elsewhere to sort this out. At least Andrew was staying in the other room to give me and my sister space. I silently thanked him, and my respect for him grew.

I sipped a breath. "Let me hear it."

Still holding the bread bag tight, I moved to the kitchen table and sat. She walked out of the room, and I heard rustling. All my irritated energy had vanished, leaving me tired. Chelsey returned and pulled up a chair a couple of feet away from me. She fiddled with her cell phone, pulled up the recording, and pushed play.

"Aunt Char, I love you, and I'm so happy you're on *Millionaire Engagement*," came Ava's voice, so full of life. "I can't wait to watch you fall in love. I know the guy you pick will be special." Rustling sounded from the recording.

"I'm back. Sorry, adjusting the cords. I have appreciated you being in my life through everything. I can't remember any time when you weren't there, when you weren't supporting me, and cheering me on."

She broke into a coughing fit. Another pause played out before she came back, voice weaker. "I want you to know I'll be watching *Millionaire Engagement,* no matter what."

My face was wet. She would miss the show that had meant so much to her. If she could only have held on. My hands cramped. I held on instead. I hadn't let her go like Chelsey had told her I had. I didn't know if I could ever do that. I could accept anything but that. Anything.

"Auntie, what the doctors are telling me isn't good." Her voice grew shakier, probably from doing all the talking to make this recording. I could hear acceptance in her voice. She believed them.

Those doctors were supposed to put only positive thoughts in her head. I had vetted them. They knew the dangers of saying anything negative. They had talked to me about that for hours before I signed up Ava. This wasn't right.

"I'm still thinking positive thoughts and still visualizing as you taught me," Ava's voice broke into my mind like she knew my thoughts. "But, I'm tired of this fight." Her voice grew weaker. "I'm so tired. If by chance I don't... I want you to promise me you'll go on. You'll go back on the show. You'll find that guy, and you'll love him for me."

She coughed again. "I will come and check on you two now and then. It'd make me so happy for you to finally find the right guy. I'll experience the love through you. Please do that for me, Auntie. And... thank you. I love you."

* * *

THE HELICOPTER MADE A SWOOPING noise as it flew us across the Pacific. Out the window, I saw choppy gray waters matching my emotions. I still needed to go on and find the sunset, despite feeling stirred up and raw.

I had warned Andrew I'd probably cry a lot for the next few days, so he and the guys would have to deal with it.

"We will," he said.

He had been strangely quiet, though still protective through this trip. He'd given me a lot of space.

"Thank you for coming with me," I said loudly into the helmet mic.

He squeezed my knee. "You couldn't have stopped me."

I tried to laugh at that, like my old self would've, but I couldn't. Instead, I nodded. "Ain't that the truth."

"Look, Charissa," he said hesitantly, "I hope you don't find it weird or creepy..."

I gestured toward the pilot. "You know he can hear you?"

Andrew shrugged. "I don't care. I want you to know that ever since my sister showed me a video of you on TV, I felt protective of you. You've been through so much... I can hardly imagine. The reason I stick so close is not just because I like you, find you fascinating, and a wonderful woman. It's also because I have this feeling you need someone to have your back. Whether you pick me, or not, for as long as I'm on the show, I'm going to watch out for you."

"I'm sure the othe—"

He interrupted me. "They don't do a good enough job. I

trust no one but myself. If you don't like it, give me a word, and I'll back away. Just know I'm concerned about your safety and wellbeing. I consider it my job to care for you."

* * *

THE LATE AFTERNOON had a nice overcast to it, and the weather was perfect, in the seventies, when we arrived back on the island. Dee really wanted us back in the morning, but I hadn't rushed.

"Three out of the five new guys opted to go home when they learned there was a personal issue going on, and you would be gone for a few days," Dee said as she escorted me to hair and makeup.

That was a relief.

"We're going to quickly shoot you meeting two more guys, and then we'll dive into the rest of the show."

"Which involves…"

My mind reeled in a fog. I needed to force my brain to work and process that I was back on an island and a fantasy world.

"Cocktail party tonight with the guys you choose, and tomorrow there will be more dating. You aren't going to like this, but we have lost days to make up. You won't have much time with these new guys. You're going to have to spend as much time as possible with them today and tonight. Try to get to know them. I'm sorry we had to cut out two dates you would've had with them."

She stopped walking and shifted her weight. "I'm sorry."

She was trying to show me empathy, but I couldn't

handle it. I looked away, unable to hear any more. Getting sympathy from Dee was a no-can-do. I wasn't up for it.

* * *

Andrew

CHARISSA REFUSED to take more time for herself and the grieving process, despite my heartfelt pleas. That woman could be stubborn at times. That was good, and maybe it would help her to stay busy so she wouldn't think much. I wasn't a shrink, and I didn't know the answers to these things.

Again, Charissa was in a daze on the plane. This time she hardly cried but spent much of the time with this long-lost look on her face. I knew she had to be thinking about Ava. Again, I gave her space. I just focused on making sure she was comfortable. Time passed quickly, and before I knew it, we were back on the island.

The moment the helicopter landed, Dee swept Charissa away, giving her instructions on what she needed to do. I heard Dee say something about new guys waiting.

Of course, there would be more guys. Of course, the show wanted Charissa to jump right into it. That was the deal, but it seemed brutal not to even give her a chance to go to her hotel room before they put her to work.

One of the guy crew members greeted me and said he'd walk with me back to my hotel room. Cords ran from his ears to his waist and over to the cameras aimed at me, waiting for me to do something interesting.

I followed the young man, anticipating a meeting with

Shawn and Forester. I was sure they'd have a lot of questions.

"Back to the competition," I said.

After being with Charissa constantly for the past few days, it was weird to be without her in the house of the pining. From the moment I strolled into the hotel room, the tension pressed in on me.

Despite the fact that a maid came regularly, the place smelled like a sweaty gym mixed with sour milk and rotten produce. Furniture was shoved toward the walls in erratic ways, with tables laden with dirty dishes and half-eaten French fries, hamburgers, hotdogs, and pies. Half-filled cups were stacked everywhere.

Hard rock blared. Forester and Shawn lay on the floor, counting through a push-up battle, complete with trash talk.

Shawn peered up, startled, and jumped to his feet. He hurried over to the music and snapped it off.

Forester climbed to his feet in one smooth step and stood before me. "How is she?" he asked.

Shawn came up beside him, looking quite small next to the hulk.

"She's upset," I said, "which is understandable. But, she's here and ready to do the show."

"That was a low trick you pulled, man." Forester extended his arms out and flexed like he might be ready to fight.

I hoped he was the lawyer he claimed to be and not the muscle man he looked like.

"She needed somebody."

"It was low," Forester muttered.

Shawn shook his head. "Well played," he said. "So, tell us about it. Did you meet her family?" He tipped up his chin.

"It wasn't like that," I said. "She was so upset. I doubted she or her sister knew I was there most of the time. She cried the whole way over on the airplane. No. More like sobbed."

Forester walked over to the counter to retrieve water in one of the last clean cups. "Glad I missed that."

"I had a splitting headache after the flight." I tossed my bag to the side so as not to contribute to the mess.

"Where is she now?" Shawn shook his arms like they hurt. "Can we go see her?"

"Production swept her away the moment the helicopter landed."

Forester slammed down his glass of water onto the kitchen table. "Man, you got to do a helicopter ride with her, too?"

I shrugged. It'd be best not to slip into how awesome that was. Better to distract them with facts. "From what I could make out, she's meeting more guys."

"Damn." Forester punched his large fist into a pillow. "This is getting ridiculous. How many more guys are they going to trail before her, tempting her? They're not letting her develop any real connection with anyone with the clock ticking onward." He looked over at me. "Well, except for time with Andrew, that is."

Another landmine. Keeping Forester caged up for days hadn't helped his mood.

"So, what have you guys been doing?" I asked.

"Hanging out." Forester's tone sounded terse. "Living in this filth."

Shawn rolled his eyes. "For being such a clean freak, you'd think you would do some of the cleaning around here instead of all the bellyaching."

Forester's eyes narrowed, letting me know this was a hot topic they'd been arguing about.

To shift the attention, Forester asked, "What's her family like?"

Fire lit his eyes. I wouldn't want to meet him in a courtroom.

I pulled out a kitchen chair at the table. It scraped against the carpet. I sat. Both Shawn and Forester watched, waiting for my answers.

"I don't know how much I should say. I'm not sure she'd want me to talk about it."

Forester punched his fist into the pillow again, this time not quite so hard. "Talk. You already have an unfair advantage."

CHAPTER 24

Charissa

*T*he production crew used the same set-up for meeting the new batch of candidates. I couldn't even muster up the pitiful amount of nerve I somehow found before when meeting the first round of men.

All the bright colors, the bench, the flowers, and the pathway where the guys decided their interest all mocked me. Ava had never been to Catalina Island, and never would.

Dee shouted instructions to the production crew with wires hanging off her like a weeping willow tree. While she stayed busy, I hurried behind a thick palm tree and pressed my back against its uneven bark. I slipped out my secret phone and, with unsteady hands, held it to my ear as I closed my eyes, letting the gentle sun kiss my eyelids. I listened to the audio message Chelsey had sent me from

Ava. I'd listened to it over and over, and now I listened to it again.

I breathed in her words along with the salty ocean air to see if I could sense her presence with me. I wasn't sure about it, but thinking about her and hearing her voice made me feel a comforting warmth in my core. So, just in case she was there, I talked to her.

"Ava, this is for you. You better be around, and you better help me pick right. I have no idea how to do it myself."

I slipped the phone into my pocket, clenched my hands and released them, and rejoined the crew. "Let's get this going." I slapped my hands together. "We're losing daylight."

Dead silence.

The crew stared. The last thing I wanted them to do was to become sappy. If they did, I'd cry, and nobody wanted that.

"Chop chop." I gave the signal to move. They needed to treat this day like any other.

My gesture kick-started Nancy into action. She hurried up and escorted me to the bench. "Let me do my introduction. I know the guys are anxious to meet you."

Nancy looked as lovely as ever and also had the sense to act like this was a normal day.

She spoke to the camera. "After waiting for a few days with increased tension, two more millionaires remain who want to see if they're a fit for Charissa." She motioned to me. "How do you feel about meeting these faithful suitors?"

Like I didn't want to meet them. I'd rather take a walk on the beach with Andrew. He'd be up for that. He wouldn't expect anything, and he'd be okay just being there. Nancy cleared her throat, reminding me I needed to answer her... America waited.

"They have delayed long enough, and I should meet them right away." I bared a toothy smile.

Nancy stepped away, allowing me to see a shadow coming down the pathway. As the man came closer, I could tell he was skinny. Not a little skinny, but super skinny. The kind of thing that made me suck in my gut to not appear fat standing next to him, but knowing I would appear that way despite my efforts. Still, I wouldn't let that rule him out because of my insecurity. He had curly blond hair tossed everywhere, which made me want to run my fingers through it. He extended his hand.

"I'm Tom, and I'm happy to meet you," he said. He had an intensity about him. It felt almost demanding.

"I'm gla—"

He interrupted. "The production company wouldn't let me meet the guys who arrived before me, but the one other guy who stayed... Well, let me tell you, he's from Idaho, and I'd pass on him if you know what I mean." He nodded his head as if he agreed with himself. "Well, maybe you could keep him around if you want to have potatoes with every meal." He grinned and elbowed me in the side.

His first impression involved putting another guy down, along with my home state? That said a lot. Waiting for me for days or not, this guy wouldn't be waiting for me any longer.

The five minutes we had together dragged on, but eventually, the producer called, "Time."

Tom pressed my hand between his hot and sweaty palms. "I can't wait to get to know you."

I gave a nervous laugh and watched him move out of earshot. I motioned to the production crew. "Really?"

They shrugged and gave me sympathetic looks.

I pressed fingers to my forehead. "How could he have been vetted and successful?"

"Thin-man syndrome," one of the camera crew guys called out.

"I guess."

That was as good of an explanation as any. Although Andrew was fairly thin, he didn't have that attitude. "I hope you didn't stack all the great guys first and leave the real doozies for last."

Nancy took her place in front of the camera again and addressed me, off-screen. "Are you ready to meet the last guy of the day?"

This needed to be over and done with. "Bring him on," I said.

She stepped out of the camera shot, and I watched as a tall, slender man strolled up. He wore a cowboy hat and held a bottle of wine in his hand. His shoulders were broad and his jeans tight. He reminded me of JT. My stomach went all jittery. I wasn't sure if I wanted to meet another confident, rich cowboy.

"Howdy." He stepped up and took off his cowboy hat to reveal ruffled black hair. He bowed, straightened up, and plopped his hat back on his head.

Warmth moved from my neck and up my face. Despite all the guys I had met, and how many times I had been through this, and despite not feeling exactly myself today, I still blushed and became twitterpated.

"Hi," I said, unable to hold eye contact.

He grinned, revealing a deep dimple on his right cheek. "You're shy, I can see. I thought that might have changed when all the fame flew to your head."

I tipped my head back and squinted up at him in the glaring sun. "I haven't gotten that famous yet, but there's still time."

His eyes sparkled as though he was pleased with my comeback. The way he looked at me, I could see how a girl would be compelled to want to please him.

"We have a little feistiness here." His dimple showed itself again.

I squared my shoulders. "I'm not sure what 'we' have, but I'd been told I have spunk."

Not enough to have stood up to JT on the last show, but I had vowed to change that, and that was what I was doing.

The sun beat down on me in bright streams, making me wonder if it was possible for a person to melt like the Wicked Witch in Oz, and my neck started to ache from looking up at this man. It was time for an assertive move. I inhaled a deep breath before diving off a high dive.

"Let's get out of the sun and sit on the bench."

I started for it, but he grabbed my right hand and jerked me toward him. Standing less than a foot from him, my heartbeat increased.

"Naw." He peered at me and reached out and brushed a few hairs off my face with a soft touch. "We can talk later. I want to see how you can ride a horse."

"What?" I asked, gesturing to the crew members for help.

Instead, they signaled for me to return my attention to him.

The cowboy stood there grinning. "My name is Jared, and I don't like boring intros or living a dull life."

Okay. Well, message delivered, in-person. Andrew had done the same kind of thing, but not as dramatically.

Seconds later, a large brown horse trotted onto the set. It even sported a blue ribbon tied to its tail.

"I thought I'd take you for a ride," he said. He strolled over to the horse and stroked his nose. The horse bumped into the touch. Jared seized the reins and hopped onto its back.

I stood there staring until he nudged the horse to side-step closer to me. Before I could take it all in, he bent over, grabbed me under my arms, and swung me up onto the horse in front of him.

I yelped. The horse took off trotting. My insides shook as my grasp tightened on the pommel.

"You okay?" Jared whispered in my ear as his body pressed against mine.

I shivered. This man was cocky and sexy. I'd definitely keep him around… if I survived the horse ride.

* * *

As evening approached, it became time again to find out who had resolved to stick around and who had decided this experience—or I—wasn't for them.

As Dee hurried me over to make-up, I turned to her. "There was hardly a choice between the two."

"We had three others," she said.

"Were they good ones?"

"What do you mean? They are all good ones. We pride ourselves on doing a good job of vetting your choices. We don't go after 'crazy' like other shows. We go after guys we think are legitimate choices. We believe the American public wants to watch a sweet romance, not just hostility and fights."

I rolled my eyes. "If it happens, though, you don't have any moral outrage about showing it on-air."

She shrugged. "Got to make a living."

"So, stop the PBS commercial, and let's cut to the chase between you and me. There aren't any cameras." I looked around just to make sure no lights shone on me. "Tell me as a friend, not a producer, did I miss out on anything great?"

Dee pushed down her hat as she walked. "For you, no. They didn't wait. Anyone who was a real match for you, or someone who would treat you well... Well, they would understand a family emergency and not use a few days waiting as a reason to leave."

She still wasn't wearing any makeup, and I doubted she had washed her hair in days, but she was good at giving advice.

"Thanks," I said. "You know, you aren't as tough as you like to think you are."

It was her turn to roll her eyes.

"You're capable of being a compassionate, caring person."

She shivered at that and grimaced.

We arrived at the makeup room. I rushed in and sat on Monique's chair to be polished up. As she worked, I considered my choices.

Tom was definitely a no-go. So, even if he chose me, I couldn't choose him.

Jared was a completely different story. Soon, I'd find out if he would join me on future adventures. I hoped he would. Something irresistible infused the cowboy under that hat. Ava would approve.

* * *

ONCE AGAIN, I stood next to Nancy, waiting for the next phase of progress. While a crew member miked her, I looked around. I could see how people developed island fever here. The island didn't change much from day-to-day. White clouds dotted the gray sky with a lightness. The temperature stayed about the same. The waves on the ocean flowed in gently compared to other ocean coastlines

"So, what did you think?" Nancy asked on camera.

"I'm grateful both of these two guys waited a couple of extra days to meet me. That was nice of them. It says some-thing about them, a willingness the three others didn't share."

Nancy smiled. She recognized my evasive response.

"What did you think about Tom? Is there's a chance?"

Really? I didn't want to diss people on national TV. That was rude and left lifetime scars. I was one to know.

"He seems like a nice guy... on the talkative side." I gave a forced chuckle. "I don't think I got a word in edgewise the whole five minutes."

Nancy nodded. "That's fair. What about Jared? He certainly didn't over-talk, and he brought a horse."

I smiled, remembering his arms holding me tight so I wouldn't fall. "Amazing. Didn't see that one coming." Before thinking about it, I added, "I thought I'd prepared for the grand gesture by watching shows like this. I have to say, though, it's a lot different being on one than enjoying it from the comforts of a couch. One of the things I find so incredible is how much I can tell about a person from just talking to them for a few minutes."

I paused. "I certainly don't know everything, but am impressed with my ability to know who certainly won't work." I held out my hand to stop Nancy from interrupting me. "Attraction can grow. I just hope I have enough time with the guys I select to see if we fit."

"Well," Nancy said, "with that, shall we see which guys said yes to you and who you'll pick to continue?"

I was ready for another hug from Jared. Certainly, I was up for that. Nancy gestured for me to walk down the familiar path of jitters to see how my life would unfold. I stepped onto the boardwalk, my sandals not making a sound, thank heavens. My footing felt more grounded.

Peering up into the whitish-gray clouds, I wondered if Ava watched. I wiped at the corner of my eye and filled my lungs with air. This walk hadn't become easier, unlike zip lining. These men had their choices. It wasn't just about mine.

As soon as I approached, I saw Tom perched at the bar counter. He slid off the barstool. Keeping his cocktail in hand, he approached, grinning.

"Where's Jared?" I asked.

"Haven't seen him. Hope I never have to again."

Maybe he stepped away for the bathroom. I looked over at the crew. "Is he coming?" I asked.

They pointed to the table where the shells had been held. Only one shell lay there. Damn. If Tom continued this journey, he'd cause more drama. After speaking badly of Jared, I could just imagine what he'd come up with for the other guys.

Tom reached out for my hand.

I pulled out of his reach. "I'm sorry, Tom, but your journey ends here."

"What? Why?" he snapped.

None of the other guys had done that. I searched my mind for a way to answer. "Because I can see we wouldn't be a good fit."

He puffed his chest out, and his eyes narrowed. "Why is that?"

Crap. He wasn't going to let this go. My legs started to give out on me, and the headache I thought was gone flared.

"I just don't." I pressed my lips together to give me courage.

"Come on, don't give me that. I hung out and waited days to meet you. I had the golden ticket and spoke with you for five minutes. You come here asking for Jared, that low-down, scum-sucking loser. Then, you tell me you aren't going to take the time to get to know me any further. The least you could do is tell me why."

His sneering face demanded more out of me than I had to give.

"First off," I said, "I'm sorry you had to wait, but there

was a death in the family. My attendance at the funeral and being there for my sister was important. It was a lot more important than creating this entertainment for America. My niece just died, and she was the most incredible person. You could've learned a lot from her. She was loving, caring, and light to all those who she met. She didn't backstab or try to hurt others. She didn't storm around expecting things and demanding things from people like she was a king. Like you are doing."

I clenched my fists. "Instead, she was grateful for every last thing she had in her life and, believe me, she had a lot less to be grateful than you do. You have your health, as well as your wealth. You have an opportunity to come on TV and make a complete ass of yourself. So, stop pushing me, and accept that you had your free vacation. Just go home and be nicer to the next girl you meet."

* * *

THE PRODUCTION COMPANY didn't tell me what came next. They just hurried me to the wardrobe and make-up. I plopped down on the chair for Monique to do my hair. She started combing and tugging at it, up high.

"Monique, are you doing an up-do?"

"Sure am. My instructions are you're supposed to look fancy."

"What's going on?"

"Don't know," she said with a sly smile. "They have apparently learned not to trust me."

"What do you mean? Dee?"

She nodded as she worked. "Tell me about the guys you met today."

"The first one was skinny, which is okay. Some girls really like skinny, but I felt so big next to him. It made me self-conscious. If he'd had a great personality, I'd overlook that, but he was so rude. He put down the other guy before I even met him."

The back of my head hurt as she pulled. "Then there was this amazing guy who looked an awful lot like JT. He had JT's confidence and a soft touch.

"I heard he took you on a horse ride."

I flushed. "He did. It was so romantic. He clung to me tight during the whole ride. I felt safe with him and knew he wouldn't let me fall. He didn't show up, though."

"What?"

"He didn't pick me."

"You have to be kidding. After all the waiting around, and work he went to arrange the horse. That's weird." She shook her head.

"I'm trying hard not to think it was me."

She patted me on the shoulder. "Don't go there. Some rich guys are impossible. There's absolutely nothing wrong with you. You're a diamond any man would be lucky to be with. You have a nice selection of men to woo you, and they're all waiting."

* * *

THE CREW HAD DECKED out another hotel room with a dazzling display of flowers, ancient pots, and stunning paintings. One, an impressionistic landscape hanging over the fireplace, featured a mixture of soft oranges and the palest of blues smoothed with white and creams. Though calming, I still needed to squeeze my hands into tight fists as I strolled into the room.

The gentlemen greeted me with smiles.

"Charissa," they said in chorus. Each, in turn, came over and gave me a comforting hug.

"Are you okay?" Forester asked as he enveloped me in his arms.

I felt very small and protected and couldn't keep the tears back.

"Yes," I mumbled.

"It'll be okay." When he stroked my arm, heat shot through me. It reminded me of our last kiss, so passionate and warm. Maybe tonight I could slip away with him and steal another.

That thought made me suddenly aware of the other men still in the room, watching.

Shawn approached next. "Anything I can do to help you?" he whispered as we hugged.

That was thoughtful and kind. I shook my head in his arms. "Have you been okay?" I whispered.

"Worried about you," he said.

I stepped back, and he took my hands. "Tell me what I can do, and I'll do it. Death can be a crazy thing." He spoke like he had experience. A reassuring squeeze of his hands reminded me what a nice man he truly was.

When Andrew held out his arms for a hug, Forester and Shawn stepped up closer, almost crowding us. Obviously, Andrew's trip with me hadn't set well with them.

He wrapped his arms around me, and I settled my head

on his chest, feeling the comfort. I closed my eyes. Being with him seemed natural, unlike with the other two, but I'd shared a lot more time with him. We had bonded while he accompanied me through some of my worst moments ever. My heater kicked on.

"It's been a long day for you," he said. "How are you holding up?"

I shrugged, not revealing how much my body longed to be in bed resting. My feet ached, my eyes hurt from the days of crying, and my on-and-off headache throbbed. If I wasn't careful, I'd be nursing a migraine.

Nancy entered the room, decked out in an attractive bronze dress suit. "Please, everyone, gather around." She rubbed her perfectly manicured hands together.

When we formed a semi-circle, I was nudged in-between Andrew and Forester, where I felt like the little weed. I was growing next to a thin pine, Andrew, and an extra-large, fully spread out spruce, Forester.

I loved how Andrew always managed to be there when I needed him. That represented love and something I could handle for years. Shawn was more secluded, while Forester was just sexy and strong. I'd have to talk to Chelsey about this when I had a chance. She'd have an opinion.

By clearing her throat, Nancy made sure we all looked at her. She posed with a professional sparkly smile, loving the spotlight.

"We've been with each other for a while now on this journey. It's been bumpier than expected," she said. "First off, everyone who met Charissa had the opportunity to choose whether they might develop a relationship with her. A few chose not to continue, including the horseman today."

Forester glanced at me. I shrugged.

"Ahh," he said and patted me on the back.

Was he trying to be comforting?

"There was an unexpected tragedy," Nancy continued.

She had to bring it up. She just had to. I was doing so well until she did that. I wished she'd stop. The camera moved closer to catch me crying. This was getting ridiculous. They would surely do a montage of all the times I cried. I was positive no other girl cried more than I did.

Suddenly, all the guys were clapping and giving me tight hugs. Wait a minute. My thoughts must have drifted off, and I hadn't heard what Nancy said.

"What just happened?" I asked.

Andrew looked at me. "It's hometown visits this week."

I took that in. I was meeting the family. I would have to answer questions. This was no longer just about me.

"You're coming to meet my sister and my nephew and niece." Andrew looked at my fresh tears and paled. "Sorry. I don't... I mean... I'm sorry."

I placed my hand on the shoulder to reassure him. Just because Ava wasn't here didn't mean I couldn't meet his niece. "It's fine. I'd love to meet them. It'll make me smile."

His knitted brows relaxed. He cared if he hurt me. What a good guy.

"Your sister on the other hand... I'm not so sure."

I wasn't. A sister could be intense. They often are more protective than moms. Andrew's sibling seemed the intense type with strong opinions. After all, she was the one who put him up to meet me in the first place.

He just laughed. "She is a handful."

Not wanting to think about it anymore, I moved my attention to Forester, "Where will I be going for your family?"

"LA. Central."

Shit.

I smiled.

He waved a dismissive hand. "Don't worry. I grew up on the rough side of town, but it has a lot to offer. You'll see."

Yeah, like gangs and gun shootings. The fact I landed on the whiter side of things didn't help, either.

My eyes moved to Shawn. "Wisconsin?"

He nodded. "Nothing but prairie, good people, and delicious old-fashioned cooking. Everyone will love you. They'll just hug you and be pleased you're with them."

"I vote for Shawn's family first," I said, dreading this upcoming week, and knowing I had no say on when or where I traveled.

* * *

THEY SELECTED Forester's place first since the producers wanted to give me a chance to recover and not climb right back on a plane.

"We'll drive with you right into the middle of Compton," one cameraman said.

When they did, the highway crawled with barely moving cars. Out of the window, a dull, ugly gray smog hovered over the area.

I looked at my hairdresser and asked, "Is that bad?"

"It's a crazy place. Real crazy. Anyone who gets out of there to makes a life for himself is real impressive. It says something about them because not many people do."

That was good to know. I could sense Forester was special. Though he looked like he did—the epitome of a jock—he made his money using his brain instead.

The closer we came to his home, the shadier and rougher the area became, and the more my heart rate increased. I found it disturbing to discover Forester came from this. There I was, entertaining courtship with these men who were practically strangers. I knew almost nothing about them except for sharing a few minutes here and there in a vacation-like environment.

My throat constricted as a group of gang bangers sauntered down the street. We passed concrete brick, chain link fences, and various displays of graffiti on storefronts. My fingers encircled the doorknob and clenched. I would be okay. I had the crew with me. There was safety in numbers.

Not much later, we pulled up to a tiny, older house that looked like it was barely standing... one harsh gust might topple it over. The warped wood had been painted pale blue sometime within the past hundred years, and sections of it remained stuck to the wood. The rest decayed in various stages. The white trim hadn't fared much better. A wooden fence had attempts of white on it. The fence outlined the house's property up to the cemented driveway, which bumped up next to another lifeless house.

Directly in front of the house, someone had piled brick posts about three feet high. Along the ground in front of the lawn, more stacked bricks guarded the house.

"That's weird," I pointed to the brick as I talked to the photographer's assistant.

He shifted the camera bag higher on his shoulder. "That's an effort to keep people from driving their cars into the house."

I pivoted my head back to look at it again. "You've got to be kidding me."

"It's Compton," he said, like that explained everything.

I returned my gaze to the house with its saggy pink and white drapes in the front room.

"Oh, my gosh," I said. "Do we need to worry?"

His eyes scanned down the street one way, then the other. A few older people lumbered down the sidewalk. "I'll feel more comfortable when we're inside," he said.

This man was tall and rough-looking, but he was still worried. That wasn't a good sign.

Nancy nodded toward the front door. "Forester's waiting. Go make a good show."

Vehicles, so low they almost dragging on the pavement, thumped by with sounds of rap music polluting the air.

"Okay."

I scooted toward the front door, anxious to make it inside and out of the public eye. Before I made it all the way there, though, Forester rushed from the house with his long steps and big welcoming smile. He engulfed me in his arms, and I pressed into him, acutely aware of my involuntary trembling.

My heart picked up speed, this time excited, as he held me tight.

"Thank you for coming... here," he whispered.

As I clung to him, I became keenly grateful for the privileged life I had come from, and he had not enjoyed. Again, before I could register any more, he bent down and planted a tender kiss on me. I immediately wanted more, but he pulled away, leaving me aching. I opened my eyes to find his mesmerizing brown eyes drawing me in.

"Let's let one feisty woman meet another."

He grabbed my hand and pulled me toward the house. We had gone several steps before my brain clicked into action, and I figured out what he just said. I was feisty.

"Hey." I tugged on his hand. I wanted to talk to him about that before we focused on family.

He kept going, and no amount of begging stopped him. I had no more chances to put this off.

CHAPTER 25

Charissa

Forester's mother was a plump older black woman oozing with a lot of love. The moment we stepped into the house, she rushed over and wrapped me in a tight hug, just like her son often did.

"My Forester is a great catch," she said. "You should choose him. My boy has the kindest heart. He'd buy me a big house and spoil me if I let him, but I refuse. I need to stay where I belong."

Forester laughed and put his hand on her shoulder. "Ma, don't pressure her. You could, at least, let me replace the furniture."

She brushed at him as though shoeing at a fly. "Don't you touch my furniture. You don't want to give your old mom a heart attack from changing everything that gives her comfort, do you? Now, Charissa here is fine with me telling her how it is. Go away so we can share girl talk."

Before I could process what that meant, she seized my right hand in a tight grip and yanked me to her weathered floral couch. Shoved up against the living room window, it looked about to collapse.

"Let's talk."

She stared at me.

I gulped and forced a smile. "Okay."

This woman was a formidable force. Forester was wrong. I was nothing like this level of feisty. She could blow me over and keep on going, full strength.

My stomach twisted into knots as she launched into a round of harmless questions about where I came from, my family, and mostly what I thought of Catalina Island and the show. Eventually, she droned on about Forester and how brilliant he had been as a child and how she always knew he was different.

"He constantly had his eye on making himself a success. He'd go to the library and stumble home with stacks of books on business. He constantly wanted to watch those boring business shows on TV instead of cartoons."

I raised my eyebrows, trying to imagine it. I don't think I'd opt for those shows even now.

His mother shook her head. "Strange boy." She reached out and patted me on my knee. "You won't go wrong with him as long as you are an extremely clean person."

Clean? How clean? This would be an important detail. "Why?" I asked.

"The one thing he won't tolerate is a mess."

What did that mean? "Just what constitutes a mess?"

She smacked her lips together. "Well, let's say you two decide to take a trip to the beach, and you have a fun day, but you happen to get some sand in his car. He won't rest until he goes to the fancy car place and they vacuum out every grain of sand."

What? His mom had to be teasing. I glanced over to Forester to see if she was serious, but he was no longer in the room. I caught a glimpse of him in the kitchen sneaking bites of food.

"Forester, is that true?" I called out to him, twisting my head toward the kitchen.

He moved to the doorframe. "What?"

"You can't stand sand in a car?"

"True."

Hmm. I wondered how far this obsession went. That could quickly become annoying. "What happens when you have kids? How will you handle it then?"

He tapped the doorframe with one hand and shoved a chunk of meat into his mouth. "They won't bring the sand into the car."

I picked up the pillow that rested on the worn couch and tucked it on my lap. "You can't keep sand off kids. That's impossible."

He stepped into the living room, taking a huge bite into his chunk of meat. "Then they'll take off their clothes before they climb in the car." His face showed complete confidence in that as a reasonable answer.

He had to be kidding. That was extreme.

"You're so funny." I tried to wave it off but knew I couldn't live with someone like that.

His straight face and his mother's mumbling gave me

the feeling he was serious. That could be a problem, so I would need to find out more about that later. Cleanliness wasn't exactly my strong suit.

The rest of the time with Forester unfolded much the same. His mother had gone out of her way to cook us fried chicken, biscuits, and bacon-smothered green beans. Seated at the table, I stared at the plates filled with the types of food that killed people. Panic rose up in me. I was expected to eat this blood-clotting, life-sucking food. Bile rose in my throat. Such food gave people cancer.

Other people stomped all over their health willingly by eating death-producing foods. Ava had gotten cancer, even though she never ate that way. She died because her body wasn't healthy enough.

I wiped at my eyes. Now wasn't the time to think about that. It seemed so unfair. Some people also smoke nonstop, drug themselves, drink themselves into waste, and their hearts keep on beating. Ava ate as cleanly as possible: all organic food, like vegetables straight from the ground or fruit plucked from trees. A doctor had explained this unfairness. "Each person's constitution is different. We have no say on how well our constitution will handle it."

"Eat up, dear," Forester's mom finally said, noticing how I spread the food around the plate. The temptation to shove a huge bite into my napkin did cross my mind, but fear of being seen stopped me.

Pressure thumped in my head. I couldn't eat the food. I couldn't betray Ava like that. She was denied living a full life. I couldn't shorten my life, too.

His mom watched. I cleared my throat. "The food is wonderful. I'm sorry, but I really don't have much of an appetite." Worried that I might burst into tears, I pushed myself from the table. "I'm sorry, I need the restroom." Standing, I looked for the direction to go.

Forester pointed the way. "Down the hall, second door on the left."

I took off and found the cluttered bathroom, where I recollected myself. When I made it back to the dinner table, Forester must've said something to his mother because she didn't say anything else about the uneaten food.

Before dessert was put on the table, someone knocked on the front door. It was a limo driver here to pick up the crew and me. I slipped over to the front entry to talk to him.

"We haven't even gotten through dinner."

The driver nodded. "You have a red-eye flight to catch. You have fifteen minutes."

I took that for half an hour. I peered outside at the sky. Stars sprinkled across it, and the pleasant temperature greeted me. Ava's gift to me. I liked to think this was a way she told me she was near, supporting me. Stepping inside and shutting the door, I found Forester and his mom waiting.

"Looks like I'll have to leave soon," I said. "Since I missed a couple of days, they have me on a tighter schedule to make up for lost time."

Forester stood up from the dinner table. "You don't need to explain."

I smiled at his mom. "I loved meeting you and learning more about Forester. I can see where his drive comes from."

She stood. "Come give me a hug."

I took a deep breath and moved over to her, afraid I'd become lost in her arms. My fear was for a good reason. She grabbed me and squeezed me into her ample breasts until I struggled for air.

As she held me, she said, "I hope next time I see you, you're engaged to become one of the family."

She was good at putting on the pressure. My face felt like a gas burner had been flipped on inside it.

Forester approached us and tugged me from his mom. "My turn." He opened the front door. "I'll be in soon, Ma."

He pulled me outside to sit on the top step of the porch. He leaned his arms on his knees, and the way his muscles moved under his tight-fitting shirt made me do several double-takes.

The limousine parked in the front driveway. It shined in black in the darkened sky.

Forester rubbed his hands together. "So, this is where I come from. What do you think?"

The tension in his body increased. I sensed it more than saw it.

"I think," I said, shifting my weight, "you are incredible. Things weren't handed to you on a golden platter. Obviously, you're a fighter and have a lot of grit. I want to know more."

He leaned into me and gently placed his forehead on mine, sending a chill down my spine. "We could share a lifetime learning about each other."

* * *

WISCONSIN. I have to admit the sad truth that The Badger State had never made it onto my bucket list. I confessed this on the phone to Chelsey as I waited for my flight. The airport was practically empty at this gate. Apparently, the part of cheese country where we were headed was not a popular destination.

The producers had gone easy on me with the cell phone rules, hoping the connection to a familiar environment and connecting with my sister would keep me together. Besides, I wanted to be supportive of her. Chelsey needed to hear from me... to know I cared. Allowing contact between us was one of the most human things I'd seen during the production.

Chelsey coughed. "From what you told me about the suitors, Shawn sounds like the best one for you."

I flushed. I wish she hadn't said that. I wanted to stay open to them all without influence. Besides, maybe I'd just pick Forester. I could live off of his kisses. The memory of our last one flooded into me, especially that lip nibble.

"You shouldn't be voting. You haven't even met them, except Andrew. The show would think you're biasing me."

She laughed. "Relax. I've never worried about the rules before. I have no intention to begin."

"Why do you say Shawn is the best? Forester's kisses are the better."

I heard water. Chelsey was at home. She was probably cleaning or getting a drink. She was never one to sit still.

"Besides," I pointed out, feeling myself growing defensive, "Andrew's the most protective and aware. I'd say sensitive, but Shawn is conscientious, too."

I tapped my finger on the terminal's hard plastic seat.

How was Chelsey going to respond to all these good points? I watched an older gentleman a few rows away nod off to sleep.

It didn't take long to find out her opinion. "From what you say, Shawn's homespun and comes from a place most similar to yours. Marriages are hard. The more things you have in common, the fewer things you have to fight about."

More people drifted into rows by me. She might have a point there.

The announcer called for my plane. "That's my boarding call. Wish me luck."

"I'll do better than that. Happy kissing!"

* * *

MY SISTER MADE ME LAUGH. It eased my mood as I settled in for my flight.

Several hours later, I peeked out of the plane window to find tall buildings reaching for the sky. I thought Wisconsin consisted of hilly terrain and trees that carried on for miles. My mental picture of the state included desolate cheese and dairy lands left mostly to wilderness, and far removed from civilization. I thought it might be a lot like Idaho, but without The Gem State's stunning beauty. After all, Wisconsin didn't have the Rocky Mountains.

The reality was far different, with those legitimate skyscrapers, one after another, forming city blocks. It looked more like Salt Lake City than Idaho Falls. We flew over a sports dome or two and lots of cars, highways, and wide-spread housing developments.

It dawned on me why these trips were so important.

Just because Shawn was a dairy farmer didn't mean he lived in the remote Walden environment, I assumed.

I should be thinking about Shawn and how I couldn't wait to see him, or Andrew and how much I missed him. Instead, thoughts of Forester consumed me. His broad, incredibly defined chest, and those lips that lost me in the world of Forester. That man could kiss. With a mental swoon, I remembered the flood of intensity accompanying the warmth of his mouth on mine, which made scary LA worth braving. With the two of us, opposites attracted. For now, that was enough, as long as I had access to his tender lips. My mind replayed his kisses over and over until the plane jolted into the landing.

Soon after, Dee, the film crew, and I were zombies treading through the disembarking process. Like robots, we went through the actions of gathering our luggage while the staff took the additional step of securing our transportation.

The moment we stumbled out of the airport, a nippy coldness—not unlike Idaho's—greeted us. I stopped, tugged open my suitcase to yank out a sweater, and layered it under my coat.

Everyone in the crew stopped impatiently to wait for me. They wanted to get on with it. I had inconvenienced them enough, but I stopped anyway because I needed to. I was changing, becoming more self-aware, and not caring what other people thought.

This place was prettier than I expected. From the shuttle van's windows, the sky appeared a deeper blue than in San Diego, and clouds were numerous, stark white, rolling around in a whimsical essence.

We would be in the shuttle van for a little over an hour before making it to Kenosha, a mysterious place I'd never given much thought to. That, along with my sister's choice of Shawn for me, made me realize she probably thought I had neglected Shawn in much the same manner as JT had disregarded me. That couldn't be true, could it?

* * *

ANY ELEMENTS of city life fell away from the farther we went out of town in the late afternoon. The more we drove, the more the landscape transformed into one familiar to me. My nervousness picked up and burst into a full-fledged dance.

We pulled into a long gravel driveway leading up to a quaint country house with a large barn off to the side. Shawn strolled up with his relaxed, confident grin, several days' beard growth, and his pearly whites gleaming. He wore cowboy boots, Wranglers, and a tan cowboy hat tilted back so I could admire his face in the fading light.

Not wanting to wait, I opened the van door before it came to a complete stop. I ran over to him, right into a whiff of rustic cologne, which invaded my senses and blurred my vision. He curled me up in his arms and held me tight like a precious item he wanted to honor.

If Ava hovered in the skies watching, she'd smile and cheer for me to go for the kiss. She was the hopeless romantic. She must've gotten that from me because, after soaking in this embrace, I pressed closer against his firm chest and slightly tilted my head back.

Shawn smiled at me, his crystal eyes amused. He leaned

down and kissed me. Our lips touched, and he pulled me closer. I kissed him back and grabbed tighter onto his flannel shirt. I didn't want to stumble, but I wanted more of him. He held me much longer than I expected, and heat generated between us as we connected. It warmed me up faster than any sweater or coat ever could. Finally, he lifted his lips from mine and looked at me.

Recovering from his kiss, my eyes fluttered.

He blinked a couple of times, too. "I missed you."

Tingles moved through me. Shawn had just climbed the chart to Forester with that kiss. Where had that come from? I wanted more.

It was amazing how much more comfortable I felt at Shawn's than Forester's. My comfort gave me strength.

He grabbed my hands. "Come on. I can't wait to introduce you to my girls."

Girls? He hadn't mentioned he had children. I wasn't so sure I was ready for that. A pang of pain pierced me. Ava. Dear Ava. Nobody, nothing, could replace her. Since my trip to Forester's, I'd concluded I never even wanted to try to have children. It had nothing to do with Forester or the other guys. It had everything to do with not wanting to feel the kind of pain I was feeling from losing Ava again.

We stomped through dirt and grass as the pungent smell of manure increased, and the sounds of cows' lowing grew. Shawn opened the door of the barn to stalls of cows. Hay covered the floor. A shiny green tractor stood in the corner.

He grinned. "Ready to milk my girls?"

CHAPTER 26

Andrew

*M*eet the family week meant I had a chance to go home for a few days before Charissa flew out. Production didn't want me to visit my sister before then, but I argued she was a single mom, worn down with kids, and needed me, so I won permission to see her. I would've visited her even if they didn't approve. I'd had enough of the show's rules. I could give over only so much control of my life.

Despite that fact, I didn't immediately call Gina to let her know I was back. Instead, I worked my way through the ferry docks and traffic and stumbled into my apartment tired, wanting to collapse on my bed.

I opened the front door and fumbled around in the dark for the light switch. My apartment smelled surprisingly like melon or lemon... maybe something had leaked.

Finally, I found the light.

I gaped at my home. Messy stacks of papers and other stuff had disappeared. The dishes were done. I wandered around the place. It looked like a professional maid had spent days transforming everything. My entire apartment sparkled.

I strolled over to my fridge to see if, magically, I would find food in it. I didn't. But now, instead of strange life forces growing inside, the fridge shined. The top shelf held a post-it note. "Good luck on making a good impression."

Gina. She must've used her spare key. I smiled. I loved my sister. She had been so thoughtful. She must have spent hours cleaning my place when she already had so much to do. She did it because she didn't want me to mess things up with Charissa, but that didn't take away all the effort she put into this—with kids, too. Maybe I'd ignore my exhaustion for now and drop in tonight for a short while.

Half an hour after that, I rang her doorbell. My extremely excited sister greeted me like a happy puppy wagging her tail. She wrapped her arms tight around my neck and clung to me... way more even than her children. After I pried her off, she stuck close to me like she was afraid she'd lose me if I ventured too far away.

"You need a haircut," she declared after a full-body scan.

"Thanks for cleaning my house." I leaned down to pick up one of the toddlers attached to my leg. "You didn't need to."

She wrinkled her nose. "Of course I did. I want this to work out for you, and there was no way it would if she saw it the way you left it."

Dragging a second squealing toddler along with my leg, I stepped into her living room.

"I probably shouldn't tell you this, but there's a high probability Charissa will never go to my apartment. The production company wants me to meet her here with the whole family."

Gina shook her head. "Nope."

She could be so-o-o headstrong sometimes. "What do you mean 'nope?'"

"Doesn't matter what the production company says, you're going to figure out a way to get alone time with her, and you're going to take her to your bachelor pad because you want her to see you're successful, and you do know how to clean. Ha-ha. And that you still clearly need a woman in your life."

So, I bent over and picked up my nephew, plopped him in my arms next to his sister, and carried them both. "What do you mean?"

"Your place is bare. You need someone to make it into a home. She'll see that and be softer on you, not even knowing why."

She pointed to the table where she had set a heaping plate of vegetables, meats, and mashed potatoes. She sat at the dining table, waiting for me to join her. I wasted no time, positioning the two children in their places and taking a seat.

"Tell me all about it. I want to know... was she every-thing you expected?" My sister dove into the roast and potatoes, waving her fork as she talked. "Do you love her? I want all the gritty details."

I don't know why she bothered with the food on her plate. It was me she wanted to devour. To save myself, I answered her questions to the best of my ability as I dug into the pot roast.

She continued to ask questions throughout the meal, and even after dinner and as we made our way into the living room. She carried a cup of coffee, and a small amount of steam floated from the cup onto her face as she leaned forward to sit in a rocking chair.

"Do you want to marry her?" she asked.

"Of course." I shoved a hot bite of pie in my mouth. My taste buds exploded with flavor. Charissa would surely love Gina's cherry pie. Anyone would.

"Be bold. Don't hide your feelings for her."

Her comment stole some of my pleasure from the pie melting in my mouth. I was completely positive I didn't want to hear her next words. To delay the inevitable, I licked my fork to enjoy the last remaining flavor on it. "When have I ever hid?"

"You're hiding now," she said.

"I'm relishing this pie." I drove my fork in for another bite. The crust was light and crisp.

Gina set her coffee down on the table and rocked forward in her chair. With elbows on her knees, she rested her head on her hands. "You're more comfortable talking about food than women."

So? "Aren't all men?"

She bowed her head farther against her hands. "I care."

"Too much." I went in for another bite. She was acting more bossy than normal, which meant she must be worried about something. "But, I'm grateful for you, sis. I appreciate you stepping up in the mom role since her passing. I also appreciate you finding Charissa. Don't worry. I made it this far without any help."

My plate was empty, and I stood. "That pie is great. Is there any more?"

"Sit," she snapped.

I sat.

"You will not be getting any more pie until we've talked."

This was serious.

"Andrew," she said, going back to a gentle voice, "ever since Chris, you've been hiding."

I flinched. "Have not."

"You are living in Temecula. A town famous for families and the Bible belt to boot. That isn't a place a bachelor goes looking to meet someone. Plus, you sell life insurance. You *sell* safety, Andrew. You can't be safer than that."

Sometimes when she became all worked up as a tight neurotic ball, it was best to ride it out until she unwound. It was going to be a while until I had more pie.

I slumped back in my chair. "I'm on a reality TV show. That's not safe." I was proud of that point.

"Have you told Charissa how you feel?"

I stared at my sister. "I don't have to." I set my plate on the wood floor. "She knows."

Gina shook her head. "Little brother, she's a woman. She doesn't. You have to tell her, especially when you're in your kind of situation."

My sister sounded so certain that she was right like it had to be completely true.

"Fine," I said, giving in. It wouldn't hurt me to make

sure with Charissa. I bent over and picked up the plate and fork. "I will tell her. By the way, she's vegetarian. So please cook something she can eat."

CHAPTER 27

Charissa

I came out of the washroom, grateful to be away from the smelly, loud cows, and found myself meeting Shawn's mom. She was of sturdy stock... a square frame filled out over the years. She wore a short bob haircut and a tee-shirt that covered her shoulders and reached an inch past her waist and jeans. Her skin was tan from spending a lot of time outdoors, though her wrinkles were few. Her friendly demeanor covered an inherent toughness.

We shook hands, and she asked, "What do you do?"

I blinked. "Currently, I sew quilts."

"You can make a living doing that?" she questioned, gesturing for me to come farther into the house and sit at the kitchen table. Its surface held a dinner spread: mashed potatoes, fried chicken, and a green salad.

My heart thundered. I was going to have the same problem over food as I did at Forester's. The potatoes were white—straight carbs for a blood sugar roller coaster. Fried chicken equaled a vein blocker. I thought I might embrace the salad, but it was layered with bacon—a wealth of health-killing saturated fat, sodium, nitrites, and nitrates. My stomach felt sick just smelling the thick, smelly aroma.

I flicked my attention back to Shawn's mom. From the way she raised her eyebrow, it made me think she suspected me to be a gold digger. Trying to ignore the food, we exchanged looks. Her chin drew tight and tipped up toward me.

I swallowed. "I live simply." My finances were my business.

Shawn hurried over to my side and plopped his arm around my shoulder. "Ma, go easy on her. She's been through a lot and has a heart of gold."

Her eyes flashed to her son, my defender. "Shawn, get your dad, and let's eat."

He looked hesitant to leave me but patted me on the shoulder as he obeyed his mother. The pat was either a goodbye or a silent message of good luck, I wasn't sure which. I now understood his haste in greeting me at the car and having me experience the cows—not to mention his chill-inducing French kisses—before the interrogation.

She halted the question-drilling during dinner, though she eyed my plate with her lips pressed together. Because of that, we made it through the meal without incident.

Once dinner was over, she dove into washing the dishes by hand. I was in the living room talking briefly to Shawn's dad—a small, bald man—who basically just asked me where I lived and if I liked it there. After we finished our chat, I stood to gather dishes and take them into the kitchen, wanting to pitch in.

As I wandered into the kitchen, I heard Shawn's mom say, "She hardly ate a thing. Did you see that? She kept circling her food on the plate. You need a woman who has substance."

That comment sent dread through me. These in-laws didn't approve. I didn't wait for Shawn to respond. I just marched into the kitchen with the stack of plates extended toward them. "Maybe I could help with the dishes?"

Shawn's eyes widened, and color drained from his face as he lifted the plates out of my hands. "You don't need to do that. Why don't we talk on the porch?"

I agreed, grateful to be away from his mom. Shawn wiped his hands on a dishtowel and led me outside.

The sky had changed to darkness, and only one yellow light cast shadows on the wooden wrap-around porch. He sat on the porch swing and patted the space next to him. I sat where he indicated and, when he took my hand, I leaned against his warmth.

"This is like a country house out of the movies."

"Maybe. So, do you see yourself living the Walden Pond life?"

His expression carried more nervousness than I would have expected. Out of all my suitors' lifestyle, his most matched mine. He was hardworking, attractive, and was a nice genuine guy.

"Definitely could. Don't know about the children, though," I said, thinking about his earlier joke.

He scratched his head. "You don't want kids?"

My fingers twisted. "Don't know if I can do it after..."
My voice trailed off. I didn't want to say her name in case
the conversation went too deep and I wouldn't be able to
recover.

His legs pushed the swing into motion, back and forth.
"You don't need to say anymore. I understand, and that's
fine."

I searched his face to see if I could spot the truth. He
seemed sincere.

"So, for a much more important question," he said.

My throat tightened as I prepared.

"Why didn't you eat your dinner?"

I sighed. "I'm vegetarian, and I don't do potatoes.
They're awful for your health."

He eyed me until amusement crossed his face. "You live
out in the wilderness, and you eat like one of those crazy
Californians? On JT's episode, you prepared a spread for
him. They showed it. I thought you would've loved my
mom's dinner."

"If you would've looked closer, you would've noticed
the entire display was vegetarian."

He chuckled. "No wonder JT freaked out."

Nerves pounded in my chest, making it hard to breathe.
"Is this a deal breaker?"

His face went blank as he looked past me off into the
distance. The night had grown quiet except for a faraway
dog barking. The moon wasn't bright, and the night darkened to pitch black.

"Does your partner have to eat like you?"

"Well, I do cook this way."

"Would you care if he ate an occasional steak and fries?"

"He could do what he wanted, but I'm not cooking it. I don't support poor nutrition."

Shawn grabbed my arms and pulled me closer against his flannel shirt. "I could live with that."

He lunged in for another round of kisses, and I didn't stop him.

* * *

THE SHOW PRODUCERS wanted to mix up the California home visits with Wisconsin dairy cows across the country, so they'd sandwiched Shawn's visit in the middle. They started with Forester's LA visit, introducing the viewers to an ethnic, different, unnerving experience. That contrasted nicely with the calm, pastoral northern beauty of a heart-land farm. Last, they scheduled us back in California with Andrew—the safe, dependable guy who had stood faithfully by my side this whole journey—all the way back in Riverside County.

I bit my nails on the way to his home visit. Self-doubt bubbled in me like boiling water. What if his sister, my super fan, turned into a stalking hater? What if he noticed the zits that just sprouted on the tip of my nose, and he changed his mind on national TV due to my obvious defects?

With my self-doubt on high heat, the limousine squealed to a stop outside Andrew's apartment complex. I bit my thumbnail. The cameras' "currently filming" lights hit red from the moment I pulled up.

My face pressed close to the window to better view his place. I gawked at the three-story apartment complex:

classic brick, trimmed yards, a spray of colorful flowers, and iron trimmings. It looked yuppie, like where young professionals would live, and oozed a calm aesthetic.

"Oh, that's nice." The words escaped, but a twist in my stomach from nausea quickly followed.

What if he was using me, the cameras, the show... for fame? Or, like I had when I went on JT's season, to increase business sales, in addition to pursuing my silly idea of finding love?

Self-questioning thoughts spread like weeds on a hot windy day. This ridiculous amount of doubting the guy's intention hadn't happened when I visited Forester. No, with him, I only feared for my life against gang bangers and drive-bys. Never once did I doubt Forester.

With Shawn, the doubts centered on my behavior toward him and if I was mistreating him by unintentionally overlooking his merits. But, with Andrew, it was completely different. I was suffering from an epidemic of worries about whether I was good enough.

"Not bad for an insurance guy," I said straight into the camera, alluding to his abode. "Let's see how bad of a bachelor pad it is. I bet its sparse, dirty, and needs desperate cleaning."

I didn't know why I said such mean things. Andrew didn't deserve it. I hadn't been like that approaching the other guys' homes. No, I saved all my judgments and harshness, for the guy who had proved the most protective and helpful. The camera crew kept shooting my every move. Hopefully, they'd edit out my biting words. Yeah right, like that would ever happen. I sucked in my cheeks to keep any fouler words inside my mouth.

Andrew peered out his window two stories up, and the moment our eyes connected, I knew I'd kiss him. Somehow, I also sensed our time together would create tense fireworks. I didn't know how, or why, or even have the faintest idea what would happen, but I knew I'd be in tears by the end of the visit. I worried, of course, it'd all be my fault.

Maybe my jitters reflected how weird it was be back in a town where all its associations reminded me of the show with JT. The town looked like any town in the USA with the green lawns, average row houses, chain grocery stores, and restaurants. The backdrop, what the locals called mountains, was what I'd call hills.

Maybe I was nervous because Andrew had been to the funeral, and there was a higher chance he'd bring up Ava. I hoped he'd have the decency not to mention her. I wasn't ready to talk about it.

I did more lip biting, not sure what I thought about Andrew. I missed his grey eyes peering at me with curiosity. I also missed the way he hugged me, pulling me so close. Even though he was protective of me, I still didn't know what he thought of me romantically. I'd really only heard his declaration about protecting me.

That thought must've driven him out of his house because, when I looked up, he headed my way at a fast clip. He studied my face as he approached, and a concerned expression crossed his features as he stretched his arms wide.

"I missed you."

I slipped into his arms, smelling his soap-clean skin,

which eased my tension once more. As always, he pulled me close in, but this time he caressed my back.

"Sh-h-h," he whispered to me. "It's going to be alright."

I didn't know what "it" was, but it didn't matter. I wasn't sure if he even knew. Maybe he simply sensed my unease. In fact, I didn't even know what I was anxious about. I closed my eyes and listened to his heartbeat, which picked up speed. He ran his forefinger and index finger along the side of my face.

"It's good to have you here," he whispered in my ear. He took a deep breath inhaling me. "You smell good."

I sniffed. "So do you."

He blushed. "Want to see my place?"

"Don't we have to rush to your sister's?"

"We will be going there later," he said. "I thought you should see how I live first. Get a better sense of me and what I'm about."

That made sense. Why hadn't Forester and Shawn done that? We had been near the towns they lived in.

"I have a bet with my sister that it's a total bachelor pad," I said.

Andrew smirked and led me across the parking lot, lawn, and upstairs to a large apartment. It looked almost empty and so minimalistic.

"Oh, you decorate like Steve Jobs," I said.

"What?" Andrew asked, eyebrows raised.

I peered around at the clean table, desk, and couch. It looked like no one had ever actually lived in this place, and it was on constant display. Andrew might be too much of a clean freak for me. I doubted he'd be as much as Forester, though. I couldn't ever keep my living conditions this clean or sparse.

"This is impressive." I walked up to him, close enough for him to grab me and kiss me if he wanted.

He pulled me toward him, deceptively slow, so I wasn't quite sure what he was doing.

"Come here," he whispered. "I want a kiss."

I couldn't resist that. I leaned my head back and let his lips find mine. He pressed firmly and kissed me with hunger. When he pulled away, he peered at me, satisfied, but with a hint of an ache behind his eyes.

"I do care for you, you know."

I teared up and blinked. I hadn't known, only suspected. "You do?"

He shook his head. "Damn, my sister was right. She told me you wouldn't know. I thought, given the way I look at you and how protective I am of you, you would know that you mean a lot to me."

Trying to shift the uncomfortable energy, I attempted a joke. "You mean you don't do that with all the other girls?" I tapped him on the chest.

"Time to go to his sister's!" Dee called out from the midst of the camera crew. I was surprised she hadn't ended our silliness earlier.

"What girls?" I heard Andrew muse as I moved to leave.

CHAPTER 28

Andrew

So far, the visit with Charissa had gone well. She appreciated my living quarters and my hugs and kisses, but I could tell the anticipation of meeting my sister was getting to her. I didn't understand. It was only my sister.

I had never seen Charissa so shaky. Maybe all the travel, meeting all the families, was too much for her. I wished she would've taken time to grieve more before she jumped back in.

The closer the limousine inched to Gina's house, the more blood drained from her face. I put my arm around her and squeezed her.

"Are you nervous?" I asked to encourage her to talk.

She nodded.

"Why? My sister loves you."

Charissa looked at me, blinking. "I have a sister of my own. I know how they can be, especially if there are no parents in the picture. They love you, but they can be awfully protective and bossy, especially if your sister is the older one. Is your's older?"

She cared what my sister thought. That meant a lot to me. "Older, yes," I said.

She shook her head. "I don't know if I'm up for this."

I didn't know if she was either. She seemed extra sensitive. To reassure her, I squeezed her shoulder with my hand. "She'll be your best friend."

She eased her body into me, melting. Warmth exchanged between us, and her shaking gently ebbed. She pulled me tighter to her, and I bent and gave her a quick kiss as the car stopped in front of my sister's house.

Gina had the place lit up like the Fourth of July with every light on. The crew stumbled ahead of us. Charissa nestled deeper into my arms.

"Any secrets to dealing with your sister?" she whispered to me.

"Shoot straight. She doesn't like it when she thinks somebody's catering to her."

Dee walked in front of our car and gestured for us to go in. I reached over for Charissa's arm and nudged her toward the car door. "I'm with you."

To my relief, she took a deep breath, pushed open the door, and climbed out. I quickly followed her and grabbed her hand. She squeezed back tight and let me lead the way in. The evening was a perfect temperature, and the air smelled fresh. I hope it helped calm her.

Charissa had opted once again to wear heels, which I

thought was over-the-top, especially because the woman couldn't seem to walk in them.

Her hand trembled, and I glanced up. She had noticed Gina heading toward us before I did. My sister walked fast, confidently.

Charissa attempted a genuine smile and reached out her hand. "You're so pretty, Gina."

They shook hands and Gina smiled the fashion-model smile she liked to use on strangers. She had thought about going into modeling work before she became caught up with her family.

"You are, too, Charissa. Even more so in person."

Charissa's whole face flushed red. "Thanks. That's kind of you."

"Come on in. I have dinner all prepared."

Gina smiled up at the camera. She was working her little chance for fame. She guided us into her kitchen, overflowing with food: baked potatoes, turkey, two homemade apple pies, fruit salad, and beans with bacon. Plates sat stacked neatly in front of the food, buffet style. Crap. She must have forgotten that I told her that Charissa is vegetarian. Or, maybe she also had vegetarian dishes, too, and I just hadn't noticed yet. That had to be it.

All the food, bowls, napkins, and silverware were set out with precision. The room smelled like Thanksgiving, and I was ready.

"Eating time." I rubbed my hands together.

I looked around for my nephew and niece, but didn't see them. "Where're the kids?"

"Neighbors." Gina flushed. "I wanted to use this time to get to know Charissa and not use it battling the kids' obsessive need for attention." She picked up a plate and gestured for us to grab one. "So, Charissa," she said, "As Andrew's big sister, I need to watch out for him. I want to make sure my baby brother is treated right. He's been awfully hurt in the past, and I don't want it to happen again. If you don't mind me asking, why is he still on the show? Is he the one for you? From the moment I saw you on TV I thought you two were made for each other."

My stomach sunk. "You don't have to answer any of that." I touched Charissa's trembling arm.

Charissa put her hand out as she blushed. She leaned toward Gina like she was letting her in on a secret and met her gaze head-on. "There is definitely an attraction from the moment we met. I can't deny that."

Gina smiled. "Oh, by the way, I cooked you several vegetarian dishes. Andrew said you ate that way." She slapped another scoop of potatoes on her plate before taking to her chair.

I wished she hadn't told her that. My eyes darted over to Charissa.

Her ears transformed to bright red as she piled salad on her plate. "Thank you."

She sank into her seat, with a plate holding a pile of goop that must have been healthy and a handful of salad. She nibbled on her food.

"Don't hesitate to pile up. There's plenty of food," Gina said. "I made fake meat goulash for you." She pointed to a bowl full of muck.

"Looks great," Charissa muttered, but didn't leave her seat.

Gina's eyes fastened on Charissa. "What do you do for work?" She was digging.

"Gina, can I talk to you?" I asked. If I could get her alone, I could remind her to go easy on Charissa. Remind her that Charissa just lost her niece that she loved very much. Remind her that she was raw.

Charissa looked hesitant. She shifted food around on her plate. "I quilt."

That surprised me. I thought she sold some face stuff for women.

"What do you think about Andrew selling insurance?" Gina asked. "You okay that it isn't more exciting?"

I leaned toward my sister. "Enough."

"It's fine," Charissa said.

"You two are sounding perfect so far. I take it you're behind his movie producer dream, too?" my sister asked.

The light in the house flickered. I couldn't believe she had just ignited a huge bomb. I had no idea what Charissa would think of that. Bile rose in my mouth.

Charissa's chin trembled, and she looked at me with wild, scared eyes. "What's she talking about?"

"His dream is to be a movie producer," Gina said. "I'm sure he's told you. It used to be all he ever talked about. Now, he's on a show, seeing how it actually works."

Charissa's fork hit the china plate with a thud. "No."

Not clueing in, my sister continued, "That has been his lifelong dream."

The cameraman hurried around the room to capture all of our expressions.

Charissa pushed her chair back and stood.

"I'm sorry, but I have to go." She hurried out of the room.

"How dare you?" I snapped at Gina.

"I didn't—"

"Seriously? She just lost her niece." I dashed toward the door to find Charissa. I called over my shoulder to my sister, "Stay here. You've done enough."

The camera spots lit up my way in the darkness. "Where is she?" I asked Dee.

She pointed to the limousine pulling away. I ran full out and threw myself in front of the vehicle. By some miracle, I managed to stop the car without getting hit. Not taking any chances, I banged on the hood and stayed in front of the car so it wouldn't leave.

"I need to talk to Charissa!" I bellowed.

Nothing happened. I stood there and waited for them to make a move as cameras zeroed in. The crispness of the evening seeped into my bones as perspiration rose from my skin to be absorbed by the chilly night. The headlights nearly blinded me. Finally, the side door opened, and I hurried over. Charissa sat there, tissue in hand and tears in her eyes. I had no idea why she was acting this way. What did it matter if I wanted to do TV?

"Can I come in?"

She scurried over to the far side of the car as I climbed in and shut the door, wanting to move away from the camera.

Maybe she thought I was using her. I had to show her that wasn't the case. "Please take us to the Temecula Duck Pond." I wanted to get us both away from here. I turned to see her staring at me. "We can talk there in private, hopeful-ly." I peered out the back window. The crew members stood in the street watching us leave. "We can walk there and talk."

She took her napkin to her nose again. When I tried to hold her hand, she pulled from me and looked out her window. Other cars passed us as I struggled with how to handle this.

"Are you okay?" I finally asked, not able to wait until we arrived at the park. It might be better this way. I doubted there were cameras in the car.

"No." She stared out the window as if to find an answer in the night's inky blackness.

"I'm sorry about my sister."

"I'm not mad about that."

Wasn't she? "Then what is it?" I reached out toward her forearm.

She pulled away and broke into more tears. "Don't touch me."

"Charissa, if it's about me wanting to produce movies, that isn't true." I leaned in toward her. "Sure, that's an interest. But, it's not why I came on the show."

The car was quiet except the hum of the tires rolling along the black pavement. My heart thundered in my chest, and I listened to its pounding dance as I waited for her to respond. I pressed my lips together and watched our car inch to a stop at a red light. More banging in my chest. What if she didn't answer me?

"I trusted you," she said into the stillness.

That was confusing. What did that mean? "You can still trust me." I moved toward her. My knee touched hers.

She pulled her leg away, shook her head, and broke into

a harder cry. "No, I can't. I thought you were the safe one. I believed in you. I thought you wanted to protect me. Now, I can see I was wrong."

"I still want to protect you. I *am* the safe one."

She shook her head. "Stop trying to fool me." She buried her face in her hands. "It makes it harder. You won. I believed in you, but now your gig is up." She wiped at her eyes and straightened her shoulders. "Driver, please take me to my hotel, then drive Andrew back to his sister's so he can pick up his car."

"But—"

Charissa snapped her attention to me, her eyes wide, wild, hurt, and angry. They held something else deeper and darker, but I couldn't quite tell what it was yet.

"I am not talking about it." Her chin quivered almost as much as her hand. "I am not."

The car jerked into motion again. The driver cleared his throat. If I said anything, it was going to make this situation worse. Disorienting lights from other cars flashed inside the car as we drove, mirroring my desperate thoughts.

"I can't believe it. Mr. Safe Insurance guy was using me to launch a movie career," she muttered. "Well, I hope it worked. I hope it gets you the connections you wanted. I hope my pain was worth something."

I'd think of something to make this right when her emotions aren't so raw. She needed some space for now.

* * *

BEFORE BOARDING the ferry the next day, I had my doctor refill my ulcer prescription. Yes, they were back, and I knew exactly why. Charissa's devastated hazel eyes giving me that look of complete shock and hurt haunted me. It stayed with me from the moment she cast them on me.

When I made it to Gina's house to retrieve my car, I didn't go inside to talk to her. Nor did I answer any of her multiple phone calls, texts, emails, and instant messages. She had her reasons for doing what she did. She did them, and now I had lost Charissa.

With the combination of LA smog and the marine layer, the skies stayed grayish black with the moon glowing in the background. Of course, the temperature was perfect, but this evening was no longer perfect for me. I was traveling all the way back to the island just to be told by the woman I loved, I had lost.

Maybe if I caught her before the ceremony, I'd have a chance. If I could explain to her, I hadn't come on the show to advance my career. Yes, I had wanted to become a film producer. Yes. That had been my life's dream. But, over the years, I had given that up. I had gotten caught up with life insurance, which was fine with me. I didn't need to become famous. I didn't need to produce movies. I could and would provide the safe and secure life she so deserved.

I bumped into Forester and Shawn on the same ferry. I nodded at Forester but decided to approach Shawn. Though a competitor, we had agreed to be friends.

"Good hometown?" I asked.

He nodded. "Couldn't ask for better. Now, I guess it's in her court. I've done all I can. Same with you?"

I shook my head. "No. It went south. I'll be the one going home."

He sighed. "Sorry to hear that. I always thought it'd be me and you at the end."

"Not Forester?"

"He's good eye candy for her, but their worlds are too different. Did you know he's very active politically?"

I didn't.

"Not saying that's good or bad one way or another, it's just dicey, no matter on which side you stand. Forester is bound to create a storm with his political opinions."

"Or, run for office," I said. "I can picture him winning. I'd vote for him. He seems strong and solid. The country could use somebody like him."

Shawn thought that over. "Maybe, but Charissa doesn't need that. She needs a quiet life."

I raised my eyebrows. "One like she'd have living with a dairy farmer?"

Shawn smiled.

Several hours later, we three bachelors gathered again in the shell room, waiting to see who would be next to go home.

Dee marched into the ceremony room. "There's been a change of plans."

I shoved my hands into my pockets, waiting to hear my fate.

"We're not going to have the shell ceremony until after the group date. Charissa wants to have one last chance with each of you before she makes her decision. Now, I have to tell you, she's not taking this decision lightly. She's really excited about all of you and sees possibilities. This is why she asked to do the group date first."

I closed my eyes and let the news settle. I celebrated with a high-five with both Shawn and Forrester, but it barely registered.

I might still have a chance!

Dee called out over the chatter. "Charissa's sister is joining you on the date. She's giving her input before Charissa makes the final decision on the two of you who'll be continuing to your last one-on-one and overnight dates."

CHAPTER 29

Charissa

*T*he day after Andrew's home visit, the show had scheduled another conch shell ceremony to send one suitor home. Andrew. Shawn. Forester. One had to go. We were back again on the island, feeling like we were able to escape the world. My pending decision, though, made my world travel with me.

Now childless, it was easy for Chelsey to get away from town and fly to Catalina Island to be with me. Within a few hours, after the shell ceremony, she'd go on the group date with me to give her insight on the remaining millionaires.

The plan involved traveling deep into the island and its wilderness. Originally, we were scheduled to visit the *Healing House* this week, but since Ava's death, the show decided it wouldn't be appropriate. Besides, *Healing House* didn't want to be promoted as the place where Ava died.

Dee had informed me the producers had worked out a deal with *Healing House* to be spotlighted on a different program and that my bills would still be handled.

I didn't like how they said, "my bills," but, as Chelsey pointed out, "It could have been worse. Take it."

The show, instead, found a sponsor that promoted cosmetics—the cheapest and worst brand. But, at this point, I was powerless to influence the business side of the production.

I needed to stay focused on who'd keep going with me after the home visits. It was hard to focus. In less than an hour, I'd see Andrew. My stomach seized, thinking about it. I doubted I could even look at his smile, grey eyes, curling hair, and natural demeanor. He had used me. He wasn't there to be my protector. Oh, what a line! I should've known better.

"Thinking about the ceremony?" Chelsey found me on the porch sipping a hot chamomile tea, which I hoped would calm my stomach.

"What am I supposed to do?"

"You know what to do."

I should leave him. "But, I liked him." Unsettling pain spun inside me like a mini-hurricane.

"I know." Chelsey plopped down on a rocker next to me. "I did, too."

My eyes flashed to her. I hadn't realized she'd paid any attention to me, let alone Andrew, at the funeral.

"He's so cute."

Chelsey smiled. "That he is."

"What a jerk," I said. "Using me to get on the show to advance his career."

She took a sip of tea. "He doesn't seem the type to try something like that, but you never know, I guess. Maybe you should talk more to him."

No way. I couldn't handle that. I gave her a level stare.

She shrugged. "Then, tell me about the other two."

"Forester is the one from Compton. He grew up there."

"That's a rough place."

It is.

"What attracts you to him?"

"He's a successful multi-millionaire lawyer who came from tough roots. Can you imagine what it took to rise from that? A lot of grit and intelligence. Plus, he looks like a fit football player, and his kisses are toe-curling. I've never been kissed like that."

"Sounds like a lot of physical attraction between you two."

More than she knew, and more than I'd admit.

"And, Shawn?"

Good old Shawn. "He is just as attractive as Andrew. Those two look a lot alike, if you ask me."

"How?"

"Both white, bluish/grayish eyes, thick curly brown hair."

"How are they different?" she asked.

"Shawn's more grounded and content. His lifestyle matches mine the most. He's rich, granted, but he doesn't act like it or even mention it. He's the most humble of the bunch and, so far... your favorite."

Chelsey smiled, but didn't convey whether my guess was still correct. "Who's going to go?"

I closed my eyes to my resolution firm. "It has to be Andrew. I should've sent him home when I found out."

"But, you didn't," Chelsey said.

"But I didn't."

* * *

CHELSEY BEAMED when she came back to the hotel room. "I got it changed!" She wore a huge smile.

My stomach tightened even more. "What did you do?" I sat up in my bed to prepare for the news.

"Got your shell ceremony put off until tonight."

"What?"

"It gives you more time to make your decision. I could tell earlier you weren't confident in what you were going to do. This will give you time to become clear, plus glean from your sister's insight."

"Perfect," I muttered. "Shouldn't you be grieving or something and not meddling in my business?"

"As, I mentioned before, I grieved for years before she died." Her voice shook and sounded full of hurt, but she looked up with determination. "Now is my time to move on."

That made sense, and I shouldn't have jabbed her like I just did. Seriously, though, she had made things a whole lot more uncomfortable. Now, I was going to spend all afternoon with Andrew... like it wasn't going to be hard enough to say goodbye.

"Come." Chelsey put on her smile. "I have some hunky men to go meet. Maybe I can pick up one of your leftover guys."

* * *

Andrew

I HURRIED onto the old 1950s tour bus we would take to the far side of the island, where I hoped we'd see the indigenous wildlife I'd read about on that first day. The buses' exterior was painted shades of brown, and yellow, with white trim. Most of its windows were jammed, and its benches' green leather was cracked, but the seats would still offer a firm place to sit.

A Sixties hippy chick with a wig of long grey dreadlocks turned out to be our tour guide.

"Peace," she said in greeting.

I mumbled it back to her and headed to the back of the bus. Forester spread out in the middle portion of the bus, while Shawn stopped and sat close to the front.

Fortunately, I found a window that worked. I stood there, letting the warm, salted breeze brush past me. I tossed my water bottle on the seat and headed to the front of the bus again.

"Where're the restrooms?" I asked the driver.

She pointed to a white building directly behind the vehicle.

I stepped off the bus and surveyed the area. To my right, about two-hundred feet away, I spotted Charissa walking with her sister. I jogged up to them. I smiled at Chelsey, "Good to see you. Glad you're with us. Do you mind if I talk to Charissa?"

She smiled and left. Before Charissa could react, I grabbed her hand and moved her over to the bathroom building's sidewall out of the bus's view. She resisted by tugging her hand.

"Please hear me out." I still gripped her wrist.

"Let go of my arm."

"Oh… I'm so sorry." I let go of her, but I remained inches away. She needed to hear me out. After that, it was up to her.

"You have it wrong, Charissa. I didn't come on the show for fame. I didn't. I came because of you. When I saw you, I knew there was something different about you. I felt a connection to you like I haven't with anyone else. I worried about you because you seem so vulnerable and helpless, and like the world hasn't been kind to you."

Charissa started to sidle away, but I stopped her with a light touch on her cheek.

She frowned. "Why should I talk to you? Even your own sister is angry at you." Charissa's hazel eyes burned into me.

"My sister is a wonderful person, but she doesn't do well on her own. She freaks out sometimes since her husband left her. I'm sorry her jealousy and fear of losing me went sideways on you. I really am. I know she feels awful, too."

Charissa stared at me, breathing hard. I wish I could jump into her head and read her thoughts.

"Do you believe me?'

She folded her arms across her chest. "Maybe."

That was a good sign.

"About which thing?" I asked.

She shrugged. "Both."

Pressure in my chest eased. Good. I had a fighting chance.

"I wanted to get to know you and see if there'd be something between us. And, for me, there is. Every time I see you, I know I love you even more than I did the last time I saw you. I care about you, and I want you happy. I'm completely happy just selling insurance for the rest of my life. Please, you have to believe me. I wasn't using you."

She looked at me with a side grin. "You just said you love me."

I flushed. I had. No sense denying it.

"I did, and I do. I've been playing it safe because I've been hurt in the past. I'm not playing it safe anymore. You mean too much to me."

"What is it that you want?"

I smiled. "Easy. To have a life with you."

Charissa's smile dropped. "I don't want kids."

I grabbed her hand and squeezed. "Being with you is what I want."

* * *

Charissa

THE OUTING WAS GOING to take place on a Scooby Doo bus. Seriously.

"Ready to go solve a ghost mystery?" I whispered in my sister's ear as we climbed on a bus that looked exactly like the one on the TV show.

She looked toward the roof of the bus. "Yes. Ava, hear

that? We want you to help us solve the mystery of who's the perfect guy for Charissa."

"Over here." Forester waved his hand.

Chelsey smiled. "Good option." She slid next to Forester, and I felt a pang of jealousy.

I had already talked to Andrew and was having a hard time getting his words out of my head. They all sounded lovely, perfect, and what I wanted to hear. Now, I need to determine if I believed him. I opted to sit with Shawn.

Soon, we were bouncing along dirt roads and learning the history of Wrigley, the island, and his heroic attempts to make this place a refuge for its endangered animals. The bus squeezed up the narrow road to find the conservatory institute.

Shawn turned to me. "I heard about the overnight date coming up. I want to say this upfront, so you know, and you don't feel like I was tricking you... I find you incredibly attractive, and I do think we'd make a great couple. My intentions are, if I make it through all these rounds with you, is to marry you, but..." He took a breath.

My stomach tightened again.

"But, I'm a guy who needs to be with a woman who feels the same way. I know you have all these other guys because this is the show, and that's what we agreed to. I get that. I'm not saying I need to have you all to myself, but I won't have any overnights with any woman without committing. That's just the way I am." He flushed and looked at his hands. "I know this is unusual for a guy, but that's the way it is with me. I have never been one for getting around."

I could see this was hard for him to say and sense his

embarrassment. I hoped the cameras didn't pick it up. I reached out, took his hand, brought the back of it to my lips, and kissed it.

"I'm actually the same way," I said.

He pulled me close to him. "Good."

* * *

Andrew

ONCE WE MADE it to the top of the island, we found ourselves at a very small airport. The rest of the crew piled off the bus quickly. I lagged behind, feeling stupid. I had poured out my heart to Charissa and in response, she sat by another man. My entire body felt tense. Clenching my fists, I slipped off the bus to see Charissa walking toward the airport building with Forester, clearly deep in conversation.

Shawn and Chelsey were busy talking, too. I wandered behind them, hoping to check in with Chelsey when they were done talking. Maybe she had a better idea what was going on in Charissa's head because I surely didn't. I scurried behind them and couldn't help but overhear their conversation.

"You two have certainly been through a lot," Shawn said to Chelsey as they took in the vegetation planted around the building.

"We have."

"Charissa sure loved your daughter."

She nodded. "She would've done anything for that child, and actually, she did. Just look how she came on the show, despite her feeling so strong against the whole TV world."

I stopped walking and found myself holding my breath, wanting to hear what came next. I had no idea Charissa didn't want to be on TV. It made sense now that I thought about it. She did shy away from the cameras. If she didn't like it, why did she do it? Did that have anything to do with her extreme reaction to my wanting to be a film producer?

Shawn stood there, face blank, not saying anything. Must have been a surprise for him, too. Finally, he asked, "Why did she come on?"

Good question.

Chelsey looked up at him brushing at hair dancing in her face from the light wind. "You didn't know?" She sighed. I sidled closer to hear. "Charissa agreed to do the show if they would help get Ava treatment in Mexico. The show paid for everything."

"She did what?"

"Crap!" Chelsey slapped her hand over her mouth. "I shouldn't have said that. Please, we're under contract not to say anything. Please." She grabbed his arm, tugging on it. "I'll get into so much trouble if production finds out. I'm so tired and upset, it just slipped out."

Shawn looked out toward the sea, and his chin drew tight. He leaned into Charissa's sister and whispered loudly, "The cameras are on Forester and Charissa. I think we're safe. Don't worry. I won't say anything."

And, I thought, kicking a rock, if being on the show didn't pay for all of Ava's treatments, hooking up with a rich man would ensure any additional expense. Charissa was as much a gold digger as the rest of them. She just hid it better.

Charissa

WITH ANDREW'S touch still on my body, the bus chugged up and around the large island. It had a lot more land and oceanfront than I expected. Most of the island was tannish brown and not too pleasant to look at, but the ocean blueness rolled on for miles.

We pulled up to an airport Mr. Wrigley had built. Still, in use, the airport amounted to a flat strip on the top of the mountain, with a small restaurant and gift shop to the left. A few planes parked off to the right. We were instructed to stay off the runaway.

Getting off the bus, Chelsey was still heavily involved in an intense conversation with Forester. My sister actually looked like she was having a good time. They laughed a lot together. The strain in her jaw was gone, and her brow crease had relaxed... something I hadn't seen recently.

"You two look like you're having fun." I forced a smile.

Chelsey returned the smile. "We are. Now it's time for me to get to know Shawn." She trotted off to join Shawn as he examined the tires on the bus.

"You sure have a *great* sister there." Forester grinned.

I did, but for some reason, I sensed he might like her more than me. I wasn't sure if it was my sister's issues coming up or if he was acting differently... more interested. I wasn't even sure if he did like her, but it certainly seemed so.

"Enjoy the ride up?" I asked.

He pulled me into his arms. I resisted, completely surprised.

"Not here," I whispered.

Forester's grin widened, showing off his pearly whites. "We have an overnight coming up." He raised his eyebrows, and, suddenly, I wanted to get far away from him.

* * *

AFTER WE ARRIVED BACK from the group date, all I could think about was Andrew. He confessed his love, then avoided me during the tour. This was the first time he wasn't naturally by my side. In fact, several times I tried to spend time with him, but he simply looked at me, said, "Excuse me," and left.

My mind spun as to the reason why. Maybe he didn't want the other guys to catch on to what we had. That was the only reason I would consider. I was *sure* that was what it was.

Well, I hoped.

* * *

GLAD FOR SOME GIRL SUPPORT, I sank into the beauty salon chair to let Monique do her magic.

"I have to look smokin'," I said, still thinking of Andrew. I wanted to look so good he can't keep his eyes off of me.

"This is your big day." Monique worked on my

eyebrows. "You're one step away from picking who will get on bended knee."

I stared at Monique's reflection in the mirror, struggling to make out what she said. It took a moment before it clicked. I needed to send home another guy, then two guys would fight on the overnight date to see who would have the chance to propose. This was getting real.

A few minutes before Monique finished her work, Dee came for me, still snapping her gum and ready to do an audio voiceover. Minutes later, I found myself saying, "I am down to three suitors, and I won't be meeting any more new men. It feels strange. I don't know how I ever got used to meeting suitors, but I guess human nature is funny that way. Maybe it is like zip lining."

I stared down at my hands. "I have developed strong feelings for the guys I am dating. I don't think I had really thought it all the way through but, if all goes well, I could become attached. I could be proposed to. Whew. That's a big step. Really big step."

After the camera people took the mic away, Chelsey came up to me.

"So, who's going home tonight before the excitement of the overnight dates?"

Monique stopped her final touch-ups to hear my answer.

I shrugged.

I should send Andrew home, but his apology had been authentic, and I felt the love from him. Shawn was such a great guy. His lifestyle matched mine the most, but sometimes it was awkward between us. He wasn't that expressive with his feelings, and we didn't share the same passionate burning fire I did with Forester. I wasn't sure, in the long run, that passion was a solid enough foundation. Forester was exotic, but I didn't know how that would translate in real life. It might, eventually, require a lot of work to make it successful.

"Don't give me that." Chelsey wanted the inside track. "I'm your sister. I know you know. You have that set way about you when you've made up your mind."

It didn't pay to have her know me so well. "Forester."

"What?" she shrieked. "Really? He's so charming."

"I know, and his kisses are fabulous. But, if I'm serious about this, which I have to be, we're on two different paths. I don't think a lawyer is the right person for me."

Chelsey gave me a funny look, almost relief, and I knew she was thinking something.

"What?" I asked.

"If you are really going to break up with him, do you mind if I date him?"

CHAPTER 30

Andrew

*S*he came here for the money. She got mad at me, thinking I was after the fame, but she was after the money. It served me right to become mixed up with a woman again. My life was so much simpler when I focused solely on work. I *so* didn't need this complication.

I waited until we came back from the group date and the other men had left to go for the shell ceremony. I told them I'd catch up with them, but it was a lie. I was actually packing my bags.

Charissa was beautiful, but I wasn't going to make the same mistake again. I had already been down this path of being involved with a gold digger before, and I knew where it led.

There was a knock at the door. I opened it for the film crews.

"You better start shooting," I said. "I'm going home."

* * *

Charissa

THE SHELL CEREMONIES hadn't gotten any easier over the weeks. In fact, I was feeling more sick to my stomach than ever before. I really liked Forester. He had opened his home to me, and he had accomplished amazing things.

I didn't want to hurt him, but my sister was ready to make him feel better, which was... flat-out weird. I hadn't seen her even thinking about a guy for years. Sure, death did funny things to people, but I didn't think she'd be like this. It was almost like she had thrown out her grieving and responsible side and reverted into an impulsive teenager. Maybe having Ava around, with the responsibility involved, had kept her anchored.

I was wearing an evening gown that floated out around my knees. It was a wavy olive green that brought out my eyes and matched my low-heeled sandals. I felt beautiful. Preparing myself to break Forester's heart, I strolled into the formal room dripping with flowers.

Shawn stood in the distance to my right. He smiled. I loved his reassured groundedness. He was good for me. Really good for me. He'd make a wonderful husband, and he was okay with me not eating meat and not having children. He knew that big thing about me. I should pick him.

Forester was over on the other side, joking with the staff. That man was a lot of fun, and he had a ton of class. I loved his fight and his ability to rise from misfortune and make something of himself.

I wasn't going to make him happy, though. I wasn't sexual enough for him. I realized that when he whispered to me about the overnight. But, maybe he and my sister...

Okay, I couldn't see it, but maybe I should give it time. Perhaps Chelsey should give herself space to recover from grieving. She could also be trying to make up for all the energy expended in helping Ava, and this was her fling. I didn't have the answers.

I searched the room for Andrew. I wanted to see him and feel the connection of his gaze. I needed his reassurance tonight. I hadn't realized until now how much I looked to him for strength during these events. I certainly needed it.

Where was he? I didn't see him mingling with the crew members or the hotel staff who hustled around.

Dee hurried into the room on her intercom, and I ran up to her. "Have you seen Andrew? I want to talk to him before the ceremony."

Dee held up a finger and turned to the room. "I have an announcement."

Something in the way she said it commanded my attention. My stomach seized. Had something happened to Andrew? Was he okay? Was I going to lose him, too? My chest constricted, which made breathing hard. I wasn't ready for this.

As though to end my misery, Dee jumped in. "I just received word from our helicopter pilot that Andrew decided to leave the show."

The room crowded in on me, dark and heavy. That

couldn't be happening. Last time I saw him, he told me he loved me. He couldn't leave.

"Why?" I whispered, unable to look at Dee or anyone. I felt sick. My head hurt. I needed a chair. It took too much energy to stand.

"He didn't give a reason. Just said he's leaving."

"Is he coming back?" I asked through another round of tears.

"No."

How could Andrew just leave with no word? One of the crew members guided me to a backless couch. I sat on it with tears streaming down my face. That couldn't be right. I remained there in a stupor, for I don't know how long when Chelsey ran up to me.

"What's wrong?"

"Andrew left."

"Then your choice is Shawn. You two are perfect for each other. You were leaning toward him, anyway. This will make things easier all around. No broken hearts and no drama."

"But, I think *my* heart is broken," I whispered.

Chelsey patted my arm. "I know it's hard that he walked away from you, especially without talking with you. That's a lot to process. But you told me many times Shawn was the best choice. He's the most conducive to the isolated lifestyle you want. He's more into the outdoor and simple life. Andrew is not that way. He's ambitious. He just oozes it."

That was true.

Dee approached us. "We need to get the show on the road. The clock is ticking."

I looked at Chelsey. She patted me again. "You got this."

I cleared my throat as Monique fussed with my make-up. My eyes felt puffy, so I knew there wasn't much she could do. When she was done, I made it over to stand in front of the two men. Each gave me a curious glance. I picked up the shell and looked at Forester, then to Shawn. "Andrew will no longer be with us."

"What?" Forester asked, face blank, unreadable.

"You didn't pick him?" Shawn asked.

I shook my head no. "He decided to leave on his own."

My voice wavered. More tears spilled. I wasn't ready to let him go. This didn't make any sense. Was it all an act?

Shawn's brows furrowed. "Is he okay? What happened?"

Was it an act when he held me when I found out about Ava? Were his smiles and glances to see if I was okay all an act, too? His kiss that challenged me to come closer. Daring me to love him. That was it. He dared me. He pushed me out of my comfort zone while at the same time protecting and guarding me... until now.

Forester and Shawn leaned in closer, waiting to see what I'd say next. Andrew had always given me that cherishing expression. He was the one I looked to for courage and support. I always went to him. He had always been there. Always gave me what I needed emotionally. He told me he loved me, and he *meant* it. I felt it. Unlike any other guy in my past, I believed his love with no lingering doubts. Now, he was gone.

Something must be wrong. This smelled like one of those bad romantic movies where the couple separates from each other because of a miscommunication. I wasn't going to lose the man I love over something like that.

Not to me. Not now. I had promised Ava I'd find love. I promised her I'd be true to myself. I had played small with JT because of my nerves... and because I was a quiet person, and the cameras, and show, and producers were intimidating. Not any longer. I closed my eyes and envisioned Andrew's encouraging smile. It filled me with the courage I needed to do what I had to do.

I put the shell back on the table. "I'm sorry guys. You're both wonderful men. Charming, smart, and any girl would be lucky to have you, but I have to go now. I have to find Andrew and see what went wrong."

CHAPTER 31

Andrew

*T*he whipping motion of the helicopter blades turned my stomach, even though I hadn't even boarded yet. The sound thundered with force like they wanted to chop off someone's head. Their nauseating motion felt much like the emotion lashing inside me.

I reviewed my plan of action. As soon as I pulled into town, I'd head for a fast-food joint and order several hamburgers and one or two orders of greasy fries. That would help me forget this whole adventure unless the TV show brought me some fame. If that happened, I'd have to find a way to hide out because I no longer wanted even to try to have a woman in my life. Life was a lot more peaceful without them. I was determined to keep it that way.

Heart thundering, I climbed into the helicopter, excited

to take another flight to take my mind off of women. The darkness of night surrounded us, and, for some reason, the idea of flying in the dark felt right.

The pilot turned to me. "Ready to head home?"

I simply nodded my head, not feeling like talking, and sat to put the headset on my head. Last time I had left the island, I had Charissa by my side. She was crying, upset, and broken. It was like seeing a wounded cat. Every part of my body felt compelled to take care of her. Truthfully, if I saw her now, looking the same way, there would be no way I'd resist her.

That was why I had to leave. I couldn't talk to her and explain. If I looked into those deceptive eyes, I'd give in to her. I made that mistake too many times. I loved her, but I wasn't going to be hooked up with someone who didn't really love me.

The moon hadn't come out yet, so a dark shadow over the island gave it a gloomy feel. I checked my seatbelt, then watched the pilot carefully, hoping he was going through the proper safety checks.

He tossed off his earpiece and answered his phone.

"Yes?" He listened for a while as I watched. His face was drawn. "Okay. Yeah… yeah. Are you kidding? Thank you. Thank you." He set the phone down. "I just love Charissa."

Charissa. Something just happened. Something big. "May I ask why?"

The pilot burst into a wide smile, turning to look at me. "Yes. Charissa took a lot of time with me, offset, to share different ways to cure my wife's cancer. She made so many suggestions. She was so awesome. I had hundreds of questions, and she was very patient and kind."

He stopped talking, his voice choking. He took a breath. "That was a call from the hospital, and they said the cancer is diminishing. They can't understand what happened but are happy with the prognosis. The diet and nutrition Charissa suggested is clearly starting to work. It is really showing promise. Plus, Charissa was able to get my wife into the Healing House. I don't how she did that. All I know is Charissa is a Godsend. I think healing could really happen."

The pilot cleared his throat. "Sorry, that was unprofessional of me. We'll get going." He picked up his clipboard. "Where were we?"

As he redid his safety check, I thought about what he had said. Charissa never once mentioned helping this guy out. The other guys never mentioned it either. I was sure they would've if they'd known. Gossip always runs through co-workers.

Charissa cared, really cared, about healing people with cancer.

"Stop!" I yelled at the pilot.

He flinched. "What?"

"I need to get to Dee, now."

I hurriedly told him why.

The pilot radioed production, who sent a limo, which arrived in the parking lot four minutes later. I thanked the pilot and hurried into the back of the car to find a man in a Hawaiian shirt, who opened up several boxes for me to peer into.

"Dee suggested I show you these. She said you would need one of them when you see Charissa."

Perfect. Now, if we only arrived at the ceremony soon enough.

* * *

Charissa

DEE BLOCKED me from walking out of the room. "You can't go."

I straightened my shoulders and eyed her. I could take her down if I had to, I hoped.

"I'm sorry, Dee. I know I broke the rules, and I'll pay whatever consequences I need to, but this is my life, and I have to do what I can. You can have the camera crews follow me if you want."

"Security," Dee called, and a second later, they surrounded me.

"You can't do this!" I yelled. "It's America. I have rights. You can't hold me, prisoner."

"But, I can."

Security stepped away to show me a man standing behind them with an apologetic grin.

"Andrew!" I yelled.

I ran to him and dove into his hug.

His strong arms wrapped around me and held me tight. His chin came down to my head.

I grabbed tightly onto his shirt. I was not going to let him go—ever.

"Why did you leave me?"

Silence drew out for a long moment. "I'm here now. We'll talk later."

* * *

EVENTUALLY, Dee was able to separate us long enough to hand me the shells. She said she wanted to reveal to me if Andrew was the person I was most compatible with from our compatibility test.

I didn't want to know. Forget the overnights and continuing this charade. I was just going to declare my love for the one I wanted to be with.

Forester and Shawn were still in the room, heads down, kicking around on the carpet. I put the shells on the table and walked over to Forester.

I looked over to Shawn and Andrew. "May I have a minute?"

The two men nodded and stepped away.

Breathing deep, I looked up at Forester, not knowing if I had the courage to do this. He was a really fun guy.

He put his hand out. "I know. I get it. Don't worry."

I glanced at my hands. "I had fun with you. Really did."

He showed his pearly whites. "Of course."

"Just in case you were thinking… If you and Chelsey… I'm fine with it."

He gave me a big hug. "Goodbye for now."

After he pulled away from me, he called out, "Dee, what are you going to do with that honeymoon suite you already paid for?"

I blew out a long breath. It didn't take long for him to move on.

I went over to Shawn. This one was going to be harder. I approached him. Andrew left his side.

"Hi," I whispered.

"I'm going back to Wisconsin, aren't I?"

I looked up at him, wiping away a few stray tears. "I always thought it would be you."

"Don't say anything. It just makes it worse. I see you two together, and I think I always knew. I wish it wasn't, 'cause you are one special gal. I'm not sure... well, let me stop there. I hope you find much happiness."

Our gazes connected. I saw his hurt and longed to make it better somehow.

He inclined his head slightly to one side. "You are going to build that Walden lifestyle you long for, aren't you?"

I didn't remember telling him about how much I wanted that. I must have at some point. Or, my sister had. "Of course, I will. I'm not giving that up, just like you shouldn't give up love. You'll probably be chosen to be the next bachelor."

He shoved his hands in his suit pants. "We'll see. If you're okay with it, Andrew and I might have some ideas for our own show, but I know he won't do a thing if you aren't okay with it."

That was a lot to think about.

"If Andrew and I somehow end up together," I said, "he can do whatever he wants as long as it makes him happy."

Shawn hugged me. "Good for you." He ran one finger along my cheek, lifted one corner of his mouth slightly, and walked away.

That left me with Andrew. I grabbed one of the conch shells and slipped over to him.

"Andrew," I said, holding the shell, "I choose you. Not just for this round. I choose you for the rest of the time. I don't know why you left me. I don't know what all the problems will be between us, but I know they'll exist, and we'll figure them out. Despite all that, I choose you. You're the right person. You're the one I look to when things become hard. Your arms are the ones I run to. My body knew before my brain did. It is you."

He looked at me, looked at the shell, took it, and set the shell down on the ground.

I bit my lip. He didn't want to take my shell. He was rejecting me. Tears came. I couldn't hold them in.

"I stopped by and visited someone in a Hawaiian shirt and a box full of jewelry before I came to speak to you, Charissa. I was able to pick up something for you. You may want to replace it at some point, but I chose something symbolic... a token with as much meaning as your conch shells."

What was this man saying? I studied his expression to determine the deeper meaning behind his words.

A butterfly suddenly fluttered past him, and I gasped.

A sign. A sign from Ava. Tears trickled down my cheeks.

Andrew reached into his pocket. "Maybe this will hold even more meaning for you..."

He knelt on the ground and held out a diamond ring.

Continue with the *Millionaire Romance* series … https://amzn.to/2YryyQB

Thank you for joining me on the *Millionaire Romance* journey. If you enjoyed the novel, I'd much appreciate you posting a review on Amazon. https://amzn.to/3ccd0Q0

Sign Up...

Romantic Rants Newsletter

and receive an ebook *Husband Shopping,* which explores what we can learn from reality tv on how to attract a man.

https://www.authoranastasiaalexander.com/

ABOUT THE AUTHOR

Anastasia Alexander doesn't have the answers to life's love questions. What she does know is that love in the 21st century is complex. There are no easy answers, and there is richness and juiciness in exploring all the complexity that love brings.

Her credentials are two failed marriages and a current successful marriage (fingers crossed), equaling thirty-one years of marriage and a willingness to believe that the benefits of flirting aren't dead. Since she loves her current husband too much to flirt outside of marriage, she pours her love for flirting into stories.